Sanford Crow

Mike Lemieux

Originally published on Wattpad.

For Jax and Adrien.

All I want is for you to see me try. Find what you love and do the same.

Prologue

By the time I came to, my palms were caked in her blood. The thickness of it had pooled and crusted in my love lines, cracking as I extended my fingers. *Love lines*, what a hokey concept.

Her blood spilled out in vile heaves like flat soda from a bottle tipped over. Its waves, hypnotic, sent my mind deeper down the rabbit hole. Puncture wounds littered her torso. A butcher knife stiffly upright, was buried in her chest.

A part of me still refuses to believe I could do such a thing. To the others? Maybe. But to Lucy?

When you suffer from a disorder like mine, reality becomes a distorted line, one that's easily crossed. My therapist calls it *psychogenic amnesia*—blackouts for the layman. Brought on from moments of severe stress or trauma, which believe you me, I've experienced plenty of. Recently, however, these blackouts have come with bodies. My worst nightmare coming to fruition, becoming alive—like a Frankenstein's monster freed, having torn itself from the table, bare to the open sky. And it all started with the flip of a switch.

But we'll get to that soon enough.

I tried to gather my wits, sift through the anger and confusion. We're in her place, which used to be our place, in the living room. I can't remember how I got here. The first thing I know I need to do is find some context in the room. A struggle, a motive, a clue, anything. Crime scenes usually open to me like a book, yet this one seems written in braille.

I couldn't move. I was in a semi-state of shock. I vomit. Bile drips off my chin in elastic strings. The only thoughts I had were those of my daughter, Sadie, suffocating the other thoughts from a darker place, the thoughts I feared led me here.

"Is mommy sleeping?" I hear Eric's voice call out from within me; the voice of a six-year-old boy; the voice of my little brother.

It was the same... the exact same, only twenty-five years earlier.

I see her head pointed to the side, her eyes staring into empty space.

I look down; my boots morph into size seven converse sneakers, tied and double-knotted. I'm eager. My backpack is strapped on, stuffed with detective and superhero comics. I hear my little brother's voice, childish and cute, whispering, "Come on, Sanford, it's time to go."

PART ONE

CHILDHOOD'S END

1969

CHAPTER 1

The ordinary man is the man to fear. The man who shows no originality. The man who is so goddamn normal that it's terrifying. Jonathan Crow was that kind of man.

He lived a simple life in the simple town of Sanford, Maine. The simplicity of it was so deeply cherished by him that he named his eldest son after the town.

Jonathan was a postman. While delivering the townsfolk its mail, he'd exchange words and laughs as a staple of the community. He was large, coltish and towering. His surprising height of 6'5, was evident even when driving, with his pointy, flattop hair brushing the mail truck's ceiling. An intimidating man by size, but the horn-rimmed glasses he wore over his dark, marbled eyes, made him innocuous.

It was late August in the summer of 1969. The Crows had taken a family trip to Ogunquit, Maine, a picturesque beach town set in the style of a Norman Rockwell painting. Rock cliffs brushed in the landscape, overlooking the endless Atlantic. The ocean rippled out waves that crashed against the mammoth rocks, creating a tumultuous yet peaceful sound. The tourists and townsfolk alike slept with their porch doors opened to better hear the natural lullaby. The smell of sand and salt hung in the air—when mixed with the heat of the overbearing sun, the town could sometimes foster an aroma of exhumed life.

The residents were as polite as could be, treating the tourists as if they were gods in a new land, grateful to have them visit. During the off season—when winter settled in unmercifully—the few people who lived there year-round hibernated until the vacation season pumped blood back into the community once again.

The Crows had gone for a long weekend, traveling in their wood-paneled station wagon, packed from window to window, mostly with little Eric's toys. Little plastic soldiers littered the backseat alongside stacks of Sanford's detective stories and comics.

Jonathan was the captain of their four-wheeled ship, always at the helm. He never let their mother, Grace, get her hands on the wheel.

"Come on Jon, we're at a rest stop, can I drive the rest of the way?"

"Grace, no."

His smile would arch in cartoonish angles when he said such things. It made Grace cringe, knowing she was getting on his nerves, and she would subsequently tiptoe the whole way.

"Daddy, when will we be there?" Sanford asked from the backseat, his head buried in the tales of Detective Artie Camper, about to solve another murder. They were a little too adult for a nine-year-old, but for his father, the sooner he grew up the better. Sanford, being the eldest, was already spoken to like a teenager.

"We'll be there when we get there," Jonathan said with one hand on the wheel and the other gripping the bottom frame of the opened window as he indignantly stared at a passing couple walking home from the beach. Their bronzing tans and whitened teeth made him sick.

"Does that mean soon? I wanna go to the beach," Sanford whined.

"What did I tell you about patience, boy?"

Sanford's head went down as he tried to remember. "Ummm..."

"Come on now. The two warriors... you know it."

"Oh yeah! The two powerful warriors are patience and time?" Sanford asked, hopeful to be correct.

"The two *MOST* powerful warriors are patience and time. *Tolstoy* said that, so it's important you say it right," Jonathan said. He'd always wield such brainy quotes like a weapon, hoping to affect an air of intelligence by repeating what smarter men had said. His own quotes were never quite as elegant, but he always got his point across.

"Yes, Dad."

"Now shut up and read your comic, I want a full report by the time we get there," he looked down at his watch, "in five minutes." He smiled from behind his horn-rimmed glasses in the rearview mirror. Sanford returned the smile with a laugh.

He knew they'd arrived when he saw two boys running with their pails and shovels, volleying a beach ball back and forth so it would not touch the ground. Jonathan stopped the station wagon at an intersection, and the boys went on ahead, haphazardly swatting the ball to each other. The jealousy in Sanford flamed, as he wanted nothing more than to leave the car and play. As they cruised forward the beach ball veered in front of the car after a bad volley. The younger child chased it down in the middle of the street.

Jonathan applied the brakes and the car came to a screeching halt; he leaned into the car horn with a Viking-like fury. The car stopped a foot away from the boy, who was frozen in terror. His skin transformed from its blistering sunburn to bone white. Finally, the boy stepped aside and averted his gaze. Jonathan kept his, shaking with anger behind the horn-rimmed glasses.

"Fucking rats," he said under his breath, but loud enough for the whole car to hear.

"Shhh, they're just boys," Grace said.

"They're reckless... Reckless rats."

* * *

The hotel was nothing to gawk at. It consisted of two rectangular buildings with space in between them, forming a broken L. In between the buildings was a courtyard, with a path of irregularly shaped rocks leading the way. Roof tiling was shattered on the sidewalk in front of the lobby doors. But it was close to the beach.

They entered their room. Sanford's nostrils flared from the musty smell, like an old attic filled with moth-balls and black mold. The popcorn ceiling was marred by water-marks in the form of big brown pools.

"Look at this garbage," Jonathan said as he threw his suitcase on the flower-patterned comforter.

"Is there a pool?" Eric asked, dragging his bag into the room; a toy truck fell out of the opened zipper as he did.

"No pool, you have the ocean. It's bigger than any pool I've ever seen."

"The ocean scares me," Eric responded with his tiny voice.

"It should scare you. But there's a lot of things in this world that can swallow you whole," Jonathan said. It was something Sanford admired about their father; his ability to tell it like it is was refreshing.

Sanford watched the fear grow in Eric's eyes.

"Don't worry, Eric. I'll be there with you and I won't let anything happen," Sanford said as he put his hands on Eric's shoulders.

"Sanford, take your brother to the beach," his father said. "Your mother and I need some alone time."

He looked towards his mother. She caught her son's gaze and smiled. But the smile stopped at her mouth. Her eyes remained stilled by something Sanford had yet to find a name for.

Grace wasn't beautiful by its standard definition, but her looks brought on vague feelings of home. Sunken eyes outlined her bushy eyebrows. Her parents were from Canada. French-Canadian—her skin was dark by nature, smooth and honey-toned. Though now Sanford detected a hint of green. It reminded him of Ava Potter's eyes, the girl who moved next door. He wished she was here now, so they could skip rocks on the beach.

"Go boy," Jonathan reiterated.

"Do as your daddy says, Sanford," Grace said.

He grabbed Eric by the hand and they were off. Their father followed them to the door and slammed it shut as soon they crossed the threshold. Sanford heard the sound of it locking. Its mechanical notes cringed in his ear.

"Come on, let's go to the beach!" Eric whined and tugged on Sanford's arm.

"Shhhh," Sanford hissed with his finger on his lips.

The door was thick, but not thick enough that Sanford couldn't make out a few words with his ear pressed against the wood. Eric copied him and moved against the door.

"Please not so rough this time." Their mother's voice was trembling.

Then Sanford's father called her something that he couldn't distinguish. Though it must've been bad; he heard his mother whimper.

Sanford gripped Eric's hand tight.

"Ss-Sanny, you're hurting me."

"Be quiet," Sanford whispered and pressed his ear even tighter against the door. The sounds of the lock unfastening came loud and fast. The door flew open, and their father stood above them, taller than Sanford had ever seen, with a look in his eyes he never wanted to see again.

He crouched down and an easy smile spread across his face.

"Boys, what'd I tell you?" His voice was sweet.

"Um, to go to... to the beach."

"Right. Now please give us grown-ups some privacy. Here," he reached into his wallet. He handed Sanford a handful of change. "Get you and your brother some french fries. We'll meet you down at the beach in a little bit, okay?"

"French fries!" Eric shouted.

"Yes, Dad," Sanford mustered out.

"Good, now go." He patted their backsides and sent them on their way. Sanford could feel his father's eyes on him as they walked down the hall, and when they rounded the corner he heard the door slam, and that metal chain lock back into place.

They walked hand in hand, the way their mother taught them to do when they were alone. Outside, the sun beat down, and the smell of the ocean filled the air. Sanford focused on the prospect of fries and the feel of sand that would soon be between his toes.

Eric tapped him on the shoulder.

"Sanny?"

"Yeah?"

"What does cunt mean?

CHAPTER 2

Jonathan's eyes peered through the binoculars. The look on his face belonged to that of a man in a forbidden place, secreted away in others' private moments.

Jonathan loved the beach. He told Sanford how he loved to watch the people, describing to him how interesting it is to watch life go on and to be a part of some stranger's world for a brief moment.

"You see that one, son?" He pointed and held the binoculars over Sanford's eyes, without letting him touch them; he never let anybody touch his things.

"The fat man?"

"Yes, the fat man," Jonathan laughed. "You see how engorged he is? Sitting in that chair on the verge of breaking it, shoving another hot dog in his mouth? What do you think his life is like at home, outside of this beach?"

"I don't know."

"Guess."

"I... I can't."

"Sure you can, it's easy. Watch. You see those tan lines on his calf? It's white next to red; he's burned. Meaning he doesn't get out in the sun much. Also, he's likely of Irish or English descent. My guess though, is that he doesn't get out because he doesn't want to. He's under that umbrella, blocking the sun because it scares him."

"Why does it scare him?"

"Aren't you the one who wants to be a detective?" Jonathan asked.

"Yeah, but—"

"It's because the world's too big for him. He prefers his own world; the little one he calls his apartment. Where he watches television, paws through his dirty magazines, and eats his endless junk food. He most likely got dragged here on vacation by his parents, so they can get him out of his cave and pretend their son isn't as pathetic as they know he is. So he sits there, staring at the ocean, seeing how big it is, and retreating into himself. It's a reminder to him that no matter how fat he gets, he's still a small turd in the grand scheme of things."

Sanford watched the fat man eat. Through his mind's eye, he saw the man sitting on his couch at home, devouring fistfuls of candy. He saw him alone, he saw him sad. In a small way, he felt his pain

"What about them?" Sanford said, pointing over to the parents of some boys he was playing with earlier.

The mother was tall and lean, with a body that a mother of three had no business carrying. Her hair was long and blond, running in waves down to her waist, revealing her curves every time the wind blew. To Sanford it meant nothing, but he saw his father's eyes widen. Unexplainable guilt rattled Sanford's spine.

The husband was built like a Greek myth. Muscles protruded at every angle. Jonathan's own body was soft and doughy, though this was obscured by his height. His teeth tightened, grinding at a volume heard over the splashing waves. Even the children seemed to be plucked from a postcard. Blond hair and blue eyes—the definition of 60's Americana perfection.

Sanford could feel his father staring through the binoculars at the family, into their lives, becoming part of it. It made him uncomfortable.

"Them?" he said, pointing ominously. "Nothing's wrong with them... they're perfect."

* * *

A cool night's wind moaned through the screen door. The boys slept outside on the porch in their sleeping bags. There was only one bed in the room, which their parents claimed. Sleeping under the stars suited the boys just fine. And on that night the sky was as full and bright as any they'd ever seen.

Sanford lay on his back. He felt the breeze and listened to the sounds of waves exploding off the rocky shoreline with his hands behind his head. His eyes were glued to the night sky. Sleep never came easy to him. It was as if his brain went into overdrive when the world became dark and quiet.

He pondered on the way his father had acted earlier. It was strange, but still, he didn't know what to make of it. The night sky was too clear for confusion; his thoughts drifted to more fantastical things.

During the last month of school, before summer break began, he learned about the sun. He became enthralled by the idea that the moon's glow was the sun's reflection. When half the earth was encapsulated by darkness, the sun still found a way to shed its light, like an unstoppable force. He thought of how Ava would be looking at the same moon. He wondered if it would be as full for her, and if so, if it made her think of him.

As he relished this thought, he heard the unmistakable sound of gravel crunching under feet. The tiny porch he slept on was above the path of loose rocks that led to the beach. Through the powdery light cast by a tilted lamppost, he saw the silhouette of a large man stumbling. The man dragged one foot slowly as if it were injured. By the way the man walked, gingerly and slow, Sanford could tell he was trying to be quiet.

Sanford propped his head up and squinted through the wooden banister of the porch. Normally, fear would have tucked him into his sleeping bag, but the bump in the middle of the night had finally found a form, and Sanford couldn't help himself. There was something about the man that seemed familiar. The man stopped, perhaps feeling the little eyes on him.

Sanford snapped his head back down as the dark man turned towards him. He lay on his side, wishing to be invisible. Still, his eyes refused to blink. He kept them peeled, staring perpendicularly through the banister. He couldn't see the man's face, but he knew who it was by the reflection from the moon. The light shined off the man's face, lighting up two flat circles with an evil glow where his eyes should be. *Glasses*, Sanford thought to himself.

Sanford sat up and looked inside to where his parents were sleeping, hoping to find two lumps under the blankets.

He only saw one.

Carefully, he got up and slid the screen door open, dragging it inch by inch to lessen the sound. It creaked and squealed, mocking his goal of trying to be quiet. Eric stayed asleep. He was the opposite of his brother that way, sleeping like an inanimate object. Sanford leaned closer to the bed, confirming what he already knew. *It was Dad.*

The *who* had been answered. But *what, where, how,* and *why?*

He found himself walking towards the beach. In the confusion, he'd forgotten to put his sneakers on. The rocky path poked and prodded his bare feet, but he endured and walked on, wincing with every step he took. Relief came when he reached the sand. It was cold and soothing.

Treading cautiously, he crouched, knowing his silhouette might be seen from the hotel lights behind him. His eyes began to adjust to the dark. Shadows formed into shapes.

At first, all he could hear were the sounds of the ocean, becoming louder the closer he moved towards it. Waves obliterated themselves against the rocks, gradually eroding them, steadily overwhelming the earth over millennia. The distant silence beyond. The thought of the alien world under the ocean filled Sanford with an oddly deep dread. Strange pallid creatures without arms and legs that could breathe underwater and drag you into the abyss. He shivered. Then he heard a sound that was even more frightening than anything the ocean could offer up.

Laughter.

His body trembled. The laughter wasn't from a group, like a band of teenagers drinking beers and smoking joints around a campfire. It was a laugh that belonged to one man, alone, and Sanford knew who that man was.

Seaweed defiled the beach, covering the majority of sand. Small lobster cages had washed up on shore, leaving the captives inside and clawing at the bars. They made terrible noises. One large rock—more like a bolder—lay forlorn on the soggy sand. Sanford snuck his way behind it and planted himself down. He peeked over the rock and saw his father, naked and dancing in the water, madly scrubbing himself with his hands.

* * *

"Can you pass the syrup, buddy boy?" Jonathan asked Sanford, as the family sat around the table at the diner the next morning.

"I think you have enough on there, Jon," Grace said before lowering her head.

"Grace, the day I care what you think will be the day I can't think at all," he said, but then smiled as if it were a joke. "I'm sorry, but it's a glorious morning and these pancakes need some lovin' too. Ain't that right, kiddo?" He gave Eric a playful noogie and they both laughed loud enough to fill the room.

"You're in an awfully chipper mood," Grace said.

"You're god damn right I am! Just take a look out there." He pointed towards the window. "There's not a cloud in the sky, I don't have a mailbag strapped around my shoulder, and I'm surrounded by the ones I love. What more can a man ask for?"

Grace laughed aloud and held his hand. "I don't know, but I'm sure you can think of something!"

"You're right! Can you pass the butter too?"

They all laughed at that one, including Sanford. He had tried to reason with himself, drawing conclusions from the night before. Maybe his father was just letting off some steam. It must be hard to cut loose as a mailman. Now that he thought about it, dancing in the ocean did look kind of fun.

But that laugh...

"Did you hurt your knee again Jon? I saw you limping this morning," Grace asked.

Sanford paid close attention.

"Yeah, I took a walk on the beach last night after you all fell asleep. I stepped on a rock and tweaked it. It's okay though, there's nothing to gain without a little pain, right Sanford?" He looked right at him, Sanford could see the shape of his own image reflected off of those horn-rimmed glasses.

"Um, yeah. Sure, Dad" he said, thinking of how his father was limping on *the way* to the beach.

A barrage of police officers plowed through the door. Sheriff Cooney led the way with six of his men behind him. The officer's expressions were stoic—faces sculpted in stone. But their bodies were slouched and shaking as they walked to the counter. Patrons eating got up from their stools to let them sit. They brought their meals to the other side and picked at their eggs while standing.

"Coffee," the sheriff said.

"Sheriff, your boys all right?" the man behind the counter said and lined up seven mugs. His apron was marred by grease.

It took him a while to answer. "All right?' I don't think we'll ever be all right again."

The sheriff sipped his coffee.

Sanford was sitting at the table across from the counter and could hear every word. He turned his attention to his father. Jonathan drank his orange juice and continued to eat.

"There's some evil in this world, Rene," the sheriff said to the cook. "And I don't wanna see no more."

"What happened?" Rene asked.

"A family," he said, perhaps louder than he intended. The surrounding patrons looked over. "A whole god damn family."

"Oh my god."

The sheriff, lost in his own thoughts, spoke softly as he stared into his coffee, stirring it with a spoon even though it was black. "Two boys," he said, "coulda been twins if they wasn't a year apart. And that little girl. A perfect looking family."

Sanford looked up at his father. *Perfect,* the word crashed from his mind like an avalanche. *"What about them?"* he had asked. *"Nothing's wrong with them,"* his father responded, *"They're perfect."*

Jonathan took another fork full of pancakes, drowned in butter and syrup. Sanford couldn't imagine why he would stuff so much food into his mouth. But as he watched his father's face he knew. His lips were sealed shut, as he chewed slow and haltingly, with the lines at the sides of his lips taut.

He was hiding his smile.

A Monster's Home

By Sanford Crow

It was on the beach when I first saw it. It was scary and had fangs. I've never seen anything like it. This was bigger then the earth it seemed like. I had this treat in my pocket I decided to give it to this giant vicious ware wolf. This ware wolf got calm as he ate. It was weird the ware wolf also got smaller.

I saw a bag from the side of my eye. I said "stay" hoping that the ware wolf would stay. I walked backwards slowly looking at the ware wolf. I ran as fast as I could, getting the bag I grabbed it and ran back. I put a treat in the bag hoping that the ware wolf would come. Well he did so I locked it up and ran back to the house.

I ran in my room and opened the bag. The ware wolf ran under my bed. I went to sleep and was nervous. I kept waking up in the middle of the night hoping I was not dead.

In the morning I got up. I looked under the bed and he was there.

"Thank god he's there" I said.

It was weird it looked like he was shedding but it looked like I saw another body under the ware wolf. I was confused and then I heard a voice.

"Help Help! Put the sun on me!"

So I moved and got up, I found a broom I got it and moved his body with the broom out of under the bed. Boom! Smoke was everywhere. Lights beeming around me everywhere in my room. Next thing I know, theres my dad right in front hugging me. I didn't know what was going on. It was my dad the hole time.

"Thank you Sanford" he said and we ate pancakes.

C + Creative story Sanford, and well written. But the assignment was to write about your family vacation.

CHAPTER 3

The Crows' house was ranch style. There were ten others on Bleecker Street just like that of the Crows. If it weren't for the subtle differences in landscaping and paint colors, they would be indistinguishable; a carbon copy of a carbon copy. It was the way Jonathan Crow wanted it: nothing distinct, nothing discernible.

Camouflage was a word Sanford found himself coming back to. *They're clothes worn to hide from your enemy, right?* But when you see the world as your enemy, what would you wear? Every morning Jonathan would shower and shave, and dress in his uniform. He would zip up in the skin of an ordinary human and affix a smile to his face. He would surround himself with orderly things: a house, a car, a job, a family—all part of his camouflage, all part of the deception.

At first, Sanford put the thoughts of Ogunquit in the back of his mind. He lived life in Sanford, Maine like a normal nine-year-old. He'd go to school, avoid all girls but the girl next door, play stickball with friends, have sleep-overs, and never dare to be the first to fall asleep.

He and Eric would build forts outside. Large sticks over rocks and logs forming a teepee. In their minds, it was impenetrable, though a sturdy wind could easily blow it down. He'd collect bugs as he explored the woods. He'd laugh without a care in the world.

Soon enough, the calendar approached October 30th—Sanford's birthday.

It was the last he'd ever celebrate.

* * *

"Happy birthday, kiddo!" Jonathan said as he walked into the dining room, gingerly gripping an ice-cream cake with its ten candles illuminating his face somewhat menacingly. The fire swayed in his glasses.

"Happy birthday to you, happy birthday to you, happy birthday dear Sanford, happy birthday to you!" they all ceremoniously sang.

Sanford froze. His family, surrounding him, waited for the candles to be blown out.

"Come on, sweetheart, make a wish!" his mother cheerily said.

Eric sat next to him, he felt him hammering him on his shoulder, eager for Sanford's wish so he could help blow. He saw nothing but innocence in his brother.

The cake beneath him was round and basic, smothered in vanilla icing and whip cream. Written in blue frosting, "Happy Birthday Sanford Maine!" It almost brought a smile to Sanford's face, thinking of the confusion it must have caused at the bakery. With that, he gathered up all the air his lungs could hold. *Just don't let it be true* he wished to himself and blew.

The candles went out and the room went dark. All he could hear was clapping; all he could feel were the hairs standing up on the back of his neck.

When the lights went on, the first thing he saw was his father's eyes. They were unemotional, dead; his whole expression seemed carved out of wood. But he held his smile firm.

After cake, he and Eric retreated to their room and to their comics. Sanford's present was a new stack of them, which he added to the stash he kept in the chest at the foot of his bed. It contained heaps of colorful adventures that he and Eric would get lost in. He needed to get lost now.

Sanford tossed Eric the new *Superman* issue. Eric stared at the cover then flipped through the pages, excited by each frame. Never reading the dialogue, he'd put in his own, filtering it through the fantasies of his own mind. It would always make Sanford laugh.

Usually, Sanford would read his detective stories. He was always thrilled when a new one came out. He took it as a challenge to solve the crime before the fictional gumshoe. Instead, today, he decided to read the new *X-men.* The premise intrigued him. A society at war with itself. Mutants persecuted and forced to be identified.

"Eric?"

"Yeah?"

Sanford laid back in his bed and put the comic down on his chest. He stared at the ceiling. "Do you ever wonder about Dad?"

"Huh?"

"Do you believe he's... normal?"

"Normal? I don't know, he's Dad."

It felt impossible to explain. He wanted to show Eric what he thought, what he felt, what he somehow *knew*, but he barely understood it himself.

"I think... he lies," Sanford said, for a lack of better phrasing.

"Daddy doesn't lie! You're lying!"

"Shhh, I'm not lying to you, Eric. I never will. I'm telling you, I think something's wrong with him."

"Stop it, Sanny, this isn't funny. I'm gonna tell Dad."

"Shhh, Eric, no! Please, you can't do that. We have to watch out for each other. Look, I saw something on vacation, something that made me think differently." He furrowed his brow, digging for the right words.

"I think he's dangerous, I think he hurts people."

"...I don't understand." Blood seemed to have flushed out of Eric's face.

"I know you don't. Neither do I, but that's okay. I just needed to tell someone, and I don't trust anyone more than you. There's some things I need to do, but I'll need help. I need you on my side. Okay?"

"To do what?"

That he didn't know. He had avoided the memory of Ogunquit like it was nothing more than a bad dream. But now he would toss and turn at night. Some nights he would just lay there, awake, not knowing why. He needed to know more. He needed to find out; otherwise, sleep would be a thing of the past.

"To find the truth."

—•—

CHAPTER 4

Thanksgiving came and went. Time seemed to alternately fly and crawl on those days Sanford would search with Eric. They'd rummage through Jonathan's closet and drawers, looking for anything suspicious, knowing there'd be a beating if they were to get caught, if not something worse.

Eric never knew what to look for. Sanford told him as little as possible. When Eric would search he'd mostly come across something insignificant: a switchblade, a razor, or a used handkerchief crusted with snot, which they'd wince at and throw at each other in a sickening game of hot potato.

Then, through pure luck, Eric found something strange underneath the bedside drawer of their father's bed. He hadn't meant to look there. It was the third time he'd checked the drawer, though this time he opened it too fast, and the drawer slid off of its rails. It fell to the ground, spilling its contents of socks, underwear, and handkerchiefs everywhere.

Something shiny caught his eye. The faux gold belonged to a picture frame hidden underneath the rails of the drawer.

"Let me see that!" Sanford exclaimed, grabbing at the frame.

"Hey!" Eric said but didn't fight it.

Inside of it was an old black and white picture of two children, a boy, and a little girl. Their forms were hazy, their faces whitewashed, nearly making them transparent. They wore black clothes. The boy seemed to be a little older than Sanford and looked remarkably like him. He was holding the girl, who looked to be no more than three-years-old.

"What in God's name are you boys doing?" Their mother's voice broke their trance.

They jumped from shock and whirled around to see her standing in the bedroom doorway. She saw the drawer, upside down on the floor. Jonathan's socks were spilled across the carpet.

"Nothing Ma. We were just looking for..." his brain froze.

Then, in an instant, his ears rang. From his jawbone to his eye he felt a hot sting.

His mother had slapped him.

She'd never slapped him that hard before. His head snapped to the right. He looked back at her with tearing eyes, trying to hold in an all-out cry; he could see that there was no anger in her face, only fear.

"Sanford, I'm so sorry!" She reached out to hold him, but he backed away, as did Eric.

"You don't understand. If your father found out you were... I'm so sorry I hit you, but you can never do this again, do you understand?"

Sanford nodded, gripping his face.

"You have to put this drawer back exactly the way it was. Exactly!"

Eric handed her the photo with a look of guilt, "Who is this Mommy?"

She took it, and looked it over for less than a second. Sanford could tell it was a photo she'd been shown hundreds of times.

"This is a picture of Daddy when he was a boy, and your Aunt Claire," she sighed.

"Aunt Claire?" Sanford asked.

"Your daddy's baby sister. She died when she was younger."

The pain from Sanford's face seemed to drop to his stomach.

"How'd she die?" he asked.

"Put the photo back, and don't tell your father about it; he gets very upset when he thinks about her."

"How'd she die?" Sanford repeated, ignoring her request.

"She fell and hit her head. It was a bad accident."

* * *

The winter was one to remember. Record lows and snowfalls encapsulated all of New England, burying it one foot at a time. Power lines and trees tilted from the snow's weight. Christmas was around the corner, but Sanford's mind was too occupied to care.

He'd become obsessed, his mind tangled up in thoughts of his father. Every day he would pursue, his what? His... *suspect?* He supposed he always knew this is what he wanted to be. All those detective stories he'd read, he'd always fantasized himself as the hero.

Detective Crow, he'd think to himself. It had a nice ring to it.

Here he was on his first case—a doozy. And he needed the right tools for the job. He'd gone through his stack of *Dick Tracy* comics and developed his own list of what he might need and strategies he'd have to know. He would learn from the master himself.

There was a magnifying glass he'd found buried in the glove box of his father's station wagon, lodged in between the roadmaps. He stole an extra powdering kit from his mother's makeup bag. He tried desperately to find the yellow hat and raincoat but realized the less bright colors he wore, the better. The one tool he knew would help more than all the others was the one tool forbidden. But he knew where it was kept.

In their backyard—thirty yards away from the house—stood Jonathan's toolshed. He had built it for himself a few years earlier, with Sanford handing him screws and nails when needed. It cast long, disproportionate shadows through the yard. It was an eyesore; their mother hated it. Her idea of a backyard was more pristine, with Adirondack chairs, wildflowers, and a garden of her own.

Sanford knew the binoculars were inside. Staring at the shed in front of him, he saw it as a monster. Icicles hung from the roof like fangs. He approached the door warily, as if he might trigger a booby trap. He calmed his breathing and grabbed the cold metal handle. He pulled the door open. The hinges wailed.

When he entered, the smell of gasoline was nauseating. Dust and pollen gathered in clumps and bundles on the floor. The lawnmower hibernated in the corner, waiting for winter's end. The plump pool pump sat next to the pool ladder. A space heater was toppled over in the middle of the room. The floor was covered in mouse droppings. The place was a mess.

The workbench was to his left. It was the only thing cleaned and immaculate. The metal top was polished and gleaming. Tools hung in order from big to small. Nuts and bolts were stored in clearly labeled containers. Everything was organized. It was as if his father was a different man in front of the bench, neat and stable, while everything around it was falling apart.

Underneath the bench was a shelf stacked with boxes. Sanford took a mental picture of what was where so he'd get it right when he'd put it back. He bent low and began moving the boxes.

He searched behind the first row and found a circular leather case matted with dust. He smiled as he reached for it. It had a leather strap from the lid to the base, which buckled in like a belt. Sanford could smell the leather as he opened it, capturing the essence of *vintage*.

Bird watching, is what his father supposedly used them for, but his father hated animals, in all shapes and forms. When Sanford was five-years-old, his mother brought home a dog. A golden retriever named Taffy. For the one week they had that dog, Sanford remembered loving it as if he'd had it forever. Then one day, just like that, the dog was gone. He remembered his father telling him that Taffy ran away. But why would Taffy run away when Sanford loved him so much?

He pulled out the binoculars from the case and held them in his hands for the first time. His sweaty skin was never allowed to touch them. In his palms, he could feel their weight, their delicacy, like some forbidden fruit always out of reach, which had finally fallen to the ground.

They were big, too big, meant for an adult. When he put them to his eyes, only one could see through the lens, the other only reached the bridge. A wave of concern washed over him as he stared through; he prayed that his father wouldn't find out that he had them.

But it's winter, and birds fly south for the winter, right?

Despite the weather, Sanford was on a mission, and unlike the birds, he'd be damned if a little snow was going to stop him. Christmas was coming and all Sanford wanted was the truth wrapped neatly in a box with a bow on top. If he was being honest with himself, he wanted more than that: he wanted an explanation, he wanted a reason why his father was the way he was. He wanted to go back, forget what he saw that night on the beach, and once again enjoy his youth. But above all else, what Sanford really wanted for Christmas was simply to be wrong.

Chapter 5

The car door slammed, and Sanford heard the grunt of his father's voice through his bedroom window. It was just past two in the morning, and it was three days before Christmas.

Sanford lay in bed and listened, waiting to hear the jingling of keys, drunkenly opening the door. Instead, there was the sound of boots crunching in the snow as they made their way through the backyard.

The toolshed, Sanford thought. *Now's the time.*

He jumped out of bed and got dressed, his clothes waited in a heap next to him. Eric kicked around in his sheets and stirred awake.

"Where are you going?" he asked, half asleep.

"I have to check on something," Sanford responded. "Another clue."

"Can I come?"

"No, it's past midnight. Get some sleep, I'll tell you about it in the morning, deal?"

"Deal," he said, and fell right back to sleep as if he was shot with a tranquilizer. Sanford smiled at him through their dark bedroom. Before leaving, he reached under his bed and grabbed the binoculars. It would be hard to see anything in the dark, but it would be better to try this way than to get too close.

He crept down the hall, careful not to wake his mother. The floorboards moaned, suggesting he stay put, go back to bed, and dream of a pleasant world. But he ignored these thoughts and descended the staircase, the binoculars dangling around his neck.

Winter gear hung from a coat hanger at the bottom of the stairs. Sanford strapped on his boots and zipped up his jacket. His nerves danced and his fingers fidgeted. They were doused in sweat and made the simple task of zippering up a test of patience. On the fourth try, he got it.

The garage was impossibly cold. It was a one-car garage, tight with clutter. The smell of dust, oil, and garbage conjured up memories of the times Sanford helped his father to clean out the garage, work on the car, and bring down the trash.

He tiptoed across the oil-stained floor, dodging trashcans and bicycles like land mines. The door to the outside was to the right of the garage door. Frost obscured its window. Sanford could only see a blur of black and gray.

He turned the knob and opened the door.

His fingers and toes went numb at once, like a light switch in his body had just been turned off. But he ignored it all. His attention was drawn to the first thing he saw: blood gleaming in the white snow. The moon seemed to make it glow.

Doubt nagged at him, so close to the truth. He wasn't a real detective; he wasn't even a patrolman. He was a ten-year-old boy afraid of his dad. The feeling grew with every step he took towards the shed.

He stopped in the middle of the yard, hunkered down behind a tree, and gazed through the binoculars. It was hard to see much of anything in the dark. The light was on in the shed, and through the window Sanford could see a shadow. His father's silhouette looked bigger, bulkier—a more threatening version of his regular self. But that was all he could see.

Sanford inched closer, realizing how loud the crunch of snow could be. But then, the sound of music filled the air, covering his steps. His father had the record player on, and he was singing along with an old Hank Williams song. It was a song about a cold, cold heart.

The languid melody would play as a backdrop in Sanford's nightmares for years to come. He was outside of the shed now and looked through the window. It was his father. Naked. Again. He wasn't dancing or howling at the moon this time. Instead, he was holding a picture frame in one hand, his penis in the other. His left arm had what appeared to be a gash on it, and blood seeped through a recently applied bandage.

It was hard to see through the frosty and dirty window, but staring from the darkness into the light helped. Sanford could make out the picture in the frame: a portrait of a family—a mother, a father, two sisters, and a family dog. It was how his father stared at it that bothered Sanford so much. Because he didn't stare at it, so much as into it, as he tugged up and down on himself.

Jonathan's body contorted with a spasm. He placed the portrait down on the bench and outstretched his arms, arching his back. He let out a growl, interrupting Hank Williams' even singing. Then, with closed fists, he raised his arms over his head and smashed them down on the portrait in front of him. Sanford's knee flinched nervously and thumped against the outside wall. He let out a gasp, then instantly smacked his palm against his mouth, trying to silence himself.

With his heart pumping in panic, he watched his father's head jerk around. His eyes went wide with fury. He stared out of the window and straight into Sanford, who was as frozen as the ground itself.

He sees me! Oh my god, he sees me!

But the light from the inside allowed Jonathan to only see his own reflection: naked, still hard. It didn't last for long; he made his way to the door in a steady march. Sanford gathered up as much courage as he could muster and quickly hid along the side of the shed. Jonathan kicked the door open. The booming sound erupted into the night as the door crashed against the wall; the metal lock clanged on its hinge.

"Hellooooo?" his voice called out almost playfully. He stood large in the opened doorway. The light from inside framed him in a powdery halo.

Jonathan stepped down from the shed and into the snow with his bare feet.

Sanford's breathing became heavy. He could feel the blood pumping through his veins as his heart went into overdrive. He clenched his eyes tight and tried to will away this nightmare he found himself in. He pictured Eric sleeping in bed, cuddled in his blankets and curling his tiny body into a tinier ball. Sanford wanted nothing more than to be in the bed next to his, dreaming about the good things that now seemed impossibly out of reach. He shook those thoughts free and opened his eyes again.

He was convinced his father could hear him breathe, that he could hear his heart beating and smell his fear like an apex predator. Hank Williams still played in the background.

Jonathan's pale body had turned to a light shade of blue. The wind ripped through the openings of Sanford's jacket, freezing his wrists, neck and face. The feeling in his fingers and toes had gone from numb to burning.

He stared at his naked father, who stood there as if the cold had barely affected him at all.

"Fucking deer," Jonathan muttered to himself through chattering teeth. His arms crossed his chest, trying to muffle the cold. He sprinted back to the shed and got inside, slamming the door behind him.

Sanford was thankful he hadn't noticed his foot-prints leading to the front of the window. He returned to his spot, knowing he could only put up with another minute of the cold. Frost-bite was nibbling at his toes.

He watched his father press his feet up against the space heater.

Then he was back to the task at hand.

The broken frame was in his hands. His fingers caressed the shattered glass. A jagged edge cut the tip of his finger. He didn't flinch.

Sanford watched him crouch underneath the workbench, moving stacked boxes and an old toolbox covered in rust. It was branded with the initials *R A C* above the lock. It looked to be from an earlier time. He put it aside and studied the floorboards that it was resting on.

He rubbed his hand on each board, searching for the right one. It was like he was playing a game with himself, cherishing the moment, making it count. A loose floor-board clattered under his hand. He pulled it free.

Sanford watched intently as his father delicately placed the portrait down into the dark hole under the shed.

What else was down there?

The wind stabbed through his jacket, and through his clothes, causing every muscle in his body to flex in agony. He had almost shrieked but stifled it with his gloves. He knew then he was done. But he had seen what he came to see, and tomorrow was another day.

He ran as fast as he could, though through the snow it became more of a waddle. The door to the garage was open. *Did I forget to close it? Or was it the wind?* The garage was freezing when he entered, seemingly almost colder than the outside. He shut the door behind him and locked it.

Wait, was it locked before? He couldn't remember. There was no time.

He burst through the downstairs door, kicked off his boots, and hung his frozen jacket on the hanger in the walkway. He removed his snow pants and climbed the stairs, his legs slowly warming. The idea of his bed, smothered in sheets and blankets was all he could think about.

Down the hallway, the creaks from the floorboard screamed at him, but he didn't care, being quiet didn't matter now. All that mattered was warmth. Bed. Sleep.

Sanford jumped into his bed and swaddled himself. The warmth radiated like a furnace. He shivered until the cold left his body for good and he lay still.

"Tomorrow I look in the hole," he said out loud to himself and became a little frightened by the rasp in his own voice.

Aside from fear, he felt something else. Pride. He was figuring things out. Detective Crow, the only one who can solve the riddle. He felt smart. Brilliant even.

* * *

Jonathan came in an hour later. The cold left his body quicker than his son's. Slipping his foot out of his boot, he cracked his toes in his hand. He lowered his foot to the tiled floor and into a puddle of icy water. His eyes squinted. Drips of water plopped into the growing pool. He put his hand out and caught a droplet in his palm. When he looked up, he saw Sanford's jacket, wet and heavy, dangling on the hook above him.

Chapter 6

"He was standing in the freezing snow, Eric, naked!" Sanford said, trying to explain the hysteria of the night before.

"But, why?" Eric responded. His body was half leaning out of bed, his hair stood up in patches, adding to his look of confusion.

"Cause he heard me outside. He's not normal!"

It felt good to say it out loud.

"I don't believe you!"

"He had a picture of some family in a frame and he was smashing it, then he hid it in the floor. I could show it to you and prove it!"

"Why would he have a picture of a family?"

"Cause there's something wrong with him! Maybe you're just too young to see it, but I do. He scares me, Eric. He scares me a lot."

"He doesn't scare me," Eric said, sitting straight now, his chin jutting up.

"That's because you don't see him, not the way I do."

Eric stopped and looked at Sanford, studying his face.

"You really think he's a bad man?" Eric asked.

"I really do. Have I ever lied to you?"

"No, but—"

"I'm not gonna start now," he said. "I think Dad hurts people, I think he kills them. I don't know why, and I'm scared to find out. But I'm more afraid that one of these days he's gonna hurt us, that he's going to—"

The bedroom door swung open before he could finish his sentence. The boom of it sent the boys back in their beds.

There he stood in the opened doorway, their father, a wolf draped in the skin of a lamb. He stood large, covering every inch of the door, of their escape. He appeared dressed for battle. Military boots were strapped on his feet, used and wet, dripping puddles on the rug. Sanford saw the hunting knife, sitting in a sheath, dangling from his belt like an idle threat. A green army, surplus jacket was zipped up to his throat. His crew-cut was bristling and tight. His horn-rimmed glasses were there as always, with his dark brown eyes, almost black, looming behind.

Sanford was terrified.

How long had he been there? What did he hear?

"Gather up boys," he barked. "We got some work to do."

"What kind of—"

"I said gather up, now gather up! Get your long johns and snow pants on. Dress warm. We're taking a walk through the woods." He spoke like he was back at war.

The pit in Sanford's stomach deepened. He couldn't help from swallowing.

His father was focused, intently, sharpening his eyes on Sanford like a whetstone.

"You all right, Sanford?" Jonathan asked. His smile arched to jagged points.

"Yes, -s-sir."

"Because you don't look too good, you look pale. Maybe me and Eric should go and you can just stay here."

"No! I wanna come," Sanford proclaimed.

He couldn't leave Eric alone with him. He didn't know what his father was capable of, or where his limits were.

A sweat broke out on Sanford's forehead as they gathered up and did as their father commanded. He could tell Eric wasn't as scared as he was; he didn't believe, but Sanford had an inkling that he would soon enough.

"Meet me outside," Jonathan stated, and marched down the hallway.

Before leaving their room, Sanford climbed a chair and grabbed his Swiss Army knife from the top-shelf of his closet. It was hidden under a pile of summer clothes. He secured it in his jacket pocket. It was dull and worn from carving on trees and digging into the ground, but it still gave him a sense of security, no matter how false it was.

Once the boys walked downstairs and opened the door into the garage they saw him. Snow stuck in his pointy hair like a web. In his right hand was the wood-axe. He stared daggers into Sanford. Sanford stared intently at the blade.

"Let's go, boys."

It was cold, not quite as cold as the night before, but almost as windy. They began their descent through the backyard. The boys resisted at first, falling behind with their heads low, feet dragging, and their hands in their pockets.

"Come on, boys! Hurry your asses up!"

Their father marched hard, with purpose, as if the snow wasn't even there. The boys had to jog to keep up.

Sanford looked at Eric and saw the fear spilling out of him. He knew that fear; he was intimate with it. To Sanford, it felt like another person inside of him, a coward, huddled against the cold.

"I'm scared, Sanny," Eric whispered. Their father was a good fifteen feet ahead, swinging the axe like a baseball bat as he walked, as if he was on deck at Fenway Park.

"It'll be all right. I'm with you, and I won't let anything happen to you, okay?"

Eric nodded, believing his older brother, who barely believed himself.

Sanford's brought his hand to the knife in his pocket and clutched it tight. The security of it began to wither, as it felt dwarfed in his glove.

Can it even break through skin?

"You know what we're doing today?" Jonathan's voice carried out with force from among the trees.

"Today we're gonna chop some wood, and you're both gonna learn how to swing an axe to do it. The cold won't quit, and the radioman said they might announce a state of emergency. You know what that means? That means we'd be stuck here, left to survive by our own wits." He pointed at his head. "Your mother's out getting food, batteries, and gas, while us men will take care of supplying the heat."

He drew a deep breath.

"You know in the hunter-gatherer days if you were a man and you couldn't make a fire, or bring back a moose for your tribe, you'd be shunned. Banned from the tribe, banned from your family. You'd have to make a plea to stay, beg for your survival. You know that's where they say the fear of public speaking comes from? Makes sense, huh? Some that would stay would even be castrated. You know what castrate means, Eric?"

Eric stood still. Jonathan stopped walking.

"Castrate means they'd take those two little marbles between your legs and..."

He swung the axe at the nearest branch, separating it from the tree in one fell swoop.

"They'd hack em' off!"

He cackled as he rested the axe back on his shoulder, then turned around and continued his march past their above-ground pool, its cover weighed down by ice thick enough to skate on.

"Then you'd be as good as a woman, picking berries, and sewing quilts. You'd see the women around you, women you know to be beautiful, but now you got nothing they want and they know it. They look at you like the pathetic freak you are."

Sanford felt as if he'd entered the rabbit's hole. The more his father kept talking the farther down the hole Sanford sunk, until his familiar surroundings became alien, and he was lost in his own backyard. The trees had a different look to them. They looked like substitutes for something that used to be real. Sanford had never noticed how dead a tree looked in the winter until then; naked in the cold. Zombies of their summer selves.

They entered the trees, into the woods.

"But that's if you were lucky," Jonathan continued. "Being exiled would be worse. You'd be left on your own in the middle of the madness. Because that's what we're surrounded by boys, absolute madness. Where it's all incomprehensible. Things that seem perfect are only an illusion. Oh, that's a good one. I just came up with that on the fly." He stopped to take a mental note. "But you see, that's what today is all about, why I'm telling you this; today is your test."

The boys nervously eyed each other.

"Today is your rite of passage."

After a few minutes walking through the woods, they arrived at a large pile of logs stacked underneath a blue tarp. Jonathan reached underneath and pulled one out. It was weathered, covered in green moss with the thickness of fleece, but still good enough to burn. He placed it right side up on a flat, wide stump. With both hands, he lifted the axe above his right shoulder. He stared at the log as if it were something else and that dead look reclaimed his eyes, like no one was home behind them. The axe came down ferociously, cleanly splitting the log in two. The boys had never seen such raw power.

In the cold air, they could see each breath out of him like an inferno was in his belly. He grabbed another log, took its weight with his hands, then placed it on the block. Again he raised his arms and brought it down. The log split precisely as if cut by a machine.

"Woo! Did you see that there?"

The boys nodded. Jonathan wiped his brow and placed another log down.

"Now it's your turn, Sanford."

"My turn?"

"Yes, you have to split this wood, you have to earn your keep now and help your family survive. You want your family to survive, don't you?"

All Sanford could do was stare. It sounded like a trick question.

"Well then, now's your chance. You're ten-years-old, it's time to be a man," he said disdainfully. "And if you can't, maybe you'll be out in the cold with no balls to keep you warm."

"But, Dad, I—"

"Just do what I say and chop the wood!"

He shoved the axe at him; Sanford's mitten could barely grip its thick handle. All he could think to do was hug the mammoth weapon in his arms. Tears started to form. He begged them to stop. Weakness at this moment would do him no favors, but he could feel the warm drops as they ran tracks down his cheeks.

"You must think I'm stupid, huh?" Jonathan asked as he looked down on him. "Take your gloves off. You won't be as warm as you were last night."

"What?"

"*What*?" he mimicked Sanford. "You don't think I know you were outside last night? When I came in I saw your pile of clothes dripping in the walkway, not to mention all your footprints outside. So, Sanford, who's the stupid one now?"

He knows. The thought was so terrifying it barely made sense.

"Dad... I," he tried to speak but could find nothing to say. He wanted to lie, but he had nothing. Incoherent thoughts zipped through his brain at lightning speed.

"Look at you!" Jonathan laughed. "You're scared shitless! You should only be afraid of one thing right now, and that's me if you can't chop this wood."

Sanford needed to cry, he needed to shit, and most of all he needed his mom.

"But, Dad—"

"There's no buts here, Sanford. Chop... the fucking... wood!"

Sanford took off his gloves as told. The cold stung his fingertips like needles. He looked at Eric, who looked petrified, frozen still. All of a sudden, as if a cord had been pulled inside him, he became more angry than scared. Demented with rage. Gripping the axe's handle, Sanford felt the violent weight of the tool in his hands. He envisioned swinging it hard, plummeting the blade deep into the chest of his father. The sickly sweet notion of murder momentarily infested his mind.

But he didn't; he couldn't.

He brought his attention back to the log in front of him and raised the axe over his head. But his imagination took hold again, the way it always had. He heard the hypnotic melody of carnival music as the snow melted to fresh-cut grass. Cotton candy and fried dough wafted their smell into his nostrils. The axe morphed into a sledgehammer. The carnival game lay in front of him, with the clown's lurid face at the top of the scale. Ava, the girl next door, was wearing her summer dress with bright yellow sunflowers on it—a beam of sultry light. She grazed through the fair and smiled at him. He wondered if she was home right now. He wondered if she could see him.

"Sanford!" his father yelled, breaking his trance.

Sanford readied himself, flexing what little muscles he had.

His father watched with arms crossed, his posture straight.

Sanford swung down.

The sharpened blade of the axe missed the log by inches and sank into the edge of the chopping block, causing Sanford to lurch forward and fall face-first into the snow.

"Ha-ha-ha!" Jonathan's laugh echoed through the woods.

"Pathetic, I bet your little brother can do better than that. Let me ask you something, Sanford. Do you not want your balls anymore? Do you wanna be out in the cold?"

"Please, Dad! I can't!"

"Can't? See, that's the problem with you kids these days; you have no confidence. I guess I wouldn't either if I was you. But you do have balls though, don't you? And I don't just mean the ones between your legs. You got courage. If you didn't, then you wouldn't have been out last night, would you? This could all be over, Sanford, just tell me, what were you doing? Were you watching me?" He set his eyes steadily on Sanford.

All Sanford could do was shake his head.

"Don't lie to me, boy!" he screamed. "What did you see?"

Sanford kept shaking his head back and forth, mechanically, as if he relinquished control of it.

Jonathan lifted his hand across his opposite shoulder and swung it around hard. The back of it crashed against the right side of Sanford's face, stopping his nodding. In the blistering cold, it felt like his cheek had been shattered and crumbled to the ground.

He didn't touch his face; he didn't dare show the pain. Sanford looked back at his father defiantly, his eyes squinting through the snowy wind. The sound of Eric crying; the smile on his father's face. Sanford had had enough.

Jonathan lifted his hand again. Sanford grabbed the handle of the axe and lifted it free from the stump with a violent yank. Jonathan stepped back, surprised. Sanford raised the axe and turned back to the log. He swung it down with every bit of anger he had, every bit of fear. He couldn't help but imagine his father's face in place of the log, with those horn-rimmed glasses over the bark.

The thick wood split in two.

He stood frozen in awe of himself, as Eric and his father did the same.

He felt invincible.

"Wow, I didn't know you had that in ya."

Jonathan calmly inched closer to Sanford and reached for the axe.

Sanford's grip tightened on the handle. His nostrils flared, his eyes narrowed, and his lips—chapped and dried with blood—curled to a sneer.

Jonathan paused and studied his son, smiling.

"How about you let me have that?" He grabbed the handle just under the blade and tugged. Sanford held on and tugged back.

Jonathan laughed. "You know, you remind me of myself sometimes."

CHAPTER 7

The day Sanford met Ava was one he would never forget. It was the last day of school, and summer started the second the bell rang, regardless of what the calendar said. Locker doors slammed as other doors opened, and adolescents blazed into the sunshine as if they'd never felt it before.

Sanford followed suit and barged out of the school, hopping on his *Schwinn*, which was chained to a pole on the side of the school. Its frame was matte black. Sanford had spray painted it in the spring as a project, covering up all indication of what brand it was, making it look like he had built it himself. He pedaled fast to get home to rid himself of the book-bag strapped to his back.

Racing down narrow streets, cutting through alleys and paths in town, made the ride quick. The town itself was condensed to a few blocks. Mom-and-pop stores, the deli, the bakery, a movie theater, all staples holding the tiny town together. He passed the pharmacy on his right. New comic books were displayed in the window, which Sanford was desperate to buy, but he only had pennies in his pocket. He kept riding.

Up ahead, standing on its own and connected to nothing else, was the post office. His father's workplace. He slowly rolled by the window, hoping to see his father inside. Sometimes he would, and sometimes his father would come out, ask how school was, what he learned, and if he got in any trouble. And sometimes, only sometimes, he would flip him a quarter to buy a comic book. But no luck today. He must've still been on his route.

The police station was after that on the right, a stodgy rectangular brick building. Officers were gathering outside of it, cordially laughing and talking with a man in plain clothes. From a distance, Sanford noticed a girl with the man, his daughter most likely, shaking hands and making introductions. He couldn't see much of her through the mass of bulking bodies, but he saw the vibrancy of her red hair, shining through the cops like a spotlight. He was too far away to see much of anything else.

He kept riding.

Through the town and out, he was on his street, Bleecker, where every house looked the same. Sanford pedaled harder, seeing his house up ahead.

He tore into the driveway, as pebbles kicked up in a cloud of dust. He'd barely applied the brakes before he jumped off the bike and let it crash into the side of the garage. He peeled off his book-bag like a scab and tossed it next to his bike with little regard. Then he started his trek through the backyard, past his father's tool shed, and into the forest, where adventures awaited.

Exploring the woods was a passion of his. To discover new terrain untarnished by concrete, and unclaimed from the ever-expanding developers. Pure and simple. In fact, it was the purest place he knew.

The quiet is what he loved the most. Winds rustled through the leaves, water from the stream babbled, birds sang and insects droned. Out there, there were no car horns. There was no yelling, no arguing. There was sound, but there was also the absence of noise.

Sometimes he would take Eric or his friends and show them the things he'd discovered: the little handmade bridge over the stream, the rotted outhouse with that half-moon carved into its door, the graves. But more than anything else he enjoyed exploring alone.

As he walked the path, he could hear the water rushing into Greenwood Lake. He followed the sound.

The water was cold. All water was cold in Maine. He stuck his fingers in the stream and watched as the water cascaded around them. He'd observed how the stream never looked the same. New rocks would appear, as old ones would wash away, changing its landscape and flow of the water. The depth would increase and decrease as storms would come and go.

Sanford had gotten pretty decent at skipping rocks. He picked the smoothest and flattest of them at this feet and flung it with a sidearm whip, watching as the rock bounced off the water one... two... three times.

Whooping and hollering he grabbed a second rock and heaved it. The throw was a dud. The rock plopped in the water without a skip, and with even less finesse. As he stood there with his hands on his waist, disappointed in himself, he heard the crunching of leaves behind him. The unmistakable sound of footsteps.

"Well, that was a dud," a girl's voice said, honeyed and clear. Sanford flinched and stepped forward, submerging his sneaker into the stream, leaving him with a soggy sock for the rest of the afternoon.

When he turned around to see the owner of the voice, he saw a girl with the prettiest face he'd ever seen, staring at him through bright green eyes.

He was mortified, but amid the embarrassment was an excitement he couldn't escape. She wore a Boston Red Sox tee-shirt, with jean shorts that went to mid-thigh, and the standard black on white converse sneakers that everyone seemed to have, though for some reason they'd never looked better than they did on her. The brilliance of her hair highlighted her rosy cheeks, with splats of freckles.

He realized it was the girl he'd seen in town.

"Hi, I'm Ava."

Sanford froze.

"Um, it was a... a bad rock, slipped out of my hand."

"It happens. You got a name there, or should I just call you dud?"

He laughed nervously and a little too hard. Then thought about how he laughed a little too hard, and then thought about thinking about how he laughed a little too hard.

"Sanford," he finally spat out.

"Um, yeah, that's where we are, all right."

"No, you see, I mean my name is Sanford, Sanford Crow."

"Really? Are you joking?"

"Nope, that's my name... don't wear it out," he said with a forced laugh.

She giggled too, but it seemed more at him than with him.

"Were you born here, or did you move here, knowing you'd have the same name as the town you'd live in?"

"I was born here. My dad always said that a man named after where he was born can never forget where he comes from, or something like that."

"Hmm, okay," she said, and Sanford could tell she thought that was cool. "Anyways, nice to meet you Sanford Crow. I guess I'll never forget your name, huh?"

Sanford smiled.

"Did you just move here?"

"That is correct, sir. We just moved here from Denver. My dad had to move us because of work."

"Oh, I'm sorry. That sucks. What kinda work?"

"There's a new sheriff in town," she said with an exaggerated southern drawl, her fingers pointed like a gun on her waist. Then she laughed. "I always wanted to say that!"

Sanford laughed too. "Your dad's the new sheriff? Cool!"

She nodded.

The words stopped there for a little while as she canvassed the area. He watched her, and every so often she would look up at him, catching his eyes before he had the chance to pull them away.

"You were doing it wrong, ya know?" she said.

"Doing what wrong?"

"Skipping rocks. In Colorado, skipping rocks is a daily activity."

He loved the way she talked. It was proper and adult, effortless. It was cool. Everything about her was cool.

"I know how to skip rocks," he said defensively. "You just s-saw me throw a ba-bad one is all."

"Okay, prove it. We'll have a skip off."

"A skip off?"

Sanford was smiling as he eagerly looked for a good rock. Ava laughed and did the same. The ground they stood on was wet. Slimy rocks and pebbles scattered under their feet as they searched. Ava grew frustrated when all she could find were bulky misshapen rocks, broken glass, and shards of petrified wood.

"I got one!" Sanford shouted.

The perfect rock was in his hand. It was flat and rounded into an oval shape. In the back of his mind, his father's voice crept up. He heard him saying, "*A woman can suck a man's pride out through his cock if he's not careful.*" Sanford didn't pay it any attention. Anyway, to him, it made little sense; he didn't even know what a *cock* was.

"Here," he said. "You can use this one."

She took the rock from his hand with a smile. "I guess you really wanna lose, huh?"

He laughed as he grabbed another rock (of lesser quality) and looked downstream to measure his shot. The edge of the water was at their feet.

At about ten yards in front of them, the brook dipped down, and the water tumbled over and around the rocks. But before that it was calm.

He extended his arm back in a sidearm motion with the not-so-flat rock loosely gripped in his fingers. Whipping it around, he let it fly.

The rock grazed the surface of the water. It bounced up and spun in the air like a flying saucer then touched down again before slipping under. It wasn't pretty, but it had height and good distance with only two bounces.

"Not bad, Sanford," she said, and he loved how his name rolled off her tongue.

She bent down in front of him and put her hand in the water, cleaning off the slime on the rock he gave her. The collar of her shirt opened, and he saw the top of her chest.

She looked up to make eye contact, but his eyes never broke from her cleavage.

"You perv!" she said and giggled as she stood up and adjusted her shirt. Sanford was unsure how to respond. When suddenly, she turned around and whipped the rock into the water. She threw it low and hard.

At first, he thought it wasn't hard enough, until he saw the first bounce and how it barely made a splash. It almost danced across the water. Five skips in all.

"See, that's how we do it back home," she cheerfully said, before her tone grew somewhat forlorn. "But I guess this is home now."

"You're amazing," Sanford said, almost involuntarily.

"Shut up!" she laughed, and playfully punched him in the shoulder. "So, Sanford, what's fun to do in Sanford?"

"Umm." He put his best thinking face on. No one ever asked him that before.

"Well, we mostly go to the lake, or the beach, neither are really that close though. Huntin' and fishin' are big around here, but I mostly like to play sports, go campin', or explore."

"Explore? What do you explore?"

"Everything!" he responded excitedly. "There's woods everywhere here. You can find all kinds of things."

"Like what?"

"Oh, all sorts of neat stuff. I have a collection of twenty or so arrowheads from the Indian days. I found a deer skull, which was whole, but I didn't take it cause I felt bad. I found a lot of rifle shells, that's why it's good to always wear bright colors out here. You never know who might be huntin', even if it's a place they're not allowed to, people hunt everywhere here."

"Good tip."

"But it's mostly the places I find that I love."

"What kinda places?"

"Well, there's an old hand-made bridge, an old outhouse, caves between rocks on the mountains, and around here is where I found my favorite place. Where I found the graves."

"The graves? Like tombstones?"

"No, not tombstones, regular stones," he said and noticed her baffled look. "Come on, I'll show you!"

The excitement in him was boundless. He wanted to show and tell her everything he knew, and pretend he knew things he didn't. He thought maybe, just maybe she'd be impressed by the discovery he had made.

They walked through the woods, towards the little bridge he had found over the stream. Every step Sanford took was accompanied by the embarrassing sound of his sock squishing in his shoe, sounding like a wet fart coming from his foot.

"I'm sorry about that," she said sincerely.

"About what?"

"Your sock. Wet socks are the worst!"

"Ha-ha, it's okay," Sanford said. "I'm just glad you didn't think it was the sound of me farting."

Ava burst out laughing. "Oh my god! You're funny!"

Sanford felt the warm glow of satisfaction growing in him.

"Now every time I hear it, that's what I'm gonna think you're doing."

"Maybe that was my plan all along, to cover up for when I actually do it."

She laughed louder this time, and a snort escaped her nose; she covered her mouth in embarrassment, making Sanford laugh too. He never felt better in his whole life.

The glow of satisfaction stayed with him as they walked along the stream, dodging poison ivy and pricker bushes like they were booby traps. To a nine-year-old they certainly were. Ava was at least three years older than him; Sanford wondered if she knew that.

The bridge stood ahead, off-kilter over the water, which was only a few feet deep. Most of the bridge was rotted away, with some of its boards completely missing. Splinters jutted out from the wood, threatening anyone to cross with bare feet. Sanford led the way, gingerly, instructing Ava to follow his every step. She did so perfectly and they crossed the bridge without worry.

They walked on.

The trees became thicker the deeper they went. The path was cluttered with growth but was still traceable. They had to crouch as they walked. Ava did so smiling, and Sanford knew then that she was not like any girl he'd met before.

Up ahead of them the path broadened as the trees and plants opened like a mouth. Ava looked around, slowly spinning on her heels as she did. Her eyes went wide, mystified.

The clearing was in an almost perfect circle, trimmed about twenty feet wide. Below them was nothing but dirt with a few fallen leaves. Grass didn't grow, the sunlight barely scraped the ground.

"What is this place?" Ava asked.

"It's the graveyard," Sanford said and pointed at the ground in the middle, where stones lined and formed elliptical shapes. "I mean, dead people have to under there, right?"

"Wow, yeah," she managed to say. "But where is all the... why is there no—"

"No weeds?" he asked.

"Yeah! There's no weeds, there's no... growth."

"I think it's because the dead won't let it grow."

She went pale, causing her freckles to pop in contrast. "Don't try and scare me, Sanford. I don't like being scared."

"I'm sorry, I don't mean to. But this place is harmless: I come here all the time. I even made up stories about these graves."

"Really? What kind of stories?"

"Well, this one here..." Sanford scampered over and pointed to the smaller of the two graves in the middle. "I believe this one was someone's kid, who got bitten by a poisonous snake when he came into the woods to explore. I call him, Reggie, and Reggie was very brave. He always wanted to know why things were and how things worked, I guess that's what got the best of him in the end, because he saw the snake and was fascinated by the way it moved, and he closed in on it. It's his courage that did him in, you see?"

"That's cute," she laughed.

Sanford blushed.

"And what about this one?" she pointed to the other, slightly larger grave next to it.

"That one is Sharon, Reggie's older sister. Sharon got namania after Reggie died, and before their parents decided to take their wagon down south they wanted to bury them together."

"Pneumonia," Ava corrected.

"Huh?"

"It's called pneumonia, not namania. Sorry, I don't mean to be a snob."

"You're not! How else would I learn? Nuh-moan-ya," he enunciated out loud to get it right.

She smiled again, and Sanford hoped he was on the verge of setting a record for it. A cool gust of wind came in, raising the loose leaves on the ground in the air.

"So why'd you make them both kids?" Ava asked.

"I don't know. They're just smaller graves, I guess. Too big for an adult."

"Yeah, I guess you're right."

They watched the leaves settle on top of the grave.

"How'd you find this place anyway?"

For a moment he couldn't recall. It was from a few years earlier, and memories of his early youth were like fuzzy dreams. But a shadow of a memory crept into his mind. It was the silhouette of a man, walking through the woods with purpose.

"My dad!" he said, as if a lightbulb suddenly and cartoonishly appeared above his head. "I remember seeing my dad walk through the woods and I followed him."

"Aha! What was your dad doing?"

"I think he had a big pair of scissors. I... I think he was crying."

The memories started to clear, and the image of his father began to develop. He saw his father standing where he was now, holding that sharp tool in his hand. His face wet.

"Scissors?" she asked, confused. "You mean hedge clippers?"

He could feel a vague uneasiness rising from his gut.

"Yeah, you're right. Must've been hedge clippers."

For a moment, they stood there in silence, listening to the faint sounds of the forest.

"Oh crap, I gotta get going. If I'm not home by five my dad won't be happy. Thanks for showing me around. I'm glad to make a friend on the first day."

Sanford stuck his hand out for a shake, mostly because he didn't know what else to do. With other friends he never shook or slapped hands, he just said his *goodbyes* and *see you tomorrows*. With her, he felt different, like he should make a gesture, the way grown-ups do.

She smiled at his hand and moved past it, closing the distance between them at an alarming pace.

Her soft warm lips pressed against his cheek. She left her mark, wet and cool when the breeze grazed against it.

He only knew the idea of love through books and movies, but as Ava turned and walked away, he knew he was under her spell. He watched as she left through the forest, and put a hand on the wet spot on his face she'd made. She waved and called out.

"It was very nice to—"

CHAPTER 8

—*meet you, Sanford.*" he said out loud in his bed as he lay there, restlessly, his hand still pressed against his cheek. Reality washed over him as the memory evaporated.

It was still dark when he rose from bed and blindly waddled across the room. The shape of Eric under his blankets moved up and down along with his little snores. Sanford opened the door and walked down the hall to the bathroom. His parents' bedroom was to his left. His mother breathed evenly as she slept, as if she were trained to do so. His father had a deep snore, rising from his chest with a roar. It made Sanford cringe.

In the bathroom, he stood in front of the toilet to relieve himself and looked out the window above it. Snow was falling steadily. It was Christmas Eve and it would be a white Christmas. Normally this was a thought that would give him joy. This was the time of year he loved the most. Christmas cheer usually ran through his veins, but this year the whole holiday was shadowed by his suspicions. When he looked out the window, the snow only seemed confining.

He'd had enough. Detective work was hard work; he could only imagine how much harder it would be as an adult. Sanford needed his case to be closed. He needed a verdict, and he still begged for it to be *not guilty.*

He heard his father wrestling in his sheets, moaning awake and rising to life. Despite the weather and the holiday, the mail must be delivered. Sanford knew what he had to do. He knew it since that night he saw his father in the shed.

He tip-toed out of the bathroom and past his parents' bedroom. The bedsprings squeaked as Jonathan got out of bed.

Sanford hurried his pace.

Once he got into his room he slowly closed the door, hoping the hinges wouldn't whine. He left the doorknob turned in his hand and quietly let it latch when the door shut. Jonathan stepped out into the hall right as Sanford did so.

Sanford exhaled in a long sigh, realizing he was holding his breath the whole time.

He climbed back into bed and waited.

The engine to the station wagon fired at 6:30 a.m. It croaked to life with a smoker's cough. Exhaust shot out of the tailpipe and filled the early morning sky.

Sanford looked out the window and watched Jonathan vigorously scrape the windshield with his ice scraper.

The second he leaves... he thought to himself, peering out to his father.

Jonathan stopped clearing the windshield and looked up towards his son's bedroom window. It was as if he could feel Sanford's hatred. It was too dark inside for him to see, but Sanford aired on the side of caution and stepped to the corner of the window.

The car reversed. By the time Sanford looked outside again, the station wagon was already on the road, a trail of exhaust behind it.

He threw on his winter coat like a cape, seeing it in bold cartoon colors as he zipped it up, the word "*ZIP*!" projected in squiggly yellow letters across the comic panel in his mind.

The bedroom door creaked as he slowly opened it, trying to be silent not to wake his mother. He gingerly stepped down the hallway. He was quiet and stealthy, until one floorboard creaked. It was loud, wailing like a ghost. He froze.

Nothing.

He carried on. For he was the hero in his story, and heroes aren't afraid.

Downstairs, he strapped on his boots and walked through the garage, where the light from the outside was shining in. He stood at the door, looking out of its window to the frozen tundra awaiting. He breathed in deep, trying to settle the nervous buzz in his body, and opened the door. The wind shot, throwing the door open and slamming it against the garage wall. The sound was explosive. He waited for the voice of his mother.

Nothing.

He stepped forward into the heart of the cold and closed the door behind him. The wind whistled through his ears, telling him to go back inside before it's too late. But *too late* had already come and gone.

The path through the yard and towards the shed was at his feet. Snow, branches, and debris covered the ground, with trees swaying back and forth, waving at him, taunting—some bent to one side with the weight of snow. Sleet pelted his face from all angles, and the wind pushed him back and forth as if it didn't know which way to blow. His legs were heavy marching forward in the snow.

What am I doing?

Lack of sleep began to wear on his mind. For the past month, his brain had been running on fumes. Delirium tugged at his neurons. He'd had enough, yet he kept going on what felt like an endless voyage; his backyard never seemed so tremendous.

Before he reached the shed he saw her house. The morning sun was just above the horizon and gave enough light to frame its outline.

If something were to happen to her...

The thought pushed him on.

As he got closer to the shed door, a glimmer caught his eye through the trees

A lock.

He grabbed the thick hunk of metal with both hands and hopelessly jerked it back and forth.

Now what? The question seemed insurmountable. His barely formed plan was backed up by a non-existent one. All he had to do was get to the pictures under the floorboard. If he brought them to Ava's father, he would see, and it could all be over. He was the new sheriff after all, and he surely wanted to make a name for himself.

He'd have to walk through the snowed-in woods and hope beyond hope that his father wouldn't come home. But he'd do it, and the sheriff would have to believe him. Ava would see to it. It's all Sanford had to go on.

In his detective stories, souvenirs brought murderers down. Cherished mementos they refused to let go of. Sanford had visions of Ava's father seeing the proof, an actual light bulb glowing above his head. "It was the mailman!" he'd say. "In the study, with the candlestick!"

He shook his head. The fatigue was weighing heavier, confusing him with every passing moment. Doing the only thing he could think to do, he grabbed the nearest rock on the ground. It was small, but heavy in his hands; hard enough to break the glass.

What if I'm wrong? How could I explain breaking the window?

He was statued in place, his arm cocked back with the rock in his hand. The one thing he knew was that he needed to know. He needed his first case to be closed, to move on, to put his personal feelings aside, and simply get to the bottom of it.

He gave himself one last chance.

I could just go back inside, be warm again in my sheets, wait for my mother to wake up, and make us a nice hot breakfast. Maybe some blueberry pancakes with maple syrup oozing off the sides.

It was Christmas Eve after all, and after dinner that night they'd be opening the presents from their parents. Eric would be awake, waiting to hear the jingling bells, the skis of Santa's sled touching down on the roof, and the bountiful hollers of *ho ho ho*, but would fall asleep too soon. They'd wake up to find more presents scattered under the tree, and they'd tear through them like wild dogs.

Did he really have to ruin that?

He took one last glimpse of Ava's house. It may have been Christmas Eve, but the childhood excitement of it seemed distant, belonging to another child, one he felt was slipping away.

The rock crashed through the window, sending the sound of shattering glass into the woods, reverberating among the trees. The rest of the glass crumbled around the frame as he swept it away with his sleeve.

His arm extended, reaching for the lock on the inside. Once he toggled the lock open he became enthralled by the moment. The fantasies had come to life; he was living them. Detective Crow was here. Sherlock Holmes had nothing on him.

Lost in the daydream, he slid his arm back and slashed his exposed wrist on a shard of glass stuck in the window frame like a tiny inverted icicle. He took a second to register the pain, but when he did it sent him flailing back into the snow, where he could do nothing but hold his wound and moan.

He lay there, on his back, swaying back and forth. He became numb, with only his pajama pants and underwear protecting him from the cold.

He glanced down to his arm, more afraid to look at the cut than the cut itself. Around his body, he saw the blood against the white of the snow in swirls and dots.

What if he was seen? Or heard? He rolled over and brought himself to his knees. He needed to see what he was dealing with. With one eye slowly opening, he lifted his mitten and saw red through the blur of his eyelashes. Then he opened both eyes. The cut itself was long, but not as deep as he thought. He prayed he didn't need stitches.

There was a first-aid kit in the shed, he remembered seeing the tiny red cross on a white aluminum box on the day he found the binoculars.

After discarding the rest of the broken glass, he pushed open the empty frame and heaved his body onto the windowsill. The weight was excruciating on his injured arm.

It was warmer than it was outside, but barely. He crawled over to the space heater, turned it on full blast and let the electric heat wash over him.

The sun rose higher, peeking through the broken window and covering the floor with its warm glow. His legs were the first things to begin to thaw. He balled himself up and rolled on to his side, letting the heat push its way into his chest. His breath came easier as exhaustion took hold. Before he knew it, his eyes were shut, his consciousness slipping away to somewhere warm.

When he awoke, he spasmed. Afraid. His body was matted in a layer of sweat. He sat up quickly, wide awake, but mightily confused. The corners of his eyes stung with the dried crust caking its way into his corneas. He rubbed them, trying to focus.

When he opened his eyes again he saw where he was. The sun was still in the midst of its rise; it had barely moved on the shed's floor. Sanford knew he must've slept minutes instead of the hours it felt like.

He surveyed his surroundings. Mouse droppings polluted the floor around him, with the smell of tiny dead things emanating from inside the walls. He pictured their various skeletons, small and fragile.

The patio furniture was in the corner, covered in dust from winter storage. The lawnmower—big and bulky, next to the pool pump covered in a tarp. The things of summer that sat and waited.

Then he came across those three letters. "R.A.C," he said out loud to himself, seeing them stenciled onto the rusty toolbox. He crawled over to it.

He flicked the locks free and opened the lid; the hinges howled, and dust scattered through the air in the rays of sunlight. There wasn't a single tool inside of it, only old black and white photos, all of which were of his father and Aunt Claire as children.

Each photo was of a different age. They started when Claire was a baby, to when she was no more than five. That's where they stopped. He put them back in the toolbox and shut the lid, then stared at those initials, wondering who they belonged to.

He slid the box aside.

The floorboard goaded him. It felt as if those little eyes from the portraits were staring back at him through their shattered frames, their fingernails clawing at the glass. He knelt down and pried at the wood with his bare hands. It took a few good yanks to free the board. He placed it next to the toolbox.

Sanford looked into the hole; into the pure blackness. He imagined his hand creating ripples as he reached into it. His fingers slowly disappeared the further in he reached. The unwelcome thought of a dead, pale hand grabbing his and yanking him into the hole came unbidden.

The thought slipped away as he touched a wooden frame. Underneath it he could feel another, then another, and another; a whole stack of frames.

He began to pull them out, one by one.

Each was of a family—smiling, happy, haunting—preserved in a moment of perfection. He kept reaching in and bringing out others as if it were a magic trick. When all were out he looked around and realized he had propped them up on their stands surrounding himself.

There were eight families all together.

A memory rose from the back of his mind. It was from a few years earlier. Eric was only three, Sanford six. *The Wolfman* was on television one night and Sanford had watched it, much to his father's chagrin. He knew it would terrify him for days, and it had.

There was a poem of folklore that the townsfolk of *Lianwelly* would recite, about how a man with the purest of hearts can be corrupted by the wolf's bite, and when that first moon is at its fullest he will become the monster himself, no matter how pure his heart may be.

The idea gnawed at Sanford, infesting his dreams, turning them into nightmares.

He'd woken up screaming for the third night in a row. Always dreaming of the moment the father killed the wolf-man and watched its dead body transform back to that of his own son's. Jonathan quickly came into the room. It was the first time Sanford remembered being afraid of him.

* * *

"What's wrong, Sanford?"

Jonathan had come in, sitting calmly next to his son in bed.

"Is it the wolf-man again?"

Sanford did nothing but nod, his face bubbling with tears and snot.

"We've been through this, son. He's not real, that was nothing but movie magic. Grown men applying makeup to another grown man, pretending to be a wolf. It's silly, ridiculous. They're playing make-believe. It's not real."

Eric was in the bed next to him crying as well.

"Look, you got your brother scared. You're the oldest, Sanford, you gotta set the standard. Be the one to look up to, not be the one that's afraid of someone else's imagination. Cause that's all movies are."

"But..." Sanford stopped himself.

"But, what?"

"Nothing." He shimmied cowardly under his blankets.

"Sanford..."

"I...I thought I heard the wolf-man scratching under my bed. And I-I heard a howl outside!"

Once the words left his mouth, he felt the heat of embarrassment on his face.

Jonathan took off his horn-rimmed glasses and rubbed at his eyes.

"Look," he sighed. "The howl was nothing but our neighbor's whining dog, who he refuses to take in at night. You know this already, you've heard that dog a thousand times before, and I'm gonna go there in the morning and drag that dog inside myself if I have to, okay? And as for under your bed..."

He'd gotten on his knees. He'd bent down and lifted the sheet, peeking underneath.

"No monsters under here, it's nothing but that mind of yours playing tricks."

"But I heard the scratching, I felt it!"

"No, you didn't, you know why?"

"No!" Sanford sulked.

"Yes you do, now say it."

"I don't want to."

"Sanford, you better say it, now." Jonathan's eyes bored into Sanford's

"Because... monsters aren't real."

"Correct!" Jonathan put his hand on his son's shoulder and settled him back into bed.

"Now, the last thing I'm going to say about this is the truth. Monsters. Are. Not. Real. But, evil is..."

"There are bad people out there Sanford and it's important that you know they exist. Murderers, rapists, and pedophiles; these are the true monsters of the world. They don't have fangs or horns, and they're not weakened by silver or sunlight. They are just like you and me, walking around wearing the clothes of a normal man."

"He could be your neighbor, your doctor, the man pumping your gas. He could be your teacher, your friend's parent, your friend. They could be anybody, even you. You may not know it, but one day you might have a certain kind of urge. You might wake up with it for the first time, but at the same time you might realize it was there all along, like another person, whispering ideas in your head."

He paused and stared off into the wall.

Jonathan continued, "The real monster is mankind. We are the most selfish beings on the planet, and we will do anything to feed our needs. And don't get it wrong, son, you don't have to be a murderer to be a monster, you just have to want something bad enough to make it all that matters."

Jonathan arched his back and yawned.

Sanford lay still in bed, frozen with terror.

"So I don't wanna hear no more about the wolf-man under your bed, got it? Good." He kissed Sanford's forehead.

As he walked out of the room—before he shut the door—he looked back at Sanford.

"Goodnight son. I love you."

The door shut and the light was off, drowning the room in blackness

* * *

The shed door burst open. His father stood in the archway. The sun lay on the snow in the background, making the world behind him shimmer. His father was a silhouette; his features, lost in the auroral. Sanford shielded his eyes, squinting past the blinding light.

He clutched the picture frames tightly.

Jonathan stepped forward into the shed, closing the doors behind him.

Bulbs of blue and red flashed across Sanford's eyes as his pupil's refocused.

Jonathan saw his toolbox pushed off to the side. He saw the floorboard removed. He saw Sanford carrying his exposed secret.

Sanford could almost see the fiery temper of his father being stoked.

Then a strange thing happened. Jonathan looked at his son standing there, holding those frames, and his anger seemed to melt away.

"Those don't belong to you, son."

Terror had left Sanford speechless.

"To be honest, they don't belong to me either. You know I could feel your little eyes staring at me through that window that night," he said towering over his son, looking down at him like a giant. He pulled down a lawn chair hanging from the shed's wall on a rusty nail and plopped it down next to the space heater, where he sat and removed his snow-covered hat. His ears were bright red.

"You're scared. I could see that. I would be too if I saw my father doing those things that you saw me do; not comprehending any of it. You're ten-years-old now, right? That's gonna have to be old enough for you to know the truth. Come here, Sanford." He patted his lap for his son to come and sit on it.

Sanford didn't respond; he didn't move.

"Okay, you don't have to sit here, just put those frames down, and grab that toolbox for me. I need to show you something. It's gonna help you understand."

Sanford was curious and scared enough to do as told. He picked up the toolbox and brought it to his father.

Jonathan grabbed it from his son. He held it up and brought it towards his lips. He blew the dust off of it and rubbed his thumb around the initials carved above the lock.

"You know what these initials are?"

Sanford stood motionless; his eyes stared blankly.

"R.A.C, these are my father's initials, your grandfather, Robert Allen Crow. He was a man you never met because he died a long time ago. Which is a good thing, I suppose, because he was a mean son of a bitch. I know you think I could be mean too, but you don't know how truly cruel some people can be. You have a walk in the park compared to how we had it."

He opened the lid and gleamed at the first picture he saw of him and his sister, Claire. Teardrops materialized in his eyes, something Sanford had never seen before.

"Look here, this was my sister, Claire, your Aunt Claire. She was everything to me, Sanford. I was her older brother, her protector, kinda like you are with Eric. But I let her down."

Sanford watched the picture shake in his trembling hands. Somehow, Sanford couldn't help but feel bad for him.

"One time, I musta been... I don't know, seven? Yeah, so she was three. Anyway, I picked her up and did the helicopter. You know, where I hold her from the armpits over my head and spin around? Like I used to do to you. She would giggle so much from it. But this one time I guess the laughter was too much, and her bladder exploded, and she just peed right into my face," he said with a growing smile.

"But don't get me wrong," he said. "It wasn't funny at the time. I mean I had piss in my mouth and was pretty pissed about it. But you see, it's the memories like that which are the funniest to recall," he said and thought for a second. "Remember that, Sanford."

He was waving the picture while he talked—animated in his stories—and brought his attention back to the toolbox as he grabbed another photo. The lines in his face darkened, becoming deeper, disintegrating his smile as if it were never there.

"She was five in this photo," he said. "She was never in one older than this."

He sat quietly for what felt like an eternity, with seemingly his mind elsewhere, intramurally adrift.

"Wh-what happened to her?" Sanford managed to ask.

"I found out," he said, still disoriented.

"Found out what?"

"I noticed the bruises. They looked like camouflage on her legs, with greens, yellows, blacks, purples. I'd hear his footsteps at night, marching down the hall towards her room. But I didn't believe it for the longest time, I couldn't. Until the day I had to believe my eyes."

"We were hosting a family gathering. A graduation, a communion, a baptism? Something along those lines. It was hot as hell. Sticky. What I do remember was at the end of the party I couldn't find Claire anywhere. I saw my mother. She was alone, sitting in the sun with a vodka drink in her hand, and a stoned look on her face. She wouldn't respond when I shook her arm and asked where Claire was. She only looked at me from behind those dark shades over her eyes, and I swear I could see the terror in them, even through that shelter of tinted glass."

"By the time I found Claire it was too late. She was in our father's work shed, crying with her head buried in her knees. My father took her in there, in the middle of the day, in the middle of a party, like it was nothing to be concerned about. I stayed with her the rest of the day. It was that night I confronted him. I told him how I'd kill him if he ever touched her again. But my father was a huge, imposing, and at that point an inebriated beast of a man. A threat from a nine-year-old was comical to him. I remember him laughing as he raised his fist and..."

Jonathan brought his fist against his knee. His mouth was contorted downward, his eyes were sunken in his face.

"I never knew someone could hit that hard."

He looked back at the picture of Claire. In it, she wore a white dress with white socks and black shoes. She had a sun umbrella in her hand, casting her face in a scattered shadow while her body glowed from the light. Her blond hair, white as ivory in the colorless photo.

"Claire got involved. She ran up to him and kicked him in the shin, hard enough to make him stop his attack on me and focus it on her. He grabbed her with one hand by her shirt and flung her like a rag doll. I watched her in the air, almost mesmerized that she could fly like that. But then... then she came down. Her head crashed right into the corner of the coffee table."

"We all stopped and looked at her laying there—lifeless. My mother finally snapped to life and broke into hysterics. She ran over to Claire and held her in her arms. Then something in me snapped as well. It was like a switch got turned on in my brain. I picked up the fire poker slowly, so he wouldn't hear. While he stood, staring at Claire's body on the floor, I swung with everything I had, connecting the poker with the back of his skull. He didn't know what happened. He barely flinched. He more or less swayed there for a second and touched the back of his head with his hand. Then he fell to his knees in a stupid surrender, shocked by all the blood on his hand."

"I could feel my blood bubbling in my veins. I'm not gonna lie to you, son… it felt good. I think that's what scared me more than anything else. But when I went back to Claire, I knew she wasn't sleeping. You see, the dead have a different look to them, an empty look, like her body was only a body, and not her's anymore, like she became just another object in the room."

"By the time any help came, they were both gone. My mother too was unresponsive. I kept trying to shake her so she could hold me, but she wasn't there anymore. I ended up in an orphanage and foster care. From one shitty family to the next. My whole family got broken, and I used to think they were perfect, naive as that was. Now… I collect those," he said and pointed at the family portraits Sanford had stacked on the ground. "You see, it helps me to know that there are good families out there, like I wanted ours to be. I envy them, Sanford."

For the first time since the whole thing began Sanford looked at his father as something other than a monster; he saw him as something the monster left behind.

"So… you didn't… hurt them?" Sanford asked.

"Hurt who?"

"The… those families."

"Hurt them? Of course not. Sanford, what is it you think I do?

Sanford rubbed the back of his neck embarrassingly.

"I have a hard time letting go of the past, son, but I promise you I try," his voice was weary. His eyes gleamed in a film of tears.

"I'm sorry Dad. I don't know what I was thinking."

Jonathan kneeled beside his son and kissed him on the forehead.

"I'm sorry too, Sanford."

They stood in silence, caught in an awkwardly vulnerable moment.

"What are you doing home, anyway?" Sanford asked as he wiped his eyes with the sleeve of his jacket. "I thought you had to work?"

"Everything is shut down," Jonathan said and stood up. "We're about to get the worst storm in ages. They declared it a state of emergency. Listen, it's Christmas Eve, and I want nothing more than to spend it with my family. How about you?"

He placed his hand on Sanford's shoulder.

"Yeah, me too," Sanford said and smiled. He realized through all of this, he'd almost let the holiday pass him by.

It was Christmas, and he began to feel like a kid again.

Chapter 9

The record player hissed as the needle laid into the groove. Nat King Cole bellowed out through the speakers. When Sanford heard his voice, it surely felt like Christmas again. Sanford was wrapped up in his red and green flannel robe. He wore it annually, only on Christmas Eve and Christmas morning. Each year he would grow a little taller and the sleeves would inch a little more up his arms. This year was no different; his spastic growth had made him look oafish. But he wore it anyway; he was a creature of habit after all, and tradition was the hardest habit to break.

Jonathan wore a green turtleneck sweater and swayed to the music as he diced onions. Tears filled his eyes. He stared out of the kitchen window, seemingly lost in the winds full of swirling snow. It was the rain in the forecast that had the town worried. Ice could encase the power lines, possibly sending them into the dark ages for Christmas.

"Sanford? How about you check the oven, see if the thermometer popped up on the turkey," Grace said, swinging hip to hip with Jonathan.

"It popped! It popped!" Sanford shouted, his mouth was watering from the sight of it. His appetite had been nonexistent the past few months, but on Christmas Eve it came rushing back. Everything around him had settled; he felt like he could eat for days and sleep for years. The nightmare was finally over.

They crowded around the table. The aroma of holiday decadence filled the air. The turkey gleamed in the tray. Green beans, mashed potatoes, and stuffing with gravy. A pecan pie sat cooling on the kitchen counter; the steam, constantly rising from it. Sanford watched his father sharpen the knife. He sipped his apple cider, savoring the tart taste. His whole body tingled in that moment. It was Christmas and everything felt right.

Jonathan stood at the head of the table and carved the turkey. The knife slid through the meat like butter. His eyes as voracious as his appetite. He stood tall, poised like a butcher.

They feasted, joyfully talked and laughed. Jonathan told stories of hearing the reindeer prancing on his roof as a child, and the footsteps of Santa Clause as he waddled towards the chimney. He gave Sanford a wink so Eric wouldn't see.

"But even if you do hear him tonight, or any bump or sound that you think could be him, you can't get up and check. Because if you see Santa, he'll know, and he won't leave you one single present. It's all part of his magic. So make sure you go to bed early tonight!"

"You kiddin'?" Eric said. "I'll go to bed now if I get more presents!"

They all laughed.

After dinner, they sat in the living room, where the fireplace was lit. Sanford felt the heat radiating on his face as he lay on his stomach. He rolled over next to the tree and put his head underneath it, staring into the vast green pines, illuminated by the multicolored lights bouncing like the Aurora Borealis across a clear night's sky.

Grace walked in, gingerly holding two glasses of wine. She handed one to Jonathan, who had Eric nestled in his lap. Her hand ran across the back of his shoulders and she planted a kiss on his lips.

Sanford looked back at his father and saw the fire reflecting off his horn-rimmed glasses. It danced in them, and even though Sanford was warm from the fire, he somehow felt a chill pulsating through his body. His father's face was expressionless as he began to whistle. Then he transitioned to singing: "Silent night... Holy night..."

Outside the wind wailed, as if it were trying to sing along with him. They could hear the ice against the house; the snow had changed to sharp freezing bullets. It seemed like at any minute the windows would shatter and the ice would fill the living room, freezing them where they sat.

"Are we all right in here, Jon?" Grace asked.

He didn't respond. Instead, he kept on singing.

"All is calm... All is bright."

"Jon?"

Eric was asleep in his lap. His father's arm lay stiffly on the chair, while his other one carelessly held the wine glass. Grace gave up trying to talk to him; it was a trance she seemed familiar with.

Regardless of what his father had told him, something in the back of Sanford's mind wouldn't let him relax fully, and couldn't help but feel his Christmas joy slowly slip away.

The sky lit up with vibrant flashes, followed by what sounded like a cannon. The bay window flashed with bright blue.

The power went out as if a chord was pulled. The only source of light in the room was the fire.

"All is calm... All is bright." Jonathan now talked instead of sang.

"Jon, the transformers blew. The power went out," Grace said, concerned.

He ignored her. His eyes were glued to the fireplace. Eric stirred restlessly in his lap.

"Jon? Did you hear me?"

His fingernails dug into the arm of the chair.

"Jon?"

"Yes Grace, I know, goddammit!" he said, erupting out of his trance. "The radio said power outages were guaranteed. We're just gonna have to suffer Christmas in the dark."

"Suffer?" Sanford asked.

"I meant celebrate," he responded, with a hint of sarcasm.

He moved in front of Sanford, above the fire. He stood still as the fire swayed, causing his shadow to move without him, almost as if it wasn't a part of him at all. For the first time since that morning, Sanford once again was afraid.

Chapter 10

Sanford dreamed about a boy that night. It wasn't a boy he recognized until he woke up and remembered the picture of his father and Aunt Claire. The boy was Jonathan, just about the same age as Sanford.

In the dream, everything surrounding him was black and shadowed. The world was quiet except for the sound of dripping. Sanford sat in bed shaking under the covers; he could see his own breath escaping from his mouth. *DRIP, DRIP, DRIP.* The sound was pestering. He covered his ears with his hands. When the boy stood over him he saw his wrists slit wide, gaping like eyes. Blood carpeted his hands. The floor—no longer visible—had become a lake of blood. The boy lunged.

Sanford woke up, feeling as if he crashed into his mattress after falling from a cliff. He was disoriented and sweating profusely, with no blankets on; he had kicked them off.

He looked at the clock; it was three in the morning. The only sounds were from the heavy wind and falling ice outside. It was Christmas morning, but his Christmas spirit was long gone.

Eric snored like always, a sound that made Sanford feel more at ease. He grabbed the blankets and tried to fall back to sleep, but he could only toss and turn. His mind raced. Thoughts with no solidity came and went, exhausting him.

Before he knew it, he woke to the sound of squeaking springs. It was morning. The sun was out and lit up the room. Eric was jumping up and down on the bed.

"It's Christmas, Sanford!" he screamed. "It's Christmas!"

He ran over to his brother and shook him until he was fully awake. "Come on, get up! You smell it? Bacon! Mom made bacon!"

"It smells burnt," Sanford said, groggily.

"Mmmm crispy," Eric said. "I'm going out—you coming?"

"Go ahead, I'll be there in a minute."

Eric ran off in a blur, his one-piece pajamas gone in a flash of green. Sanford couldn't help but smile. It helped the memory of that dream float away, becoming a fuzzy recollection. Sanford got up and put on his annual robe, letting the warm flannel hug him.

Why is it so cold in here? He thought. His father usually had the wood-burning stove overly stuffed on winter mornings, and the heat would drift through the house, making it a sauna.

He stretched and yawned. Sanford took one step towards the bedroom door—then he heard it.

A scream.

His mother's scream.

He froze. It was over almost as soon as he'd registered it.

Sanford slowly walked towards the opened door. He stood at the doorway. The hallway never seemed so long; the kitchen and living room loomed ahead. One step and the floorboard moaned. He stepped back, hoping it would erase the sound from existence.

"Hello?" Sanford called out in a mouse-like voice.

No answer.

He tip-toed down the hall.

A breeze washed over his parched skin, cooling it. If he weren't so afraid it would've felt nice. But instead, it felt wrong and out of place.

Why is a window open?

"Mom?" he croaked.

No answer.

The portraits on the wall were tilted in dramatic angles, as if an earthquake had shaken the house. There was a large blank spot on the wall. A portrait was missing. Sanford knew which one it was. It was from a few Christmases ago and the four of them were gathered around the tree, staring blindly at the flash from Jonathan's camera, sitting on its tripod. In it, Sanford was looking off to the side and Eric blinked his eyes. It was far from perfect.

"Eric?"

No answer.

There was only the hiss of the record player, as the needle tried and failed to find a groove. Beyond that was a muffled sizzling sound coming from the kitchen.

Sanford felt his adolescent hairs standing, his heart thudding—an electric charge through his core.

The closer he got to the kitchen the more he gathered his senses. The smell of bacon still hung in the air. He turned the corner and entered the kitchen. A pan was sitting on the stove, with the gas turned on high. Fat sizzled in the pan with only black meat to cling to. Sanford turned off the burner and listened as the house got quieter.

He called out one last time.

"D-Da-Dad?"

The wheeze of the record player stopped. Sanford strained his ears, flexing muscles he never used. He wanted to hear anything: a whisper, a giggle, something to break the spell. But there was nothing.

Sanford stood at the kitchen door; the one that swung open like an old saloon's. He was waiting; for what, he was not sure. But he was afraid to open it.

Is this a dream?

He begged that it was and that he would soon wake up. But the cold was too sharp, the fear was too extraordinary.

The sound of whistling broke the quiet. Sanford jumped from the high-pitched noise. It came from his father, beyond the closed swinging door. Sanford pressed his head against the wood and pictured him sitting there.

He recognized the melody. *Silent Night.* His father whistled it in the same deranged way he had the night before.

Sanford breathed in deep and pushed the door open an inch, holding his breath as if he was plummeting underwater. He prayed and pleaded to any god that could hear his thoughts. All he wanted for Christmas was to open the door and see his family sitting around the tree, waiting for him. His mother would turn when he'd walk in, the smile of Christmas morning on her face and holding a cup of hot cocoa for him.

He cracked the door further, feeling the nerves in his body twisting into fisherman knots. At first, all he could see was feet.

Why would Mommy sleep on the floor?

The hinges squealed over his father's song.

Sanford froze in the doorway, leaving it ajar. He was afraid to move; petrified to make another sound.

"Sanford?" Jonathan's voice carried through the house.

A lump formed in Sanford's throat. He tried to swallow it down but felt he might choke. His hand shook on the door.

"Come!"

The authority in his father's voice was impersonal. Robotic. It was a command to a dog. Sanford obeyed. He had no say in the matter and nowhere else to go. He needed to know. He needed everything to be okay.

The first thing he saw was her. Except she didn't look like his mother anymore. She lay on the floor with one hand tucked behind her head, as if she were watching television propping her head up to see. Blood filtered through her fingers helplessly. Her eyes stared blankly at Sanford with no thought or emotion behind them—the eyes of a doll.

Sanford could feel his father watching him. He saw more blood from her chest, her head, and stomach. She was motionless.

Dead.

Jonathan sat in his favorite chair with his legs crossed beneath him, watching his son. A hammer rested on the right arm of the chair, a knife was run through the left. A shotgun lay at his feet.

Sanford saw Eric. He seemed smaller than usual, miniature, curled up in a ball and underneath the tree, surrounded by presents.

Sanford went over to him. He collapsed to his knees, next to his brother, crushing a long rectangular gift.

It's probably a sweater. Mom always gets me clothes. Sanford thought. *She knows I hate that.*

Eric was breathing quickly. His arms were wrapped around his knees. His face wet with tears.

Sanford placed his hand on his little brother's shoulder. He pleaded to God to stop this. But at that moment he felt God was nowhere in that room, or in that house. God was gone from the world.

He looked up at his father, whose eyes stared wildly into his. Unblinking. Yet to say a word to each other, Sanford's eyes said it all. *Why?*

Suddenly, Jonathan gripped the shotgun, whirled it around, and pointed it at Sanford.

Sanford stared into the barrel, into those two long holes running like tunnels. There was no light at the end.

"I never wanted this," Jonathan said. His voice was groggy, as if it were the first words he'd spoken all morning. "Not here... This is your fault, Sanford... You did this."

In one motion Jonathan fell to his knees and gripped the shotgun upright. He was no more than ten feet in front of his children, listlessly staring into Sanford's eyes. His chin rested on top of the barrel.

"Maybe none of them were perfect... maybe there's no such thing."

Jonathan closed his eyes and pulled the trigger.

Sanford covered his ears from the blast.

When Jonathan fell, Sanford saw the missing portrait of their family, standing on the end table next to his father's chair. It was splattered with blood. In it, Jonathan's smile was wide and infectious, with his eyes gleaming behind his horn-rimmed glasses. The same ones that he wore now.

PART TWO
DELIRIUM

1994

CHAPTER 11

It was a strange case, and Detective Crow had lost all hope in solving it. He put his mind inside the killer's. Let the shadows creep over his thoughts. They've been there before.

The killer's pattern was predictable. The only way to complete the cycle was to be where Detective Crow was at that very moment... waiting.

He didn't like using Abigail as bait, but desperate times call for desperate measures, as he was overly fond of saying. She didn't object; she knew what she was in for. The maniac had butchered her sister and she wanted nothing more than to put him behind steel bars, or better yet, deep into the ground.

The alley was confining, slick, and streaked with oil marks. It reminded him of a cave. Abigail stood there shaking, nervously puffing on a cigarette. She'd dressed for the occasion. Six-inch stilettos. Fishnet stockings. Dressed as a prostitute. Dressed like her sister.

Loud footsteps echoed down the alley. Abigail was afraid; Detective Crow could see that. His finger caressed the trigger on his standard-issue Glock. *Don't worry, Abby. I won't let anything happen to you.*

A dark figure appeared: broad shoulders atop of a muscular torso, with slim, long legs and wide oversized feet. Only his face was covered by the dark cast of the alley.

It's him, Crow knew it. Intuition told him so. The man was draped in black; his long raincoat flapped as he walked. This is when most men would feel the panic creep into their consciousness, screaming "*RUN!*" But Detective Crow lived for these moments. He thrived on them.

The stranger crept closer to Abby's exposed back. He could see something in the suspect's hand, shiny and pointy.

This is it, Crow thought. The man in black lunged, knife in hand. Crow emerged from behind the dumpster with his gun raised.

"Get down!" he screamed to Abby, but she didn't move. She couldn't. She saw the man—the same man that murdered her sister. She froze.

All she could do was scream.

Detective Crow got off one shot; one loud *BANG!* The sound pierced through the alley and trailed off. The man turned.

And everything went black. Silence. And a sound rose in the distance: heavy guitars, loud drums. *"Get vertical! Get vertical! It's the power of Dew!"* Teenagers then screamed into the camera and were drinking *Mountain Dew.*

Sanford shot upright in his seat. The soda jingle struck him like ice water to the face. Reality came rushing back. He had been lost again, his mind adrift in a TV movie.

Most of the time when he'd watch a detective movie or show he'd transform himself into the main character in his mind. He'd perform the heroic acts, recite the cool lines, affect the same bravado. In those moments, he was everything he wanted to be. But an itch on the back of his neck, his back stiffening up from his slouch, or the scratchy cushion under his ass would too quickly bring him back to reality in his one-bedroom apartment.

Popcorn bits and kernels littered his shirt and the couch. He could still taste the salt on his lips and feel the butter slick on his fingers. He ran his hand through his thick and wavy hair. Then he moved on to scratching his beard; it had gone from trim to shaggy in record time and itched like hell.

The fantasy had lasted longer than usual this time, taking him deeper than it ever had before. He believed therapy had a hand in that, opening doors that were meant to be shut and unlocking memories that should've been caged forever.

It was five in the morning, and Sanford had been awake for two hours. Instead of confronting the day ahead, he had put on the television. The sun outside was yet to rise, and the only light in his apartment was that from the movie.

Detective Crow couldn't even pass a goddamn psych exam, he thought to himself. He turned the television off; it had started to depress him. The coffee in his cup had cooled to room temperature but he sipped it anyway.

A half-eaten slice of chocolate cake lived on the coffee table. It was part of his birthday celebration, which he'd had with Sadie. Turning thirty-five felt like nothing to celebrate, but it was an excuse to be with her. The gray in his beard had become his calendar, and he knew it was almost time to shave. Maintaining a respectful appearance was only done for her sake, so as not to embarrass her any more than he already had.

He wouldn't see her for another three days. Every other weekend was simply not enough. Through the times spent without her, he could feel himself slipping.

It's only three more days.

But that's another seventy-two hours.

Which equals another four-thousand-three-hundred and twenty minutes.

Jesus Christ, that's forever!

The lamp was just in reach. He turned the knob and a blue flash erupted from under the shade. It blew. His heart began to palpitate. The darkness in the room seemed to grow.

The phone... I need to call her. Now! He picked up the phone, disregarding the clock. He had her number memorized. The phone rang twice and went straight to her answering machine.

"Hi, you've reached the offices of Dr. Diane Wesley. We're sorry but the offices are closed at this time. If you would like to—"

He hung up.

The clock said 5:14 AM. His session with Diane was at nine.

He'd been walking on a tightrope since their last session when she asked him to do something he was yet to even try. A stack of blank pages sat on the coffee table in front of him—next to the old cake—with a pencil lying across it. It had sat there untouched for seven days.

How could she ask me to write it down?

It was absurd to him. How could writing down what happened possibly help? She had him write about other moments in his life that he chose to forget: embarrassing moments in school, sexual failures, but she had never asked this of him. This was too much.

He supposed he knew it was all leading to this moment. She used his own hobby against him, insisting that he write to unlock the trauma instead of to escape it. The more Sanford thought about doing it, the more he knew...

A picture of Sadie sat on the end table, her eyes followed him as he moved. She had her mother's eyes, blue and animated like the bottom of a flame. But she had his dark hair, his nose, his ears, his everything else. He was just happy that she didn't have his memories.

It was his goal as a father to give her only good ones. It was a difficult goal, becoming harder and harder to do.

But he tried. For her, he would try his best.

The pencil was in his hand, lazily dangling. He let his mind drift.

It was Christmas morning. 1969. The last Christmas Sanford would ever celebrate. He heard a sound, and he knew it was the only way he could start the story. The last sound his mother ever made, followed by the worst sound of all.

Deafening silence.

He wrote.

Chapter 12

The snow flurried steadily outside. It reminded Sanford of that day; every time it snowed it reminded him.

His fingernail dug into his cuticle and he began to peel away a raw layer of skin. It was a compulsion he developed in his early teens, picking and biting until the skin came loose and blood formed, mixed with a sharp and adequate pain.

It made him uneasy to be in her office, it always had. *Shouldn't you feel comfortable in therapy?* His eyes stayed fixed on the window as white flakes fell from the sky.

"I should have moved to California."

"What was that?" Diane asked, and Sanford stared at her like she was in his head. "Did you just whisper something?"

Did I?

He was always getting lost in his mind. It was bad when it snowed, and it was even worse around Christmas. Moving to New York hadn't helped. But he'd established himself in Peekskill; he had a job, an apartment, and a beautiful daughter who was his whole reason for trying, for existing.

I wonder what Sadie is learning in school tod—

"Sanford?" Diane broke his train of thought.

"What? Oh, did I? Oh, I was just...just saying, I don't think I can do it."

"You can do it. You already wrote it, right? That must've been the hard part, no?" Diane said, sitting in an armchair across from him. Her black, pinstripe jacket with those enormous pads hugged her shoulders, where her black hair ended. A matching skirt dangled inches above her knees. Sanford wondered how she'd walk through the snow in such an attire. *And in those heels?* She looked good though, as always.

Her notepad was in her hands. She looked at Sanford through her green eyes, then jotted something down. That always annoyed him. How can you have a conversation with someone who's always judging you?

"What'd you just write?" he asked.

"Don't be concerned with what I wrote, this is about what you wrote. Writing is what helps you, Sanford. You know this. We know this. This is important, the most important breakthrough we've made yet in our sessions. But you still have to face it, and reading it out loud is the best way to do that."

He leaned back on the couch which was overly stiff. He stretched his neck and looked around. Her office was pristine; everything was in perfect order. From her psychology degrees on the wall, hanging at a perfect right angle, to her pencils and pens standing upright in a cup on her desk. Sanford had to fight the urge to rip the story he wrote in half and storm out of her office.

Breathe, he said to himself, *just breathe.*

"It's been twenty-five years, Sanford, and you've only moved on from what happened to you, you've never faced it. I think that's the main contribution to your psychogenic amnesia. If you—"

"That sounds like a disease," he interrupted.

"It's not a disease, Sanford, just a state of mind right now. It's only a clinical term: don't be afraid of it. I believe if you can move past your past, those blackouts of yours will stop." she said, and then bit her lip, afraid to push him too far. "First, just tell me how you wrote it."

"With a pen."

"Don't be a smart ass, that's not what I meant. When did you write it? Where? How? In what format?"

"This morning," he said looking at his watch, "about three and a half hours ago."

She sighed. "Did you write in the third person again?"

"No," he said, "the first."

"Okay, great! That's a humungous step. Did you think about doing that, or did you just start writing?"

Since his younger days of reading comics, the adventures of good versus evil had always intrigued him. He remembered the first day he'd made his own. *Where was I?* Sitting at a table surrounded by children. There were adults too: men and women wearing... *white?* He'd made boxes with rudimentary sketches inside. Word bubbles popped as his caped hero flew around. It was then he realized the power of imagination. The escape. And soon writing had become it.

He wasn't sure what he was angrier at: the fact that Diane had him write for therapy or the fact that it worked.

"Well?" she said, breaking the silence. She motioned to the stack of papers next to him on the couch.

"Fine," he said and inched over to where it lay and picked it up. It sat heavy in his lap. He ignored the weight and grabbed the first page. He bit down on his lip, just hard enough to taste the copper tang of blood.

Christmas morning started with my mother's scream, and ended with my own...

When he finished, he put his story down on the coffee table in front of him. His hands shook and the pages were wet from his sweaty fingers. Diane watched Sanford come back from where he was.

"It's hard for me to remember what happened after that," Sanford said. "When I try, it's like... my brain won't let me. And as far as the dialogue: I think it's more or less what was said. Who knows..."

"That's okay," Diane said quietly. "It must have been hard enough for you to write what you could. Things like this shouldn't be simple. You're in a tug of war against yourself, your own subconscious, for your own sanity."

"So you think I'm insane?"

"No, of course not. If I thought that you'd be somewhere far less pleasant than this office of mine, and wearing a jacket far less comfortable than that one." She smiled.

Sanford couldn't help but smile back; he liked the way her dimples punctured her cheeks.

I wonder what her lips taste like, he thought and an image of Ava Potter swam in his head. He hadn't seen or even imagined her face since he was ten.

"Look, we've made some incredible progress today, Sanford," Diane said.

Sanford's visions of Ava slowly dissolved as the room he was sitting in crept back into focus. "But..." she continued.

There's always a *but.*

"...I think we should dig further. Now, I know how you feel about trying this, but it could be the key to help you face your demons and mend your wounds."

"You're talking about hypnosis again?" he said, and his body tensed up. "Why would I want to face my past? Shouldn't I just move on from it?"

"Just look at what you wrote. When you face your fears you can relieve yourself of them. It's a form of exposure therapy and it can help to heal you. You should want to be healed for Sadie, no? You need control, Sanford, for her sake, you even said so yourself."

"You sound like my ex-wife."

"Well, your ex-wife is only trying to put her life back together. And if you want Sadie to be a bigger part of yours then you need to do the same."

He thought about that, but mostly he thought about *her*. Sadie, every time her name is mentioned a glimmer of light breaks through his clouded mind. *Are you that afraid? You shouldn't be afraid of anything anymore.* It was her he needed to be strong for. Fearless. She was the reason he was here in the first place.

"Okay," he said.

"Okay? Just like that?"

"Yes, if you think it could help... I need to get better. I had another dream last night. This time... when I woke up... I was punching the bed frame." He showed his hand, which he'd kept hidden. It was bruised, with several tiny cuts on his knuckles.

"Eric again?"

"Yes, Eric again."

She looked up at the clock, calculating what they had time for. Her nose crinkled.

"Well, time's up for this session. I'm sorry, Sanford, but we're going to have to discuss this next week. Maybe by then you'll have finished the rest of your story. And I do believe that with the hypnosis we could put an end to those dreams as well."

You mean nightmares.

"I hope so," he said.

But *hope* had lost its meaning. Hope was for children, and along with his childhood, hope had been lost.

Chapter 13

The roadwork had started very early. Drills plummeted through concrete, sending tiny tremors through the whole house. The brutish voices of the road workers bellowed in the background.

As Frank lay there, hearing those voices carry through his bedroom window, he watched the clock flash—4:48—and groaned, sandwiching his head between his pillow, but he couldn't drown them out.

"Hey, Billy! I got one for ya'. What tastes good on pizza but not on pussy?"

Frank could imagine many things not tasting great on it. Pretty much every topping that normally goes on pizza he'd prefer not to be on a pussy.

So let's see... It's a joke, so pepperoni, sausage, onions, peppers, out. What? Cheese? Sure, that would be pretty disgusting, but no, not good enough.

"I don't know, what?" number two asked.

He concentrated, the answer floating on the periphery of his mind, and sharpening his focus, cutting through the morning fog. His lips formed a smile as he lay in the dark bedroom. He had a way of silencing the world when he needed. It's what made him the successful detective he was, with the most solved cases in the district.

"*Crust,*" he whispered to himself and chuckled.

"What, hon?" Nancy said, waking.

"Crust!" the first man shouted, and the rest of the crew laughed.

"Nothing, Nance. Go back to sleep," Frank said with half a smile. And just like that, she was snoring again.

Morning routines were the same every day. He'd wake up, tell Nancy to go back to sleep (because it's not like she had anything to wake up for), pull his feet out of the blankets, and plant them in the slippers he had set up perfectly perpendicular to the bed. It was his days in the military that instilled such monotony. He had weeded out most of the habits, but his mornings were filled with robotic motions like his waking mind was on autopilot. Grind the coffee beans, brew the pot, take your medication, make the eggs, eat the eggs, sip the coffee, read the paper, take a shower, brush your teeth, etc.

Frank Waters had become a bore. He knew it and his wife knew it more. Predictable as the rising sun. He supposed he'd lost something along the way, losing the biggest piece of himself when he lost *her*. But she had been dead for thirty years now, and that seemed like a lifetime ago. Now he had Nancy, and he did love her, sure, but not enough to try.

The house they lived in was built in the twenties. It stood on an angle, as if it had one drink too many. The exterior paint would peal, leaving black sickly patches underneath. Every time the wind blew, flakes of carnal white blew through the sky like dead skin. Frank had no desire to repaint it.

His favorite room was the bathroom. Mostly because of the window, which was inside the shower.

The shower was his domain. For him, it was a time of self-reflection. Warm water washed over him; the suds would cling to his short, stocky body and near-paunch. The military gave him many deep-rooted habits, but exercise was not one he maintained. Boot camp had left that foul taste in his mouth. It was then that he'd have his morning cigarette, leaning out of the shower window, which gazed out to his small backyard and beyond, where the Hudson River flowed between the mountains. Even then, in the winter, he'd have that window open. Cold air rushed through as hot water rained over him.

It was his one of three cigarettes a day (on a good day). The first was always in the shower, more ingrained than a cup of coffee. The second would be on the job; if he'd stumbled into a new case or had to revisit an old. Sometimes it woke him up to some new detail, or took his mind in a new direction on a stale case. His third and final cigarette (on a good day) always came in the car ride home, in quiet contemplation of what the human animal is capable of.

Deer grazed in the backyard as he puffed away. Normally, the sight of deer meant nothing to Frank, especially in that part of New York where they could amass like a plague. One of the deer felt Frank staring and turned around. Its unblinking eyes peered into his like black, polished pebbles. Frank kept his eyes fixed on the creature, wanting to win the game.

"Frank!" Nancy called out from behind the bathroom door. He jumped from the interruption and his cigarette fell into the stream of water. The deer scurried off.

"What?"

"Phone call, it's the station."

"Be right out."

"Uh-huh."

He stepped out of the shower, dripping wet, and put the towel around his waist. Nancy waited on the other side of the door, holding the phone with its extra long cord that stretched from the kitchen to the bathroom.

Frank opened the door and grabbed it.

"Yeah?" he said into the phone and listened.

Nancy watched her husband, soggy and dripping water all over the bathroom floor, which she'd no doubt have to clean. His chest hair was wet and curling, his gut protruded and swam into his love handles, his bald spot shone from the overhead light.

"My god," he said. "I'm on my way." He handed the phone back to Nancy and shut the door.

"What's going on?" she asked.

"Work," he responded.

"Come on, Frank, you can tell me more than that."

"Jesus, Nance."

"Please..."

"Fine, but I don't like telling you this stuff. It's not healthy."

Frank took a deep breath.

"A family was murdered, okay?"

"A family?" she said, shocked, but wanting more.

"Yeah, looks like the father did it, but they need me to come in and confirm."

He waited for Nancy's follow-up question. He didn't like how curious she was about such things. To him, it screamed of desperation. For most of the day, all she did was watch television and eat. It was one talk show after the next, with white trash, would-be fathers, baby-mama drama, and cheating spouses caught on camera. Occasionally she would clean and then eat, or go shopping... then eat. Frank knew it was hypocritical to judge, his weight was starting to get out of control, but she still held the belt in the heavyweight division; at least he got some exercise on the job.

"Wow, how could someone kill their own family?"

"I don't know."

He listened as she walked away, and thought about how untrue that was. He did know; he'd felt how cold some hearts could be.

Chapter 14

Traffic moved inch by inch going south towards the city. The rat race, stuck in a crawl. Sanford drove north, without a car in front of him.

He had no briefcase to carry, no secretary to greet, no water cooler to stand around and discuss the ball game he hadn't watched from the night before. As he passed their cars he thought about this, and thought about how he would like to have those things, but knew he never could.

He thought about his father, how he blended in and played the role of the everyman. How he'd wave at the residents in town as he delivered their mail; how he fooled them all with a smile on his face. Sanford's own personality prevented him from doing such things. If he waved at a stranger, he'd feel awkward and obtrusive. His hand would be twitchy and his smile crooked.

How'd you do it, Jon?

Jonathan's brand of crazy was his own. Still, he played the role and was never himself unless he was alone. Sanford didn't want to pretend. Playing make-believe was a child's game.

Anytime Jonathan's face entered his mind, it did so with a shotgun underneath it, and his chin pressed against the barrel. Eventually, the image would dissolve, and a new face would appear. The blue eyes of his father would morph into the green of his own, and he'd see his own face resting on top of the gun.

No, not like that. Too messy...

His mind drifted back to the drive, and to his work van, which was also his car. Its rusted, maroon-painted body was wearing thin, and he could feel its malfunctions from under his ass. *Dead Crow Cleanup* in big bold letters, half peeled away, and not to mention the U was completely missing, was emblazoned on the side. He'd take the van to the grocery store, to therapy, to the movie theater; he'd take it to pick up Sadie. He always felt bad about that, especially after she requested he to pick her up a block away from school so her friends wouldn't see her get into "that creepy van."

The commotion of the van was the soundtrack to his drive. The muffler sputtered with smoker's cough. The tires clicked as they spun, slapping their worn-out rubber against the pavement. Sanford gripped the wheel as he thought about his daughter and all of the ways that he failed her. He did so until all that clamor dimmed to the point of nonexistence.

The radio turned on.

It was a song where a man was singing about how he was a loser, baby, so why don't you kill me?

"There, that's better. I don't know how you drive in silence like that, man. I mean we could at least talk, but you'd rather listen to the sounds of this shitty van," Panda said, and Sanford jumped out of his seat, forgetting he was even there, which was generally a hard thing to do.

Panda, or Vic Carol, was a beast of a man. He was large, but not in a muscular way. A layer of blubber coated his entire frame, so no one part of him was fatter than the other; he was just overall *big*, and bearish. That, with his pale, blotchy skin, led to his nickname. He was Sanford's only employee and only friend.

"Sorry, kinda forgot you were here," Sanford said.

"How could you forget that? I'm sittin' right fuckin' next to ya, and I'm as big as the van."

Sanford couldn't help but laugh. "I just get lost in thought sometimes."

"Well, just don't forget you're drivin', cause the airbags won't put a stop to lil ol' Panda here flyin' through the windshield," he said, chuckled, then threw a cigarette in his mouth and lit it.

"Come on, man. I gotta pick up Sadie after school today. The van is bad enough as it is, I don't need her breathing in that shit too."

"Really? It ain't like the smoke will be around in six hours." He took an elongated drag and blew it out.

"I'm not talking about the second-hand, I'm just saying the stench of it. It smells like shit; furthermore, you smell like shit," Sanford said and smiled.

"Ha-ha, fuck you, Mr. High and Mighty because you quit smoking, what, two months ago? I'll hold it out the window, aight?"

"Fine, if she smells it and asks if I've been smoking, I'm blaming you."

"I've never seen someone so afraid of their own daughter, you pussy."

Am I? Sanford thought to himself. *I'm just afraid of losing her.*

The rest of the drive was filled with Panda playing DJ. The conversation dwindled as he jostled the dial back and forth between rock and hip-hop stations, all of which Sanford couldn't bear to hear. He was an eighties metal fan through and through. To him, this new age *grunge* and *gangsta rap* was just a fad, and he'd always say how hair metal was making a comeback.

Then it happened. This time of year it was inevitable. Panda had stopped on the easy listening station, where Christmas music played from Thanksgiving to Christmas night on a twenty-four-hour loop.

They were three-seconds into *The Christmas Song* by Nat King Cole when Sanford screamed, "No!"

He jabbed the power button, punching the radio silent.

Panda looked at him curiously. Sanford was taking deep, ambiguous breaths while a steady stream of panic began to shake his nerves.

"You okay, man?"

He could barely hear the question over the pounding of his heartbeat. It was the first panic attack of the season, and though it was a small one, it was still a nuisance. He gained control of his exterior through breathing methods and counts of six. The jitters had settled down to minor jolts, but his insides were still twisting and turning,

"I'm fine," he finally got out. "Just hate that fucking song."

"Enough said. Turn right up ahead. This is the neighborhood."

Finding the house wasn't too difficult. They were on the prosperous side of Westchester County, and this development they drove through, in particular, shone with considerable wealth. Acres separated neighbors. Gates separated the road from the driveways, and the driveways were more like roads themselves. They saw the house from around a bend. It was in a vast cul-de-sac the size of a baseball stadium. Yellow crime-scene tape riddled its front gate.

Sanford parked at the top of the driveway. Panda got out and walked to the control panel at the gate. He pulled out a folded piece of paper from his pocket, read the code, and typed it in. The crime-scene tape snapped and fell to the ground, dragging open with the gate, which moaned ghoulishly. Sanford pulled the van through, letting Panda hop in and take the ride up the prolonged driveway. The house stood on top of a hill. The driveway seemed to take unnecessary curves and turns to get there.

At the top, it turned into a circle. Sanford parked in front of the path, which led to its castle-like doors.

"You ready?" Sanford asked.

"Always am."

“Start getting the supplies together, I’ll see what we have in store.” He began to walk down the path.

“Go get em’ Detective Crow!” Panda shouted, smiling.

It was Sanford’s tradition. He’d go in alone and check the scene, putting the story together in his head of what went down and how. Usually, around those parts, it was nothing more than suicide or an accidental overdose. But once in a while, they’d get a murder, and those were usually crimes of passion. Sanford would never get to be a real detective, but something about this job got him as close as he could.

Panda watched him as he lifted the tape and walked in.

“Crazy fuck,” Panda said, loud enough for him to hear. He lit another cigarette to give Sanford extra time.

He figured he would need it.

* * *

The smell hit him first. When he opened the door it walloped him in the face. The bodies must have been in there for quite a while, barricaded behind closed doors and withering away while the rest of the neighborhood went on living.

Sanford was never told what happened. When he would get a job like this it would come long after the case was closed and the house was no longer an active crime scene. The facts were available, but he’d never ask for them because he never wanted to know. He’d see how the bodies were drawn in chalk, where the bloodstains were, and interpret the stories they told.

His game was to imagine the details, put them together, and develop a suspect and motive. When he was done he’d make his deduction, then

Panda would tell him how close to the truth he was. His record was 4-18, but that didn't matter to him. It was the stories he loved.

Whoever lived here was rich, he thought and laughed at the obviousness.

Every room was pristine, and he grazed through each one carefully. At the top of the steps and at the end of the hallway were double doors made of oak with golden handles—doors he knew would open up to a nightmare. He opened them and stepped in.

Feathers—the first thing he thought because it was the first thing he saw. The room was covered in them. They stemmed from the bed, covered in dried blood, much like the headboard and far wall. It appeared the pillow had exploded. *As did the head that rested on top of it*, Sanford thought. Bits of skull and brain stained the bed, end table, and a family photo of the three of them: the father, the mother, and a teenage boy. The father wore glasses; Sanford knew it was him from the start.

He was disappointed, to say the least; it didn't take a brainiac to figure out what had happened here. *Jealous lover*, he thought, *only jealousy would cause someone to shoot their lover in the face, so they wouldn't have to see it anymore.* At least his record would advance to 5-18.

From the corner of his eye, he saw a blur of red. The master bathroom's door was open a sliver, and the blood inside was bright against the white marble tiling. He walked towards it, careful not to step on any skull fragments that happened to be on the rug. Most people couldn't make the approach with such calm, but Sanford Crow wasn't like most people. His father's parting gift to him was a life of desensitization. To him, stepping over human bones was as easy as a normal man stepping over shattered glass. It was a minor inconvenience.

He paid little attention to the bathroom, or to the fact that it was bigger than his own apartment. His eyes were drawn to the bathtub. The morning sun crept through the skylight window, accentuating the depth of the tub.

Pools of blood had coagulated on the inside, and on the tiles surrounding it. Dust particles pranced in the air through the beam of sunlight, giving the blood a look of movement.

He knew what happened here. The husband came to his senses of what he'd done. He might've looked in the same mirror Sanford was looking through now, seeing the same tub behind him. He entered it with the gun in his hand.

Sanford looked up at the ceiling—splatters of blood.

He could see it now, the man in the glasses—forlorn—couldn't face his son again. He placed the gun under his chin. Sanford's own chin itched as he turned away from the tub and back towards the mirror above the sink. In its reflection, he saw the man turn his head and look at him, though it wasn't the man from the photo anymore. His once circular glasses turned into horn-rims. His curly hair straightened and shortened.

"This is your fault, Sanford... You did this."

The gun went off and Sanford yelped. He covered his face with his trembling hands, blocking his eyes, but it didn't stop the visions.

"I'm sorry," he whispered to no one at all. When he removed his hands and looked in the mirror his father was gone. There was nothing but an empty, blood-filled tub.

The front door opened with a creak, Panda was coming in.

Sanford turned the sink on and threw his face underneath the rushing water, washing it madly.

"Hey, Crow? You all right?" Panda said in a concerned voice from behind the closed bathroom door. Sanford looked at himself in the mirror, his eyes were mildly bloodshot, and his face a little pale.

"Yeah," he responded, "just got a little sick."

Sanford opened the door and faced him.

"You need to go outside, maybe get some air?"

Sanford shook his head.

"Okay, if you say so, man. You're the boss," Panda responded, knowing not to pry any further. "So, what you got?"

"Murder-suicide. It was a pretty easy one. Husband shot his wife then offed himself in here."

"Ooo! Close but no cookie! It was the wife who did it."

"The... the wife?" Sanford asked, confused. He'd automatically assumed it was the husband.

"Yeah, I read about this one in the paper. I'll still give it to you though; you just got the genders mixed up. Looks like you're what? 5-18?" Panda looked for a glimmer of pride but found none in Sanford's eyes.

"You sure you're okay, man?"

Sanford found himself staring back into the mirror. There he was again, staring back at him through his own eyes. When he moved his father moved as well. He couldn't escape him.

I am him...

His mouth opened wide to a hollow circle as he let out a gasp inches away from the mirror, fogging up the reflection.

Panda stood there and watched, dumbfounded.

"Hey, Crow?"

Sanford didn't respond. He could only hear the acute sound of dripping. He looked for a leak in the faucet; there was none.

"Crow?"

Sanford heard his name from a distance, muffled over the dripping sound. He covered his ears with his hands to silence them. But they were there, louder than ever.

"Sanford!" Panda yelled again and lurched forward, grabbing Sanford by his wrists and removing them from his ears.

Sanford screamed, seeing his reflection in front of him.

In one barbarous thrust, he slammed his head into the mirror, shattering the glass and splitting his hairline open.

"What the fuck, man?" Panda panicked.

Blood trickled down Sanford's forehead, around the bridge of his nose, and crept into the cracks of his lips. His vision blurred as his eyes rolled back. Then Sanford fell towards the ground.

* * *

His eyes crept open; he rubbed at them. The walls around him were covered in posters, stickers, and doodles of random comic book characters in an all-out war with each other. The flannel sheets on the bed were not his own. He inhaled the aroma of incense trying to mask the scent of old weed, mixed with the stale smell of dirty clothes. It was the smell of a teenage boy.

Where am I?

At first, he thought he was in his own room, but from twenty years earlier, when he was fifteen and living in his third foster home, hosted by foster parents who for once weren't total assholes. Though the posters on the wall were of bands he barely knew. *Nine-inch Nails, Alice in Chains, Nirvana*; he knew the latter.

Didn't that guy just kill himself? With that thought, the befuddlement of what happened began to dissipate. He was in the son's bedroom of Mr. And Mrs. Murder-Suicide. With that realization he felt a connection to the kid, who'll be forever changed, joining Sanford's club of lost childhoods.

That seething guilt settled back in, and he quickly jumped up from the bed, hoping the sudden movement might dull the feeling. All it did was bring on the headache. His ears were ringing. He pressed his hands against his forehead to try and subdue the relentless thumping. It stung. He felt a bandage on his head. Two bandaids desperately clung to sweaty skin. Next to him on the bedside table were four *Advil* and a tall glass of water.

Panda...

Sanford slugged them back and swallowed the whole glass of water in two gulps. He hadn't known how long he'd been out. Furthermore, he had no idea how to explain himself to Panda. In fact, he feared the conversation. It felt like a scene in a comic book, when the hero's mask slips off and his long-time friend discovers his true identity. Only instead of being seen as the hero, Panda saw him as the undercover freak he was, hiding among the normal, only being himself when alone.

He hated being alone.

Putting it off wasn't an option. But how much could he say without freaking him out?

If he dove into his upbringing, Panda would probably consider it insane, in a good way. He'd relish the story, repeat it to all of his friends, and his questions would come quick and constant. Sanford got enough of that from Diane; that was another conversation he was not looking forward to having.

The thought of her made him angry. It was all her fault, he felt. If it wasn't for her, poking, prodding, and digging, opening doors that should be welded shut, he wouldn't be on the edge like this; he wouldn't be this close to falling off.

Outside of the boy's bedroom, he heard the sound of scrubbing—Panda, cleaning up the old blood along with the new.

Sanford got up and got himself together the best he could, which was never good enough. He opened the bedroom door and walked down the long and gaudily decorated hallway. The double doors at the end were opened wide, and he could see the king-size bed stripped to its bare mattress. He tiptoed in. Inside, the room was largely clean. No more bits of brain and skull on the floors, only a massive bloodstain on the wall behind the bed, which would need a fresh paint job.

"Crow? Is that you?" Panda's voice echoed out of the bathroom.

"Yeah," Sanford said, the word crackled out of his dried throat.

Panda waddled out of the bathroom, covered in latex and rubber.

"You good?"

Sanford had to think for a bit before answering. "Yeah, I think so."

"Good."

"Look, I should probably explain—" Sanford started to say.

"Don't worry about it, man," Panda stopped him and waved him off. "Tell you the truth, I'm kinda relieved,"

"Relieved? How so?"

"All this shit we do, man—cleaning up a murderer's mess—it's like it never bothered you. It's like you liked it. Honestly, it always freaked me out."

Sanford's face drooped, weighted by shame. He was always oblivious to his own vibe and seeing how it affected his friend brought on a whole new perspective.

I am a freak.

"But don't worry, man," Panda defended. "After that shit, I could see how it really does bother you. It's good a thing, man. It turns out you're human after all."

Chapter 15

The last school bus pulled away. The silhouette of her little body emerged in a cloud of exhaust. He was late again; she knew it and sighed. Her friends had stood with her for as long as they could, waiting to see the van round the corner with its loud and abrupt sputtering engine.

"You guys don't have to wait," Sadie had said to her friends. "He'll be here soon, and I could do without the jokes anyway."

Her friends giggled, knowing they were the only ones who could joke, unlike Susie Strang, who Sadie popped in the face.

"Okay, Sadie, we'll see you later. Are you with your dad all weekend?" one of her friends asked.

"Yup! It's the best, cause he doesn't get I'm a kid. So I eat junk food all weekend, I have ice-cream for breakfast, we watch rated R movies and I go to sleep past midnight."

"Whoa! That's so cool. I wish my dad was like that."

Sadie thought about the other side of her father—the side that's only seen when he thinks he's alone. It was a side of him that scared her. But she wasn't scared for herself; she was scared for his well being, like one day he might do something to hurt himself.

"Yeah, he's pretty cool," she said and meant it. She knew that he always tried, and that meant more to her than anything.

Though as she stood alone in the cold, his *trying* seemed to be a bit less. The wind carried from the east with a chill, making her time waiting extra miserable. She wore her new *Air Jordan's*, in which her twig legs shook.

If you compared pictures of her and Sanford as a child, you'd swear it was him dressed as a girl. Her green eyes glowed like his when they caught the sun off the snow. She even dressed somewhat boyishly; on the verge of a tomboy but not quite there with her pigtails tied in pink scrunchies. So when she wore her New York Yankees t-shirts (that drove her father mad), she did so with the dainty quality of a beauty queen.

Where is he?

"Sadie? Are you okay?" Mrs. Mackenzie asked from behind her. She was a tall, lengthy woman, bundled up in layers, leaving the school to warm up her car for the long drive home.

"I'm okay, Mrs. Mack, just waiting for my dad."

"Well, why don't you come inside and wait by the door, so you don't freeze to death out here?"

"I think I'm already frozen in place!" she yelled back.

* * *

The van puttered as Sanford pressed harder on the gas pedal. All that time passed out in a newly made orphan's bed had delayed the job, and now here he was—on the one weekend he had Sadie—late again.

He raced down the Taconic State Parkway. The pedal was pinned to the floor, his grip on the wheel like a vice. It was past three o'clock on a Friday, and the road was thankfully clear, but Sadie's school let out at two, and an hour alone is a long time for a kid. He prayed she didn't call her mother.

By the time he pulled in it was close to 3:30. The buses were long gone, as were most of the cars in the teachers' parking lot. A steady wind blew a loose sheet of paper through the air like a schoolyard tumbleweed. He felt a nervous sweat take hold, layering his skin in a clammy membrane. As he pulled up to the front of the building and saw no Sadie in sight, the slight sweat became a downpour.

The walk to the school's door was a long one. Schools had always bothered him. He saw them more as prisons, where you're forced to read books you'd never read, solve problems you'll never have, and are only let out in the sun for an hour. Growing up, Sanford bounced from school to school, as he did from foster home to foster home, inhabited by a lonely captivity.

He opened the door; Sadie was not on the other side like he had hoped.

She called her mom, I knew it, he thought to himself, and instantly ran through a running list of excuses to give her.

I got into a car accident, Lucy, I'm sorry.

I saved a baby from a fire, Lucy, it was incredible!

Lucy... Panda's dead.

Each was more ridiculous than the last. *Just tell her the truth; you blacked out.* But he knew he couldn't. Another blackout would be a red flag, one that would wave high in Lucy's mind.

He thought about after their divorce, he thought about his alcohol addiction, he thought about the court-issued supervised visits with his daughter, and how he wouldn't be able to stomach those again. That lady with her clipboard, her judging beady eyes, taking notes as he played with his daughter.

It made him feel dirty.

"Mr. Crow?" a voice asked from behind his tense body, causing him to jump.

"Oh, I'm sorry. I didn't mean to scare you!"

It was Sadie's homeroom teacher; her name he couldn't recall.

"Mrs. Mackenzie; Sadie's homeroom teacher," she said.

"Right, right. Mrs. Mackenzie, how are you? Is Sadie here?"

"Her mother picked her up twenty minutes ago. I brought her in, and I waited with her for you to come, but it got to the point where she didn't think you would, so I had her call her mother."

"Fuck!" Sanford said a little louder than intended. Mrs. Mackenzie stepped back.

"I'm sorry, that was meant to be internal. Did her mother say anything?"

"It's quite all right," she laughed. "I'd rather not repeat it. But you surely know how to get her upset."

"Yeah, getting Lucy upset is second nature to me. I've had a lot of practice," he nervously laughed. "All right, well thanks for waiting with her. I gotta go kiss some feet to get her back."

Sanford turned and walked away, knowing that a confrontation with Lucy wouldn't play out in his favor. He didn't care, all he wanted was to take Sadie home; he would take any verbal lashing she had in store to do so.

* * *

"What kind of father leaves his kid waiting out in the cold like that?" Richie asked. They were sitting in Lucy's kitchen drinking coffee like water, the way recovering alcoholics tend to do.

Lucy's face was grim.

"Richie, he has his issues. But Sanford is a good dad to her," Lucy said. She didn't like when Richie spoke like that. She could see the jealousy in his posture.

He exhaled out his frustration, then guzzled down the rest of his coffee.

She and Richie had been together for seven months. Each month was celebrated with a dinner out and the clinking of glasses filled with soda.

They'd met at a meeting. In AA, approaching anybody in the group was considered taboo. But Richie didn't care. He'd seen Lucy a few times before, striding through the room in a shawl around her shoulders and long dresses that cascaded down to her ankles and waved off of them. It was hypnotic. She'd float through like an apparition. Drunks and addicts alike would watch her glide with a Styrofoam cup of coffee in her hand. She'd always sit in the back, listening to tale after tale of drunks hitting rock bottom. It was on the first day she stood up to speak that Richie knew he was in trouble.

"Hi, all," she said and waved.

"My name is Lucy, and I'm an alcoholic."

"Hi, Lucy!" the room responded in comforting synchronicity.

"Wow, that's what that feels like. It's strange saying that out loud for the first time. I've said it in my mind for what feels like years, but saying it out loud like that? It's pretty damn freeing."

The crowd laughed. Richie's smile grew.

"I am, though. I'm an alcoholic. Vodka and gin were my Achilles heel. Anything clear really."

She cleared her throat. Richie could tell she was thinking of where to take this, or thinking of how great a drink would be right about now. He knew that look well.

"I've had a rough go at it lately. Well, for my entire life I guess. I can tell you my sob story of why I started drinking, the trauma I suffered as a kid, the violations done to me, but I realize those are just excuses. I was weak, so I drank to be strong, until the drink made me weaker. I have a daughter. Sadie is her name. She's the reason why I'm here. What they say is true, you know? About having a kid. It changes you. It changes your whole view on life itself. It makes you see yourself from a different perspective. I guess it just took longer for me to pay attention." She stopped and took a long sip of coffee.

"She made me see it, though. She tends to do that. She's only six-years-old, but sometimes she's more mature than me. I divorced her dad last year. It was hard on her. But the drink was hard on him too. He never hit her or anything like that. If he did, he'd be dead, not divorced. But he'd drink till he was gone, and you can't be a father when you're no longer there. It was the worst around the holidays, Christmas in particular. The last one was the one that did it. He woke up, hit the bottle right away. Before I knew it he was gone again. Obliterated. And he lost it. Before Sadie got the chance to open her presents or even see them, he flipped his switch and destroyed the tree, stomped her gifts, pissed himself, and passed out."

The room groaned.

"Believe it or not, I understand his actions. If you knew what he'd been through, you probably would too. But that's just an excuse. They're all excuses, and like excuses tend to do, they wear thin. It wasn't the environment for a little girl like her. She's special, you know? So, we divorced, and it got better. It took time, but it did. Though I still drank, usually only when she went to sleep... until I didn't. Slowly but surely the vodka found its way into me earlier and earlier. Eventually even into my morning coffee.

It was the beginning of last year, Sadie's seventh birthday. She was at school during the day, excited because the night before the two of us had baked a ton of cookies for her in-class party. They do that at her school, celebrate each kid's birthday, it's nice. So I had a late start at it. Usually, I'd finish my drinking by eleven, pass out, wake up at seven and be good to go. We finished the cookies by ten. I got her to bed. I remember my hands shaking as I tucked her in. I turned off the light, shut the door, and then I remember running to the kitchen, reaching for the freezer, grabbing the bottle. I didn't make a drink; I just drank from the bottle straight. I don't know when it went to. It just went on and on. No one reason in particular, nothing set me off, I was just in the drinking zone.

When I woke up, Sadie had already left for school. I never got to wish her a happy birthday, prepare her lunch, and send her off. I never got to be a mother on her birthday morning. That set me off further down the hole. I hit the bottle again. I'll skip the in-betweens here and let you know how it ended. I never picked Sadie up from school. I left her waiting for me there, on her birthday, alone. One of her friend's moms drove her home. Mrs. Thompson. She walked Sadie to the door and opened it. They found me on the floor. Fucking alcohol poisoning on my little girl's birthday. Mrs. Thompson called 911. Sadie had to spend her birthday in the waiting room of the ER, while her lush of a mother got her stomach pumped."

Richie sat and listened intently. He was in awe of her courage, her honesty, her humility. Afterwards, he approached her and told her so.

Now, here they were seven months later; the urge to drink lingered like a third wheel. Sadie, the source of their mutual strength, their reason to be strong. Richie never knew he could feel that way about someone else's kid.

He wondered what kind of father he'd be from the jump. He had stepped into the role when she was already past the rough part. That was convenient. No dirty diapers, no lost sleep. Only *hey kiddos,* and noogies on the head.

Maybe one day she'll call me dad.

He hoped so. He never had a family of his own. But he knew Sanford was her real dad. Always on her mind, always in his way.

Cause, what? He blew a load in Lucy and Sadie came out? It takes more than that to be a father.

His own father was one of the good ones. Taught him how to ride a bike, throw a ball, be a man.

Sadie likes the Yankees, maybe I'll take her to a ga— his thought was cut off by the obnoxious sputtering of Sanford's van pulling up outside. He looked out the kitchen window.

"What a piece of shit," he said.

"I think it would be better if you go upstairs, Richie," Lucy said as she stood next to him and watched Sanford get out of his van. She could see the anger fuming from Richie. She gently placed her hand on his chin and turned his face to hers. "Pretty please?" She placed a kiss on his nose.

Richie sighed, defeated, and looked one more time out at Sanford, the piece of shit he was with his piece of shit van. He turned and walked out of the kitchen and up the stairs with his fists in tightly wound balls.

Christ, he hated Sanford Crow.

* * *

The house looked worse than it had the last time Sanford seen it. It was dirty and dilapidated. Its once-white shingles were wreaked by yellow mildew. The lawn was long and uncut with patches of burnt grass. Overgrown weeds extended through the snow that tried to bury them. It was his house, and he felt ashamed even looking at it. It reminded him of a haunted house he'd seen in a horror movie; though the only ghost living in this one was his own.

He parked on the road, where the front walk to the door began. The walkway stretched straight across the short front yard. The tall weeds waved in front of him. As he walked he had to brush them away. A felt-like green moss grew through the cracks of the walkway.

How could she let it get like this?

The sound of the doorknob turning brought his heart rate up. Lucy had been watching his approach, making sure she'd open the door before he had a chance to ring the bell.

He rang the doorbell anyway.

The door crept open and Lucy's head poked out. She stood on the welcome mat with her arms crossed, looking very unwelcoming.

She was still beautiful; Sanford always thought so, even in her stern resolve. Her clothes—full of static—clung to her skinny frame, with clumps of cloth hanging in loose bundles. Her eyes carried baggage, deep and blue. Her hair was messy, with strands jolting in different directions as if she just came out of a wind tunnel. It was a chaotic kind of beauty. The kind that comes with age. She had a lit cigarette in between her yellowing fingers; Sanford was unaware that she picked up the habit again.

And here I was worried about Panda smoking in the van.

God, he wanted a cigarette. Just a drag.

"What are you doing here?" Lucy said.

"And a hello to you too, Lucy. I'm here to pick up Sadie."

She snickered at his comment and took a deep drag. She dropped the butt to the ground, smashing it under her slipper with purpose. Two spirals of smoke exploded out of her nostrils like a bull readying to charge.

"I think you missed that chance, asshole."

"Look, I know, I fucked up. Something happened at work, and I couldn't get out of there in time. But please, Luce, I need her."

"Don't call me Luce!" she shouted under her breath. How a whisper could be that loud he had no idea.

"No more nicknames, no more excuses either. It's not the first time you left her stranded like that. Do you know how that makes her feel, Sanford? Fucking worthless."

He pictured Sadie standing alone outside of her school. Other father's sweeping their children off their feet and into their arms, Sadie watching. Sadie alone.

"I know, but no one can feel more worthless than I do right now," Sanford said. Lucy heard the compassion and felts shreds of empathy. But then she thought of the other times.

"Are you drunk again?" Her posture straightened as she asked it.

"No, Lucy, I'm not." He was offended. "I'm six months sober now."

He reached in his pocket and pulled out the blue chip, and flipped it to her. She caught it and read the words engraved on the back: "*To thine own self be true.*" A subtle smile grazed her mouth; he always loved her smile, even the little ones.

"Good, Sanford, that's real good."

"How about you? Still holdin' strong?" he asked, knowing the answer already. She'd been a year clean and going to a different group than his. It was a deal they struck after he started going, and after the one night he ended up in the same group as hers. The result led him to a week-long binge, where'd he wake up in the morning and finish off the quarter-filled bottles of beer on the bedside table. His breath reeked. His eyes had bags beneath them. And he showed up drunk to pick up Sadie. That was just over six months ago. He hadn't had a drop since.

Lucy reached in her shirt and grabbed the gold chain around her neck. A sobriety chip was on it, also gold plated.

"Richie got it for me in gold,"

"Ah, good ol' Rich. Tell me, Lucy, how's it a good idea for a recovering alcoholic to be a bartender?"

"Fuck you, Sanford. Like you have any right to judge anyone. Your shit to deal with is piled a mile high."

"I know, you're right... you're right, I'm sorry," he said. "Look, I didn't come here to fight, or to be a colossal dick, even though that's how it's coming off. I came for our daughter. I need her, Luce. Without her, I just don't see what the point of..." he stopped for a second and collected his thoughts. "And I'm sorry I was late, I won't let it happen again. Please, just let me be with my daughter. Please, Lucy."

He meant what he said, she could always tell. The fact of the matter is that he was a good father, perhaps because his own father may have been the worst father to ever walk the green earth. She always thought about that, with what little she knew of the man. Lucy nodded and stepped to the side, giving Sanford a clear path to the door.

"Thank you," he said and smiled as he walked around her. "You know, you should really get someone to take care of the lawn. I guess good ol' Rich doesn't really know how to do stuff like that, huh? How can Sadie even play outside?"

"Hey, there's snow on the ground, and don't make me change my mind, prick," she said with a laugh. "If you wanna cut it in the spring, go right ahead."

"All right, I will." He smiled and opened the old screen door, browned to the point where he couldn't see in. "Sadie honey? Daddy's here!"

The quick pitter-patter of feet came rushing down the stairs, with a tiny voice shouting, "Daddy!" Sanford closed his eyes and let that sound fill his mind. To him, it was the greatest sound he had ever heard. When he opened his eyes he saw her charging towards him; her pink and blue jacket already on, her little duffle bag packed and wrapped around her shoulders. She knew he was coming and she was ready to go. The warmth of that thought could keep Sanford docile through the coldest of winter nights.

He embraced her in his arms and spun around. Her legs and tiny feet became propellers through the living room.

"Can we go to the movies tonight, Daddy?" Sadie asked as her feet retouched the ground.

"Of course, sweetheart. We can do whatever you want."

"In that case, I wanna go to the movies, I wanna get popcorn, I wanna get ice-cream, I wanna go to the pet store and pet the puppies, I wanna build a blanket fort, and then I wanna sleep in the blanket fort!"

"Ha-ha! Sounds like one hell of a night. We better get started then, huh?"

Everything that happened earlier that day seemed to melt away. He grabbed her hand as they walked towards the door, and loved the feeling of her tiny fingers through his. *I helped make her; I helped make these fingers.* She was Sadie Crow, and she was the greatest thing that he had ever done.

"Don't I get a goodbye, Sadie girl?" the voice came from behind them and ruined his pleasant thoughts. It was raspy and thick; Sanford knew who it belonged to. He felt his blood boil, his body flexed with hatred.

He turned and saw the brute leaning in the archway from the kitchen into the living room, like a James Dean wannabe. Richie's hair was a mess, standing up with blond spiky strands in the back. The fact that he colored his hair made Sanford hate him more. He was large, but shapeless, minus the oval beer belly leftover from his days on the bottle.

"Bye, Richie!" Sadie said cheerily, running over and slapping him a five.

Sanford was thrilled she didn't hug him.

"Hold on, Sadie girl..." Richie said and got down on a knee to get closer. His face grimaced as his knees cracked.

Sanford watched him whisper something in her ear. His brown eyes stared through Sanford as he did. The right corner of his mouth lifted in a smirk. Then Sadie nodded and ran back to her father.

"What'd he whisper to you?" Sanford asked, lowering himself to Sadie.

"Ah, it was nothing. I just told her to have a good time with her dad," Richie interjected. The smirk on his face grew larger.

"I was talking to my daughter."

"Okay, sorry, pop."

Sanford rose from Sadie and stared daggers at Richie.

"Richie, just go upstairs, please," Lucy urged.

"Alright, babydoll," Richie said and walked towards the stairs.

Sanford never broke eye contact, drilling invisible holes through Richie's head.

"Bye, Sanford." Richie smiled and walked up the stairs.

Sadie squeezed Sanford's hand. "It's okay, Daddy. Richie is nice to me."

Somehow that made it worse.

"Okay, Sadie. It's time for us to go."

Lucy grabbed his shoulder on the way out and turned him around.

"Wait, I wanted to show you this," she said and handed him a piece of folded paper. "Sadie, can you go wait for your father by the car, I need to talk to him for a minute."

"Okay, sure."

Sanford watched her go down the walkway without a care in the world.

That must be nice.

"Look at it," Lucy said.

He looked down.

Lines made of green, red, yellow, and blue in crayon, forming nothing. At first, he thought it would be a cute picture that Sadie had drawn in school. Perhaps a picture of him? Her father, in the armor of a knight. Her hero?

He unfolded the paper and saw the spectrum of colors decrease to only red and black. There was a picture crudely drawn, as if whoever drew it held the crayon in a closed fist and dragged it across the sheet. There was a man without a head, blood spouting from his open neck. A woman lay on the floor with an object sticking out of her. Two children were drawn to the side, huddled and watching.

The paper shook in his hands as he felt a dark cloud forming over him. It was his past, calling to him, demanding to be heard.

Fucking Diane, this is all her fault.

Why couldn't she just leave it alone?

The fear of a looming blackout collected around his nerves, thrumming them.

"Hey," a voice whispered from his side, and a cool hand gently cupped around his, steadying its shake.

"Are you all right?" Lucy's familiar voice helped his mind slide back into his body.

"What?" he said, short of breath. "Yeah... yeah, I'm fine."

"So, what do you make of it?" she asked.

"Make of what?"

"Sanford, the drawing in your hands. Are you sure you're all right?"

"Oh, yeah, I'm fine, I'm fine. Just lost in thought," he said with a slight smile, trying to mask the panic.

"You lost in thought I'm used to. But... your eyes went blank there for a minute. Like no one was home."

"Well, this isn't my home anymore anyway, right?" he shot back.

"Really? You're gonna start with that now?"

"No," he sighed, aware of himself. "Look, I wouldn't make too much of this, okay?" he said, folding the paper into his pocket. "I'll talk to her about it tonight. I'm sure it's nothing. Probably just some kid playing a prank, or maybe it's something she saw on TV."

"Well, I hope you're right. It scared the hell out of me when I found it. It was like I could feel its malicious intent just looking at it."

"What are you, a psychic now? Tell me, Lucy, what color is my aura?"

"Fuck you, that's what fucking color. Just take care of our daughter."

"You know I will," he laughed. "Seriously, don't worry about this. I'll take care of it." He waved to Sadie, who was outside, waiting by the car. But something told him he wouldn't take care of it at all. He had to cherish every moment with Sadie, and bringing up crayon drawings seemed like a waste of time.

Kids will be kids after all.

Sadie came back to him as he turned to leave. He picked her up and put her on his shoulders; she loved it every time. She was much heavier than the last time he did it; he felt each pound as a moment he missed and could never gain back.

Lucy watched the two of them as they walked down the path. Once Sanford got Sadie into the car, she smiled at her mother through the window, and they both blew kisses as the wind blowing outside increased to a howl. The blue skies above became darker as the sky stretched south.

There was a storm coming, all three of them could feel it.

"Be careful driving!" Lucy shouted from the doorway.

"Daddy?" Sadie looked up at her father.

"Yes, sweetheart?"

"Can we go to the movies now?"

He peered back into the mirror, steadying his gaze. He was with Sadie, and that's all he cared about.

"Sure, anything you want, sweetheart."

CHAPTER 16

When he was with her, he was with her; his troubles melted away. The constant static of his mind dulled to a hiss that he barely heard. He had Sadie next to him, and he watched her more than the movie, which hadn't captured his attention anyway.

Explosions, gunshots, and the occasional use of *fuck* filled his ears. He wondered if this movie was appropriate for his daughter. But whatever Sadie wants, Sadie gets. And Sadie wanted action.

Sanford watched her watch the screen; her eyes as big as gumballs. She ate her popcorn, handfuls at a time, licking her fingers for the butter after.

She gasped as Keanu Reeves yelled something to Sandra Bullock, who for some reason was driving a bus that couldn't go under a certain speed. *They'll make a movie about anything*, Sanford thought. He wondered what a movie based on his life would be like.

Who would play him, when he had a hard enough time playing himself?

"Daddy, I need to go to the bathroom," Sadie whispered.

"Okay, sweetie, I'll take you."

"No!" Her whisper was now loud and horrified. "I'm eight, I can take myself you weirdo."

He never liked being called a *weirdo*, but coming from her it was more like a term of endearment. Still, he didn't like the idea of her strolling off alone.

But what Sadie wants...

"Okay, okay, just make sure you come right back, all right? To the bathroom and back."

"To the bathroom back," she repeated with a smile, then got up and began to scurry away in the dark.

"Sadie!" Sanford whispered loud enough for her to hear; she turned around. "Don't forget to wash your hands!"

The blush on her face was pure embarrassment. She turned and ran out giggling, and he watched her, laughing himself as she disappeared into the shadows.

He brought his attention to the screen. Another dramatic bus chase. The bus narrowly escaped crash after crash, as Dennis Hopper mocked Keanu Reeves. *"Pop quiz, asshole..."*

Sanford laughed and gorged on more popcorn. The movie was kind of exciting, he supposed. The hair on his arms rose when the bus made a death-defying leap—completely unrealistic, but isn't that what movies are for?

He ate more popcorn. One buttery handful after the next, until his fingers touched the bottom of the cardboard. *Shit, when she gets back I'll have to buy her more.*

Wait...

How long has she been gone?

Paternal panic began its lurk in. He had let himself get lost again. Nervously, he stood up and scanned the dark theater, thinking she must have sat in the wrong spot. Dark faces occasionally lit by on-screen explosions stared back at him.

"Hey, sit down, buddy!" a voice echoed out of the blank faces, none of which were his daughter's

"Sadie!" he hollered out, only to be responded with a heavy, sustained, *SHHHHHH!*

He looked at his watch, tilting it towards the screen so he could see it, wishing he looked at it before she went off and knew how long she'd been gone. The more he thought about it the longer it seemed. Time moved slowly, seconds felt like minutes, and minutes became hours. The door to the theater opened, Sanford leaned over to see. Two figures entered, one was a child, a girl, about the size of Sadie, and the other was a tall man, featureless, his face turned away from the screen. One arm was held close to his chest; it appeared to be in a sling. The smaller figure pointed towards where Sanford sat, and the tall, dark man bent low, whispered something in her ear, and sent her on her way.

The little girl walked to Sanford, and the closer she got, he realized that it was Sadie after all. A warm wave of relief washed over his entire body.

"Where were you? Who was that man?" Sanford asked the second she sat.

"Sorry, I went to the bathroom. When I came out he was outside, trying to tie his shoe with one hand cause his arm is broke. So he asked me to help, and I did. Then we talked a bit, and he bought me a soda," she said nonchalantly.

"What do you mean you talked a bit? Talked about what? Who is he?"

"I don't know, he never said his name. He looked kinda familiar though. And we just talked. He sounds funny when he talks. I told him about school and my friends and stuff."

"Familiar? How? And he bought you a soda?"

"I don't know, just like... familiar. Yeah, want a sip?" she said and handed it over to her father. "It's cherry."

Sanford opened the lid and smelled inside, not knowing what he'd expect to find, but knew he would dump it on the floor either way. Then he did.

"Hey!"

"Look, sweetie, you never ever talk to strangers, I thought you knew that. And you sure as shit don't take anything from them. I thought your mom and I taught you better than that. There are people out there, Sadie, that are not good people. Strangers can be dangerous, you have to remember that." He recalled something his father said to him a long time ago, something about people being the real monsters.

"But he said he's not a stranger."

"What do you mean?"

"Well, since I just met him, he said he's no longer a stranger. Makes sense, right?"

He stood up quickly to see where the dark figure was, but he was already gone. The feeling of being watched sunk in—a thousand tiny eyes upon him. Anxiety was brewing, about to take hold. His heartbeat pounded in his ears. He was still standing, facing the crowd of faceless movie watchers, when he heard the sound of something dripping.

It was going to happen. His eyes scanned back and forth. Horn-rimmed glasses formed around the crowd's eyes; the reflection of the screen filled each lens. Sanford could feel Jonathan Crow spying through each and every one of them.

Surrender felt like the only option, and at the moment it was an appealing one. He would let the anxiety take hold, and take him to a place where the blackness covered him whole.

He was about to let go, and give control over to whatever forces were at hand, when he felt another hand—a tiny hand—grip his own.

"Sit down, Daddy. It's okay," Sadie said in her voice, three feet off the ground.

The pestering drips began to quiet. His pounding heart eased to a steadier beat. His flesh cooled as the sweat retreated. The theater became a theater again, and the featureless faces of the crowd turned to normal Dicks and Janes, scowling at him for blocking their view.

"Hey buddy, sit the fuck down!"

Sanford obliged.

"No more going off on your own," he said, trying to calm himself. There was still the thought of that stranger in the back of his mind. Who was he? What did he want? How did he know Sadie?

"Questions with no answers are the worst kind to ask yourself," Sanford thought, but not in his own voice. It was his father's words, spoken in his father's voice.

What's happening to me?

CHAPTER 17

The gun was far too big in her hands. Its weight felt disproportionate to its size. She chose it on purpose; she wanted to feel this power. It was an IMI Desert Eagle. A hand cannon.

The clunky metal was heavy to lift. The scent of gun cleaner carried off of it sharp as ammonia. She followed the instructions she was taught. Dealing with real power such as this made it important to follow the manual. Jake Hardy, the ex-Special Forces Sergeant who owned the gun range, had taught her the ropes. And proper safety was the sturdiest rope of all.

The air was crisp with a bite each time the wind gusted.

"It's a good thing," Jake had said, "to perform under distraction."

The field was long. During the spring she'd see it like a meadow. Wildflowers grew along the sides among tall, beige grass. But in the winter it was nothing but snow and ice, with targets protruding at different eye levels. The farthest was five-hundred yards away. That was for the snipers. Sometimes she'd watch them from behind as they'd prepare to take their shot. It was their preparation that was calming. Long and methodical. Even a slight breeze would have to be accounted for, or their shot would be ruined. They'd never succumb to the pressure. They'd let their training do the work for them, like they were tying their shoes. It was second nature.

With all the snow, Jake and his sons had set the targets as snowmen. Diane counted fifteen in all. She imagined them giggling the whole time as they rolled the snow, set the base, the torso, and put the head on. A few even wore top hats.

Most of them were already blown away; the regular targets stood behind them.

She took her time, waiting for Jake to make his rounds.

She wondered what it would be like if her targets were made of real flesh instead of melting snow. She wondered if she'd be able to pull the trigger when it counted, when adrenaline coursed through the body like electricity.

"How we doing?" Jake said, approaching her, his scruffy voice matched his beard. It was near thirty degrees, but Jake walked around in a t-shirt. His hardened body was immune to Jack Frost. He never slouched, always standing straight, as if his muscles wouldn't allow him to bend.

"Good, just getting ready to shoot, doing it how you told me."

"Let's see."

Her target was fifteen yards away. She stood sturdy. Her right foot dragged back to a forty-five-degree angle. Knees slightly bent as she readied to aim. Her trigger finger lay against the barrel, waiting for the proper moment, itching. Her hands joined together, the way Jake taught her, thumbs married on the other side.

"Looking good, Diane. Let me just make one adjustment," Jake said.

She felt him slide against her from behind. She closed her eyes and savored the touch. The bulk of his arms wrapped around hers. His calloused hands, rough on her biceps, loosened her arms. They were the hands of a man.

"You don't want your arms this straight. We're gonna bend them a little bit to give some flexibility. I'm still not sure why you chose the Eagle to shoot, but as long as you're prepared for the recoil you'll be fine."

Diane felt the eyes of Jake's wife on them. She was rifle shooting in the distance. Vanessa. The woman was gorgeous. Blond hair and hazel eyes, with the sporty body of a goddess. It was like she was manufactured instead of born.

Diane raised the gun to eye level and her body became alive with the memory. She was in California's Berkley College at the time, a dumb sorority girl, naive to the world. With the gun in her hands she felt the wooziness of the spiked drink she'd been given that night. She felt the sweaty grip of the boy on top of her. The confused thrusting. The paralysis. The sounds of the other boys chanting as they gathered around them. The confusion. The smell of his hot breath over her, reeking of pizza and cheap beer. She became part of the pledge's hazing, much like forced chores and hundreds of push-ups. The flash from the camera went off.

The snowman looked at her with a crooked smile of buttons. Its cheeks made of snow grew the shaggy stubbles of the boy's attempted beard.

Jake was still behind her.

She fired, yanking the trigger instead of squeezing.

The sound was that of dynamite exploding in her hands.

The heavy gun recoiled and almost busted her in the face. Jake, surprised, held her from behind to limit the force.

"What the fuck, Diane! I wasn't ready!"

He grabbed the gun from her. Her hands were trembling.

The snowman stood unscathed, but his top hat was gone. Diane saw it tumbling down the hill, carried by the wind. A mammoth-sized hole straight through it.

It was then she laughed.

"This isn't funny, Diane. You could've hurt somebody. Me for one," Jake said sternly.

"Aw, is the big, bad soldier scared of lil' ol' me?" She laughed harder.

But then she stopped when she noticed the time on her watch.

"Shit, I have an important patient coming in. Same time next week?"

"You're fucking crazy," Jake said. "But yeah, sure."

Slipping off her earmuffs, she noticed Vanessa glancing over. Diane handed Jake the earmuffs and put her hand on his shoulder. Slowly, she moved it down to his bicep and squeezed, then planted a kiss on his grizzly cheek.

"Bye," she said cheerily, then looked at his wife and smiled.

Vanessa just stared.

* * *

The fraternity party lingered in her mind. She thought about it when she got into her car. She thought about the way it changed her, how she went from a dolled-up beauty with makeup and flowing, layered hair, to wearing sweats and a tightly wound ponytail.

Then, as always, she thought about Natalie Gleeson, a girl who came into her life when Diane needed her most.

After it happened, Diane buried herself in work—it was all she had left of herself—and she'd focused on it, razor-sharp. But at Berkley, she had struggled with her dissertation. In fact, she was late in even starting it. A subject, a concept, a tiny glimmer of an idea, escaped her mind on greased wheels.

Interning at the hospital hadn't helped either. There, she'd see the first of the many patients to come. She'd observe them as others observed her. It was hard. Everything about who she was was hard. But when a girl named Natalie came in for help, everything seemed to fall into place.

That a patient as complex as Natalie Gleeson had fallen through the cracks of the mental health system and landed on the doormat of a struggling student was a sad, yet common event. Involuntary hospitalization became unlawful in the 1980s, and patients like Natalie wound up either cared for at home or wandering the streets like vagabonds. Natalie was the latter.

When she first walked through Diane's door, she didn't come in alone, far from it. She had a twin sister named Gladys. Identical look-wise but not in terms of temperament. Natalie was mild-mannered. Gladys was the rebel, spewing cliche sayings like *rules are meant to be broken, it feels good to be bad,* and *good girls go to heaven, bad girls go everywhere.* She stole the last one from Mae West, but would adamantly deny this if asked.

Then came Little Petey Goodman with his little Converse sneakers, triple knotted because that's how his dad taught him to keep the laces from going under the soles. Strands of his white-blonde hair would fall over his bright eyes. He lost his mother when he was a baby, but his father had brought him up right. Petey is only ten-years-old; he'll never turn eleven.

Trevor Flowers was a gay, black man, politely waiting his turn to speak. Alice Whistler was a punk chick, Missy Smith became a Buddhist, Michael Withers was an abstract artist, and Candice Shane was a businesswoman.

Then there was Dick Marrien, the pervert, and Mary Halls, the self-described *Black Widow, and* Channing Floyd, the heroin addict.

The worst of them was a man named Malcolm White, or Mr. White, as he liked to be called. He had a peculiar taste for blood; more like an unquenchable thirst for it. Mr. White considered himself a vampire.

He'd spend the daytime sleeping, or *hibernating,* as he'd call it, waiting for the others to sleep. Nighttime would fall and he would rise. He'd slip on a black suit, a black shirt, a black tie, black shoes, and black leather gloves. With his black hair, he saw himself as nothing but a floating face in the night. He was once arrested for biting the neck of a young, beautiful girl, outside of a bar.

Diane wrote vigorously about all of these individuals and treated them each as separate patients. It was a long and tedious process, though she was invigorated by it. She saw Natalie as a means to an end, and she wrung her out, exploring her various personalities. With each new session, Diane felt a little bit of herself coming back. She started dressing better, wearing makeup again, fixing up her hair. She felt herself gaining power.

Diane found her way into Natalie's past, to when her parents died in a car crash when she was five, and how she was left to be raised by her grandmother—a nightmare of a woman.

Natalie had been beaten, starved, tied up, and left alone for days. The basement became her dungeon. The sunlight became a memory. She once spent an entire summer down in that basement.

Diane's dissertation was the best in her class. It was so good, that her professor submitted it to be published. Diane followed the code of ethics. She left out Natalie's name but bared her story for the world to read. Worst of all, for Natalie to read herself. She hadn't known she was the subject of a dissertation. All Natalie wanted was help.

When Diane presented to her the *Time* magazine with her story as a three-page feature, she was already out of school. Natalie read about her life, broken down into 4,000 words. In retrospect, it was a terrible miscalculation. It had gone against every oath she'd taken as a doctor to show her that article, yet Diane convinced herself that she was only trying to help, believing that if Natalie read about her other lives from the outside looking in, it may open some doors to that steel trap in her head. Meanwhile, in the dark corners of Diane's own mind, where the light was rarely shone, even that excuse was littered with holes.

Natalie had filled up her bathtub with warm water; the *Time* magazine sat on the closed lid of the toilet, opened to the article about her. She stepped into the tub, laid back, closed her eyes, and grabbed the razor to her side. It took the permission of all the lives inside of her to do so. They all agreed, and she slid the blade down her wrists.

You can't save them all was what her friend, Dr. Francis Abbot, said to her the day the news reached the door of their practice. She was sitting in her tall leather armchair, inserting the *Time's* publication into a glass frame to hang behind her desk. It was the last time she had really cared about her work. But once the notoriety wore off, so did her passion, and the proceeding years of monotony had left her jaded.

Diane thought about this as she left the gun range and drove to her office. She thought about how long it had been since her last publication. She thought about how since then, she'd never felt so revered, and how she's been savoring that taste for well over a decade.

Then, she thought about Sanford Crow.

Chapter 18

When Frank arrived at the scene he perused the apartment hesitantly at first, edging around the corners.

It was the second murder of its kind in a row. Much like the first, it was the slaying of a family. Though his first case seemed open and shut. The father was sitting behind bars, awaiting the process of a trial, screaming his innocence. But here, the father was with the rest of his clan.

In the center of the room, Frank stood amongst the bodies, gingerly stepping over them, gracefully for a man of his weight. He'd never once disturbed a crime scene. His fingernails dug into his scalp, scratching in the middle of his horseshoe bald spot. It was a habit of his that Nancy pestered him about. "*You're gonna bleed if you keep at it like that, Frank!*" But it helped him to think, and the job was based on thinking. Murders such as this were an irregularity in Westchester County. But Frank was an irregular man—a homicide detective who transferred from New York City for a calmer life. It seemed as if violence had finally caught his scent.

None of it added up. The upper brass knew it. The running theory was that it was nothing more than a coincidence. Two terrible fathers who had finally had enough and called it quits on family life. But Frank didn't believe in coincidence.

The apartment itself was charming, or it used to be. The white living-room couch, which looked cozy and comforting with the suede-like material and high-back cushions that Frank could imagine the family sprawled out across, perhaps during movie night, had been recolored with dark maroon stains. The leather reading chair and the bookshelf next to it had been toppled over. The glass coffee table was smashed in. Shards of glass crunched under Frank's shoes at any given point in the room. The thirteen-year-old daughter was through the table. The multi-colored rug had transformed into one deep shade of purple.

Frank hated how desensitized he'd become. It scared him. It was the only thing that did scare him anymore. In his childhood, everyday brimmed with a new fear, a new worry, a new monster. Now, at fifty-four years of age, he'd opened every closet door, peeked under every bed, and seen every horror film brought to life. Now, here he was, standing in a room full of slaughter, his stomach empty and rumbling with hunger.

A bacon, egg, and cheese on a roll would be nice for breakfast, he thought as he scanned the room again. *Or maybe on a bagel.* He paid little attention to the murders themselves; they didn't tell him what he needed to know. His eyes were glued to the far side of the room. Where the answer was in an empty space on the wall.

Hmm.

The door opened. Frank heard the grunts of the man before he entered.

"Oh, Mary, Mother of Christ!" Sergeant Harrigan said after he walked into the room. He regained control and spoke again. "Detective Waters, what do you got?"

The sergeant was a tall man, broad, like a knight without the armor. His hair was thin and peppered with gray, but his mustache was thick and white.

Frank despised him.

He didn't respond, he was fixated on the wall where surrounding photos hung.

"Waters!"

"What?" Frank responded, annoyed.

"What... do... you... got?" Sergeant Harrigan spoke in a slow, frustrated tone. Frank sighed before he answered, smothering the urge to strike the man as he did. Sergeant Harrigan, or Sergeant Arrogant, as he'd been affectionately deemed down at the station, was one of Frank's ex-partners, who had lasted a mere six months before his undue promotion.

"I got another photo missing," he said plainly.

"What the fuck does that matter?" Sergeant Arrogant said.

Frank went back to staring at the wall, inhaling through his nose with his lips pressed together. He was immune to violence, but stupidity, he couldn't stand.

"They're trophies, Serg. Just like the first family, someone collected a trophy."

"You can't know that. We have the father dead to rights for this, just like the first one."

Frank walked over to where the father lay, dead to rights. He kneeled down next to the man and took out the pen he had in his inner jacket pocket. Frank loved his pen. He pointed. He could see the blush rise on Harrigan's pale, Irish face.

"You see these?" he pointed back and forth between the hands of the deceased. On each wrist was a faded rim of raw skin.

"Those lines?"

"Yes. They're a sign that he was tied up, most likely with zip ties. And you see how the blood runs through certain parts but not between others?"

"Yeah? What of it?"

The fact that Frank had to take orders from this arrogant invalid was maddening. He sighed again and clawed at his scalp.

"Well, that means that what was tied on his wrists were cut off after he was dead."

Harrigan combed at his mustache with his finger and thumb, spreading it apart and back again in strenuous thought. It would have made Frank laugh if he wasn't so enraged by Harrigan's presence.

"Well, fuck. The upper echelon wanted a bow on this one. We're gonna have to keep this out of the press for as long as we can. Lieutenant is gonna have a shit fit."

Frank didn't respond. He let his silence do the talking.

"Shit. You really think he might be innocent?"

Frank stood up slowly, feeling the weight of his body unmercifully on his knees. It was in moments like these he desired to be a thinner man; a healthier one. But as he rose, his insulin dropped, and his cravings for something cheap and filling clouded those thoughts. *Cheeseburger, I could definitely go for a cheeseburger,* he thought as a fresh cigarette touched his lips. He lit it, paying attention to the raw details of that first drag: his lungs ballooning with warmth, the smoke dazedly escaping his mouth, rising and dancing in the stale air, the comforting feeling of the lit stick between his fingers, rolling back and forth. He did it purposefully, dramatically. He liked making people wait for his answer, especially the sergeant.

Chapter 19

I'm not even sure I blinked; the shock was too great for common impulses. My ears kept up with a steady ring for an hour after the shotgun blast. It was like dynamite exploding in the living room. Eric's eyes were opened and saw it all.

We sat there, for how long I can't say—maybe an hour, maybe twelve. All I knew was that our parents were dead.

Something wet touched my naked toe. I watched where it trailed from.

Drip, drip, drip.

Scanning the room it didn't take long to find its repugnant source. My father, who's blood trickled from his erupted head, was dripping into the ever-growing pool of blood on the floor, into an odious amalgam of Mother and Father.

Drip, drip, drip.

The steady, metronomic pace finally broke my trance and perhaps my sanity. You see, there was this dream I had of my father as a boy, his wrists were cut wide, and his blood dripped into an oceanic flood on the floor. The recollection of it was sinister. It was as if this were all preordained. Like it was all meant to be. It was then I started to scream, loud and incessant, and it filled the room in panoramic waves.

Drip, drip, drip.

Voices filled my head.

"You have to get up."

"Save Eric."

"Save yourself."

"Kill yourself."

My father's voice.

"They were perfect."

Then Eric's, faint and trembling.

"Sanford, I'm cold."

I gathered the blanket from the couch and wrapped it around him.

I paced down the hallway slowly. I looked down at my feet. I saw my footprints tracked up and down the hall in crimson.

I looked outside of the sliding glass door. The snow had piled up to over two feet, and blistering gales mounted it against the house.

"You can't walk in that. You're too small. You're too helpless. Just give up."

I sat on the floor and tucked my knees into my chest, and rocked back and forth.

"This is your fault, Sanford. Your fault!"

As I sat there on the cold wooden floor with my family behind me, I thought about that. I thought about how this was all some life lesson that he wanted to teach. I thought about how I did nothing to stop it. I thought about how I wanted to die. Then I thought about nothing.

I don't know how long I was out for. When I awoke the sun had gone down.

Eric moaned.

I had almost forgotten all about him. I went back to the living room. I put my arms around him, making sure he was still there.

"Sanford, my head hurts," he said in a tired voice. "I'm hungry."

Food? I could barely breathe, nonetheless chew and swallow. I brought him into the kitchen and sat him at the table. After cleaning his face I placed a bowl of cereal down in front of him. It was the easiest thing to make. He shoveled spoonfuls of Sugar Smacks into his mouth.

I looked outside, through the backyard, and I saw her house lit through the trees.

Ava! I thought, if I could only get there. Her father is the sheriff and he could save what's left of us.

"I'm going to get help."

I didn't want to leave him, but the best thing I could do for him was to go. While putting on my snow-gear a terrible thought came to mind. It had all happened because of these clothes. I didn't put them away the night I spied on him. The snow-pants, winter jacket, gloves, and boots—I left them dripping downstairs.

Drip, drip, drip.

A backdraft of wind hit me and toppled me over once I opened the door. I got up and moved forward. The snow was up to my waist at times, and the trek—visibly short—became biblically long.

Ava's backyard was tiny. A swing set lay propped on my right, with its metal poles and chains covered in snow, skeletal. It creaked as the wind blew its seat back and forth.

As I approached the house, other sounds formed. I heard a piano being played with voices singing along. I heard Christmas caroling.

Tears rushed my face in a flood. I sat there staring, freezing in the cold. The cry was long and hard; my cheeks solidified with icy tears.

They must have heard me in between songs. The back door opened and her father towered above me, staring with curiosity.

He approached me wearing his flannel pants and boots, with nothing but a teeshirt on top, and a mustache on his face.

"Sanford?" the voice called from behind him, but I was too choked up to respond. "Dad, that's Sanford, our neighbor," Ava said, poking her head

from the sliding glass door. With her red hair and green eyes, she looked like Christmas morning. I felt guilty for having the pleasant thought.

The sheriff lifted me to my feet, but I fell immediately. My legs were numb. He picked me up again and carried me into the house.

"It's gonna be all right, son," Sheriff Potter said.

I was plopped down on a wooden chair in the kitchen. Mrs. Potter washed my face, scrubbing away the ice that had crusted itself to my cheeks. Tiny splatters of blood washed off; she looked at her husband with dismay. My eyes—still wide with shock—continued to rain down tears like my eyebrows were vicious thunderclouds.

"Are you okay, Sanford?" Ava asked, and I stared.

"What's wrong, boy?" Sheriff Potter asked, and I stared.

Later in the hospital, Ava would tell me what I said. I only stared at her blankly and noticed fear in her eyes. She looked at me the way I looked at my father, as someone to fear. I was the victim, the one who was broken; yet she was afraid of me.

How does that happen?

* * *

A large breath escaped him; he pushed it out slowly. He put his story down on the table in front of him. He breathed in again, letting his lungs expand to the count of six, the way Diane had taught him.

Diane studied him. His quest for self-improvement was something to admire. Her notepad was filled with phrases. There was a drawing of stick figures at the bottom of the page. Two were dead on the floor. Next to them were two tinier figures, sitting with sharp-angled knees tucked into their straight-lined chests. They were watching their dead stick parents.

Diane's palm tickled. She imagined that large gun inside of it, the ferocity of it. The power.

She glanced at the clock above his head. Their time was almost up, but she had one more seed to plant, and she'd let it grow in his mind until their next session.

"Sanford, that was great. I'm very proud of you. The steps you're taking every week are turning into leaps. It must have been difficult for you to rehash all of that, but the only way to heal is to reopen the wound, so it could be stitched up right this time. But..."

Sanford let out another drawn breath.

"But..." she continued, "what about Eric?"

"What? Eric? What about him?"

"Sanford, you never talk about him at all in our sessions. What happened to him, after? Where has he been the past twenty-five years? I feel like you locked him away somewhere up in that mind of yours, and you don't want to unlock the door."

Sanford listened; his breath was labored again.

Eric? I always talk about Eric. Don't I?

He hadn't seen or talked to Eric since the hospital, since they were both there, since the promise he made.

"Sanford?" Diane said.

Eric?

There he was in front of him, sitting in the chair, his hair a chaotic mess, his eyes wide. There was a straight-jacket laced around him; his arms were crisscrossed.

White, the color was everywhere. It painted the walls of his mind.

Sanford fell back onto the couch and rolled off onto the floor. The thump of his body rattled the jar of pens on Diane's desk. Diane stood over him calling his name. His eyes were pinched shut, yet tears managed to break through the surface.

WHACK!

His eyes flew open to see himself sprawled out on the rug. Diane was on top of him, her legs mounted around his, holding them down, her hand cocked back, measuring for another slap.

"Stop! Stop!" he screamed with his hands up in defense.

"Jesus Christ!" she said.

She rolled over and off of him on the ground, staring at the ceiling alongside of him.

"That was fucking intense," she said, catching her breath, covered in goosebumps.

Forget an article, he would be perfect for a whole book. Career defining.

"How did you do that?" she asked, barely containing her excitement. "You just put yourself into a state of hypnosis, Sanford, on your own."

"Is that a good thing?" he asked.

"I don't know, I don't know what that is. I've never seen it before, but it was... fascinating. I think for the next session it's best if I try to put you under myself."

Sitting there on the floor, confusion had set in and taken hold of Sanford; he had blacked out in front of her, but for the first time, he was able to remember it. He remembered the white, the padded walls. He remembered Eric.

Chapter 20

"Another day, another dollar, another corpse," Panda said, as they pulled up to another crime scene. It was in an apartment building, tall and impersonal, towering over the surrounding community, a dilapidated rectangle.

Sanford sat in the passenger seat, inwardly buried.

The thought of Eric had grown like a cyst in his mind; he was all Sanford could think about. Every motion felt like it occurred in a dream. Eric's face was everywhere. The face of a child on every stranger rounding the corner, on every actor on TV, in every picture he'd see.

I need to find him. Would he even remember me?

"Yo, man!" Panda snapped his fingers in front of Sanford's face. "You're not going bonkers on me again are you?"

He looked at Panda and wondered if Eric might've gained weight. He was always scrawny as a child. He could've grown to look like anyone. Was his hair long? Was it shaved?

Does he have a beard like me?

"Hey, am I talking to myself here?" Panda asked and Sanford heard the concern in his voice.

"No, sorry, I'm here. And I'm good."

"All right then, well good is good enough for me. Let's get to work. You wanna go in first? See if you could solve it?"

"Nope, I don't think I want to do that anymore," Sanford weakly laughed.

They gathered their equipment from the back of the van. Cars idly drove by and watched. Pedestrians walked along and speculated. The massacre had been in the news. It was all anyone could talk about.

They walked into the building. The lobby was bland. Prints of city buildings and nature scenes. Ahead of them was the elevator. Fake plants surrounded it. A sign was taped to the elevator doors.

Out of Order.

"Gonna have to take the stairs," a man behind a desk to their left said indifferently.

"What floor?" Panda asked. Sanford could tell by his tone that he wasn't in the mood for exercise.

"Sixth floor. Apartment 631."

Panda grunted. They walked towards the stairwell.

When they got to the door a tall black man came out and held it open for them. He towered over them with his long skinny physique. A black leather jacket clung awkwardly to his skeletal frame.

"You boys got your work cut out for you." He smiled, revealing a mouth full of rotting teeth.

Sanford only nodded as he walked through.

"Crow? You coming?" Panda was already up the stairs on the next level.

"Yeah," he said, and began his ascent, "what happened here anyway?" Sanford's voice traveled up the stairwell with a faint echo.

"With our line of work, you should start paying more attention, man. There was a straight-up massacre here."

"A massacre? Jesus. In Westchester?"

"Yup, a whole goddamn family."

Sanford felt his heart drop to his stomach.

A whole family?

"Wait, then why are we here? If it were something like that they wouldn't want the crime scene cleaned up yet. Unless..."

"They have the father nailed for it, covered in their blood like a sick fuck." Panda's voice was getting further away as he talked. Sanford slowed his pace.

"Of course the guy is saying he's innocent, but he won't stand a chance on trial. There were even words written in blood on the wall, used by his own fuckin' finger. It said something like..."

Sanford knew the next words that came out of Panda's mouth before he spoke them. He saw them drawn in imperfect letters; he heard the genuine threat.

"Nothing is perfect," Panda said. "Can you believe that? It's like, no shit man. Who the fuck thinks anything's perfect?"

Drip.

Drip.

Drip.

"Jesus, Crow, you don't look too hot," Panda said waiting at the top as Sanford finally appeared.

"I'm fine, just a little lightheaded... all these steps," Sanford managed to say. His breath was shaky.

"You don't look fine, dude. Maybe you should sit this one out. We don't need what happened last time again, huh?"

Sanford ignored his suggestion and continued to walk down the hall.

631.

He stared intently at the bronze numbers on the door.

631, why is that so familiar?

He rifled through all the meaningful numbers in his life in his head. Old phone numbers, lock combinations, passcodes, birthdays, his social security number, but none of them lined up.

Panda opened the door. The apartment was dark, besides for inches of light creeping through the sides of the drawn shades.

Panda flipped the light switch. Nothing.

"Shit," he whispered to himself. "They must've turned off the power. Hold on, I'll open those shades."

He walked off into the darkness; Sanford watched him dissolve into it until his body completely vanished. He waited in the hallway, holding the bucket of cleaning supplies. Readying himself.

Light pushed into the apartment as Panda ripped open the curtains. What Sanford saw hadn't surprised him. He had already seen it in his mind before his eyes had the chance.

There was blood… everywhere.

"Holy fuck!" Panda screamed as he looked down to where he was standing. The whole room around him was maroon.

Sanford felt strangely calm. In his mind, he saw his parents sprawled about the floor. The Christmas tree was in the corner, decorated with ornaments. Then he saw himself, huddled in a ball with little Eric in his arms.

He shook his head free from image and looked up at the pictures hanging on the wall. Portraits: tiny photos of the two children, some by themselves, some of them together. There was the husband and wife on their wedding day. One photo was of the father and his baby boy, another of the father and his eldest, and the same went for the mother with each of her children.

At the center of it all was a vacant rectangle. The blank area was filled with a white two shades lighter than the rest of the paint. Sanford didn't need to be a real detective to know what was once there.

Sanford stared at that empty rectangle on the wall and saw an image forming. It was of him and Eric, sitting calmly with their hands on their laps and smiles on their faces, just as the photographer instructed. She came next, his mother, standing behind them, with her hand on his shoulder. He remembered her touch, like a warm blanket, settling his persistent chill. He put his hand on his empty shoulder. Then out of the haze, Jonathan Crow. He stared at Sanford, bringing his pointer finger up slowly and pressed it to his mouth.

"Shhhhh," he hissed with his sadistic smile.

The bucket fell loose from Sanford's hand and crashed on the floor. He saw the number again.

631.

He shuddered. It was a mailbox... it was *their* mailbox.

The address was the same as his old house.

"Nothing... Is... Perfect."

Involuntarily, and uncontrollably, he began to laugh.

CHAPTER 21

Her finger stayed still. His eyes focused on the tip and nothing else. The rest of the room became a blur. Her voice was the only thing heard, instructing him to close his eyes, but to still imagine her finger where it was. His eyelids closed like a vault door, heavy and sure.

Diane's voice was soothing down to his core. Whispers. He followed each instruction without restraint, feeling his head getting heavier, his chin burying down into his chest. He barely felt her hand as it touched his shoulder and rocked his body like a cradle. She was in control, and his mind belonged to her.

"Now, when I say 'one' and snap my fingers, you will be totally asleep, and more comfortable than you've ever been in your entire life," Diane said, as she subtly rocked Sanford's body back and forth. "Five, your limbs are heavy as boulders, you can't lift them, no matter how hard you try. But you're okay with it, you're comfortable with it, you've given up control. Four, you feel yourself floating towards sleep, as if it's a destination or the next stop on a train. Three, the train is completely empty, except for you, because it's your train, and it's traveling back in time. You look out the window and you see the scenes of your life whizzing by. All of the moments that define who you are, all the moments that have made you. Two, you feel the train slowing down to its last stop, and you're getting ready to depart. As the train screeches to a halt you look outside, and you see the house with the numbers 631 bolted to the mailbox. It's your house, where it all began. The train comes to a complete stop at the top of the driveway, and the doors open. One..."

Her voice was gone the second he stepped off the train. It pulled to the top of his driveway as if it was a school bus bringing him home. He felt the weight of a book bag strapped to his shoulders.

He began to feel uneasy. This house numbered 631 was not the same as his childhood one.

The stairs to the front door had a different banister—silvery and thick, like those seen in a handicap bathroom stall, or a hospital.

A hospital, he thought as he opened the front door and saw the shiny, white linoleum floor, the white walls, and smelled the ominous scent of disinfectant covering up the deeper stench of death. This was not his house at all. He closed the door behind him and watched the last of the sunshine dissolve away.

Why am I here? The answer came to him once the door was completely shut, and he was surrounded by the fluorescent shine of hospital halls. When he turned back, the door was no longer there, it was only a long white corridor.

Eric, he thought, *I'm here to find Eric.*

Each footstep clicked on the floor as he walked, leaving a clatter of echoes. He saw doors with little windows along each side of the hall. He passed room after room and looked inside. There were patients locked away, some spitting out gibberish. They gawked at him as he rushed by.

The last room he passed held a man strapped to a bed, staring at the ceiling while whistling. Sanford moved to walk on by but was stopped by the man's voice.

"Look who's back! The prodigal son returns."

Sanford didn't think he looked familiar, only crazy—trying to gnaw at the collar of his shirt with his arms restrained.

"Who are you? You don't know me." Sanford said and listened to his own voice. He caught his reflection in the glass of the door. He was a ten-year-old boy again.

"Oh, I know you all right! Ha-ha-ha!" The man's accent was thickly Bostonian.

"Who are you?" Sanford demanded.

"You don't recognize me? I suppose you wouldn't, after all this time."

The fluorescent lights in the hall began to dim, then one by one were violently shutting off. Some exploded with sparks of blue and orange, pillaring the hall into darkness chunks at a time. Sanford looked down to where the last of the light shone. The figure of a man stood. He was holding a shotgun over his shoulder like a baseball bat.

Sanford turned back to the door. The patient inside was out of his restraints and pressed against the glass, his face twisted in anger.

"You left me, Sanford! You were here!" he yammered, spitting foam against the glass.

"How would I leave you here? Why?" Sanford's voice trembled.

"Sanford Crow, the brother of a lifetime!"

"Eric, I didn't leave you. I was let out."

Eric's lips curled in a snarl.

The last light above Sanford's head exploded. Sparks rained around, some seemingly getting inside. He slipped deeper into his mind. They were both children, surrounded by white. Neither was speaking. Neither could.

Sanford realized he couldn't move; he was in the room with Eric, and he was bound to a chair. The straps were tight, too tight to move. Air came in spurts, and hysteria sunk in when he felt the electrodes pressed against the sides of his head.

"They shocked me," he said from outside of the room, watching himself through the window.

"They shocked both of us," Eric responded. "But it worked on you. It got you talking. For me, it dug me deeper in my hole."

A chill passed through Sanford.

"Do you remember what you said to me before you left?"

Sanford looked back through the window of the door. He saw himself sitting beside his mute brother on the bed: he saw the tears in his own eyes. Eric wouldn't look at him; he only stared at the wall straight ahead. Sanford moved in front of him until they were eye to eye and said, *"I'm coming back for you, Eric. You are the only family I have, and I won't leave you behind, I never will. I promise."*

Hands, cold and dead, clutched his shoulder and turned him around. What stood in front of him was appalling, mutilated, and too horrible to be real. Half of his face was blown to hell. The right eyeball was missing. Its optic nerve dangled out of his empty socket like a shoelace. His mouth was ajar, permanently yawning, with a black tongue peeking out of what little teeth remained.

Jonathan lifted his hands to Sanford's face and dug his fingernails into his skin. Sanford was immobile with fear, the same way he felt twenty-five years ago. The nails tore downward.

"Time for you to remove your mask, son."

"No! It's not a mask!"

"Sure it is, I'll show you. Your's is just on a little tighter." Jonathan said and ripped a layer of skin away.

Sanford screamed.

* * *

Diane stared in wonder as Sanford lay on the couch, clawing at his own face through violent fits and spasms.

She knew he didn't belong on her couch; he most likely belonged back in a padded room, zipped up in a straight-jacket.

But where would that get me?

She pictured what her photo would look like gracing the back pages of her book. Would she go with the studious look with her glasses, or would that be too pretentious? Perhaps an elbow on a desk, and her fist under her chin, contemplating the mysteries of the world.

Maybe.

That was enough she supposed. She couldn't let Sanford tear himself to pieces.

No, I still need an ending.

Diane grabbed the glass of ice water from her oak desk. She noticed it wasn't on top of a coaster. A ring of water formed on the oak as she lifted the glass.

Ugh. She'd have to go at it with some vinegar and olive oil later.

She brought her attention back to Sanford.

The ice-cold water hit his face, bringing him back to reality. He saw his father's face on Diane's body. His blown apart head, sitting atop her feminine shoulders. Sanford looked at his hands, covered with specks of blood; his skin caked underneath his fingernails. Before Diane could say a word to him he got up and ran to the mirror.

"Sanford..."

His fingernails hadn't dug too deep. It was the one time he was glad that he had a habit of gnawing at them.

What do I tell Sadie? What do I tell Lucy? Is she going to think I lost it? Did I? Am I gonna lose Sadie?

He could see Diane's reflection through the mirror, behind.

"Why'd you let me do this?" he asked her.

"I didn't let you do anything, Sanford. I had no control over you. I tried to sway where your mind was going, but you went on your own course and wouldn't take my directions. When you started doing that to your face is when I threw the water on you. You weren't responding to anything else."

Sanford looked back into the stranger he was. He was sick of it, the feeling of having control, then losing it all. The constant back and forth felt like he was at tug-of-war with himself, and the rope was wearing thin.

"I left him there, you know?" he said, wiping away the now pink tears and bits of shredded skin.

"Who?"

"Eric," he said slowly. "I just left him there, and I never looked back."

"That's not your fault, Sanford. It's from what you both endured. It was your mind's way of protecting you, of trying to heal you. The subconscious is funny like that. It can make you forget things, forget people because it knows that those thoughts could destroy you. It's a defense mechanism."

"Yeah? Well, that's all well and good, but I was his older brother! I was supposed to protect him, not myself! What kind of selfish asshole does that make me?"

"Don't be so hard on yourself, believe it or not, these things happen. The wonderful part is that it's not too late. If you would allow me, I could find out where he is, or if he's still where he was."

"You'll do that?" Sanford said, turning away from his own reflection.

"Of course I will."

"That would be great. Thank you, Diane... thank you."

"You're welcome. Now, this crazy session is out of time. You need to go home and get some rest, okay? Doctor's orders," Diane said gently.

Sanford nodded and began walking towards the door.

"You know, it felt like I was really there, like I was really talking to him," he said before walking out of the room.

"Maybe you were." Diane smiled, and Sanford tried to return it, but couldn't. He slumped out of her office and shut the door behind him.

At the window, Diane looked out and watched Sanford get into his van and drive off. She floated across the room, fighting the urge to pirouette. She stood in front of her bookshelf and moved an artificial plant in a miniature orange pot aside. Behind it was a hidden camera; its red light was blinking.

Chapter 22

When Diane called him and told him what she'd found, he couldn't believe it. He still couldn't. Even now, as he stared lifelessly at the phone.

It wasn't possible, it couldn't be. How could he not have known?

Because you are a horrible brother. You didn't even bother to visit, to make sure he was taken care of. In fact, you didn't even bother to care.

Ten years—it had been ten years since Eric's release from the hospital. Diane carried on to calmly explain deinstitutionalization. The Mental Health Systems Act of 1980 was repealed once President Reagan came into office. Federal funding was dropped, and patients thought to suffer from severe mental illnesses were let loose—most of whom became homeless.

"Why?"

"Never mind, Sanford, that's neither here nor there. My point is that Reagan messed up, and what he created was an epidemic. Millions of patients were released, your brother being one of them."

Sanford saw images of his brother panhandling on the streets. He only knew him as a little boy, and that's all he could picture him as. An innocent six-year-old, afraid of his own shadow, living among the trash and drinking from a bottle in a paper bag.

The shades to the window were opened. The outside was dark besides for the streetlights balefully glowing through the plate-glass window. He felt eyes on him, staring through the black with perfect clarity—a predator of the night. An odd sound invaded the silence.

Huh?

It was the phone: he had forgotten he'd been holding it.

"Hello? Dr. Wesley?" Nothing but the dull whine of the dead line responded. He hung it up. How long had he been sitting there? He didn't know, but he felt his feet prickling with pins and needles as they slowly awoke.

He walked over to the opened shades. The window was black, reflecting the night's sky. He saw his own reflection and the cuts on his face. In the seconds before he pulled the curtains shut, he felt that someone was there, and they were laughing.

Eric? No, he wouldn't know where to find me.

He'd continue to feel eyes on him for the rest of the night, even after paranoia had caused him to shut off all the lights. In bed, he lay and he wept. Sleep would not come easily that night. In fact, sleep would not come at all.

* * *

The next morning was no normal morning; the night before had seen to that, and the headline on the first page of the newspaper cast him deeper into the twilight zone.

A SECOND FAMILY MURDERED, A COMMUNITY LEFT IN SHOCK.

A family has been found dead in their apartment at the Crescent Towers in Peekskill, New York.

The deaths of Christopher Serra, 41, Ann Serra, 39, and their children Miles and Melinda Serra, 9 and 5, have been ruled as murder.

Sanford stopped reading; his face turned the same color as the newspaper—a pale, lifeless gray. *Crescent,* the name hit him like a cannonball to the gut. The Crescent Towers is where he lived. Where he was currently sitting, reading the newspaper with his coffee.

If a murder took place in his own building, wouldn't he be aware of it? Wouldn't he have noticed the cops, detectives, and reporters?

Am I that oblivious?

He continued to read with a strange sense of inevitability. Something was coming.

Links to the Battista murders a week earlier have been found.

Detective Frank Waters says, "The investigation is still open," and added no further comment.

Sergeant Raymond Harrigan added, "We are at the early stages of our investigation and are trying to piece together what has happened. If anyone has seen or heard anything suspicious on or leading up to the day of the murders, please don't hesitate to contact us."

Anthony Battista still sits in jail, awaiting trial.

When asked about Mr. Battista, Sergeant Harrigan said, "Anthony Battista isn't cleared. Evidence points to him. This could be something done by more than one person. All possibilities are on the table. But we have our finest men on the job."

Regina Hill, who initially called the police, is the neighbor next to apartment 20C, where the murders took place.

"I heard them screams. They woke me up when I watched my shows. But I ain't seen nothin'."

Dread covered him like a wet blanket.

Apartment 20C was directly above his own.

There were two little kids up there that constantly scurried across the hardwood floor. It seemed like they wore steel-toed boots as Sanford tried to watch his bland murder mysteries on the television. The mother, always on the phone with her sisters. The father, constantly "trying to get in shape," as he'd hear him tell his wife, gliding back and forth on a rackety row machine directly above Sanford's bedroom at the earliest hours in the morning.

All the times Sanford mouthed *FUCK YOU* towards his ceiling with a pillow wrapped around his ears came back to him. A feeling of guilt radiated through his body as he remembered how he'd wish they would die, just so he could get a moment of peace and silence—an hour of blissful sleep.

As he sat there alone in his kitchen, realizing the family was gone, he listened and found himself hoping to hear that vicious squeal of the row machine, the mother's nagging voice telling her sister Mary that their sister Kathy could be a real bitch sometimes, and most of all, he hoped to hear the children, and the awful din of their feet.

He dug deeper into his already bleeding flesh.

* * *

Frank left the prison with fresh scratch marks on his scalp. He had gone to visit Anthony Battista. The evidence against the man was extraordinary, but Frank's suspicions refused to quiet down. A man who murdered his family and was caught at the scene of the crime covered in their blood would never deny it. They'd want the whole world to know, or they would simply cave under the weight of what they'd done and try to put a bullet in their head. Battista did neither. He screamed his innocence all the way to lockup, through his arraignment (much to the chagrin of his attorney), and behind bars, as he awaited trial (without bail).

"I didn't hurt my family—I could never hurt them! You have to believe me!" Battista shouted in turmoil. His hands were shackled to the metal table and created a grinding sound when he moved them for emphasis. It made Frank cringe.

"How about you just tell me what you remember?" Frank said, even though he'd heard the tale numerous times before.

"Come on, detective! It's like how I already told you, man. How many times do I have to fucking say it?"

"Humor me, Tony, one more time. If you want me on your side that is."

Tony sighed, "Okay, fine. It's like I said before, I was leaving work, and when I got to my car it was... fuckin' weird. It was already unlocked. I never leave my car unlocked, especially not in the shitbag district I work in. It was that feeling when I was driving, you know? Like someone else had been in there, in my car I mean; it felt violated. It was when I got home that I really freaked out, cause the apartment door was also unlocked and slightly opened. Man, before I even pushed the door open an inch, all I could see was the color red. Alarms were buzzin', man, and panic—it was like a full-body panic I've never felt before. I pushed in and saw it; I saw... I saw th-them." His eyes became liquid glass. "My babies, they were..."

Tears exploded from the man's face, and Frank watched emotionless, taking notes in his mind.

"What else do you remember, Tony?"

Tony pulled himself together the best he could and went on. "Nothing, besides waking up to the paramedics and the police cuffing me."

"You passed out?"

"Maybe, but this felt more… what's the word? Subdued? Yeah, I woke up with my head groggy, kinda like I was hungover."

"Were you? Cause we know you have quite the issue with alcohol."

"Sure, I drink, but I have it under control. I did drink that day, but only a few sips from my flask I keep in the car. Just enough to keep me balanced, definitely not enough to blackout. I know my fuckin' booze."

There it was. He'd have to go back to the evidence and test the flask found in Tony's car. And when he did, he'd bet his bottom dollar it would come up tainted.

"Are you gonna get me out of here?" Tony shouted as Frank got up to leave.

"Don't get your hopes up Mr. Battista, this story's just started to form," Frank said before he walked out the door. His plans for the day had changed. Dinner with the wifey would have to be put off (a common occurrence). Instead, he'd be going back to the secondary crime scene to see what other parts of the story he could fill in.

"The story?" Tony said as Frank left. "This ain't no fuckin' fairytale! Get me out of here, Waters! I need to bury my babies!"

Frank paid no attention. It was not his duty to care. He scratched at his scalp until he was outside of the prison and inside of his car. There was something he missed; he knew it. A crime scene that chaotic was too messy to be clean. A killer will always overlook the little things because they thrive on impulse and think they're smarter than they are. That's how Frank always caught his man.

Besides for the photo missing from the wall, the killer had left nothing to the naked eye. Forensics came back empty for fingerprints. The place was only cluttered with the markings of the family and friends. The father's being more pronounced, placed in a way that shouted his guilt: on the knife, on the hammer, on the gun. *Too ideal,* Frank had thought. His gut is what drove his instincts; it's what was driving his car back to the crime scene now.

"I don't get it, detective," the officer riding along with him said, sitting on edge in the front seat, hoping not to sound inferior. "If it looks like the father did it, why are we going back?"

Frank didn't mind such questions. The whole there's *no such thing as a stupid question* was always a half-truth to Frank. Asking was learning, and he appreciated it when rookies did so.

"Because..." Frank looked at the officer's shirt to get his name. "Hemick, in this line of work nothing is as it seems until it is what it is." Frank smiled, pleased with his truism.

"Huh?"

"The father's dead, right?" Frank asked, and Hemick nodded. "Well, then we don't have a confession or a smoking gun, because we weren't there. All we have is a crime scene that points a finger. But you have to realize crime scenes can also be manipulated to point that finger."

Hemick made an involuntary sound of befuddlement. Frank's words settled in, and he finally understood. In one light-bulb moment, he realized he was never destined to be a detective. He swallowed his newfound knowledge along with his pride, and spent the rest of the ride without a word. This was another decency Frank appreciated.

As Frank drove, his fingernails clawed at his scalp with his elbow against the window. His mind kept going back to that wall, that empty space, its white paint, bright, unmarked by dust.

* * *

It was late in the evening when Sanford climbed the stairs. The less attention he drew the better. This was still an open case, and what he was about to do was highly illegal, not to mention highly suspicious.

He ascended slowly on weary legs. Whatever was behind the door of 20C would surely be nothing to help his sanity. More likely than not it would break it, and send him to the deepest depths of psychosis, maybe to where Eric was. Nevertheless, he continued to climb, feeling the grains of the wooden banister on his fingers. The open stairwell amplified every sound.

Above him, the door to the third floor flew open and crashed against the wall. The racket was sudden, causing Sanford to freeze. He expected a man to appear at the top of the staircase, like looking through a funhouse mirror and seeing a bizarre caricature of himself staring back. He held his breath and waited. Instead, two boys ran out of the doorway, galloping down the stairwell with high-pitched laughter. They were brothers, Sanford knew immediately. They were racing, and the older of the two was well in the lead, but playing at a slower speed to give his younger brother the hope of catching up, only to quicken his pace when he did.

When the boys ran by they stared at Sanford. Sanford saw what they saw, reflected in their eyes. With his detached eyes and scratch marks down his face, he terrified them. It brought on a feeling of shame.

By the time he got to the next floor and opened the door those feelings were gone. The hallway was identical to the one he lived in. The same two fiddle-leaf fig plants introduced themselves when he opened the door. At his feet, the same red-checkered carpet ran from wall to wall. It was as if he entered a world where everything was synonymous, but just a little off; it felt unreal.

Apartment 20C would be the same on the inside as his own; he figured they all were. He stood in front of the door, knowing beyond it may lie answers. He covered his hand with his sleeve and turned the knob. It was unlocked. Sanford took a deep breath and stepped inside.

There was a musty smell, the same he remembered as a kid, when he went on family vacations to the beach and came back to a stale and unused home. The windows were closed, causing the house to be filled with dead, stagnant air, as if it was suffocating until they'd opened the windows again to let it breathe.

He opened the windows; the cold winter air blew in. He had to be careful not to disturb anything. For someone who wanted to be a detective his whole life, he had a certain respect for the job, and for the law, both of which he was disrespecting just by being there.

But this was different.

This might be family.

He supposed he could have gone to that Detective Waters he read about in the papers. He could have told him the whole story from the beginning, see if it sounded as crazy out loud as it did in his head.

Waters would make the connection eventually, Sanford figured, and look at it himself. He'd discover the old story of Jonathan Crow, that black Christmas of 1969. The Crow's had become folklore in Maine, stories that teenage camp counselors told children around campfires to scare them silly. Facts were twisted and misinterpreted, like the longest game of *telephone* ever played. It went from the horrifying truth to an exaggerated tale, where the Crow family had transformed into Satan-worshiping cannibals.

Time passed and stories died until they were nothing more than whispers. But here, inside apartment 20C, he felt as if he were home again.

Home sweet home, he thought unbidden.

* * *

The car screeched to a halt outside of Crescent Towers, jolting Officer Hemick as he tried to sip his coffee. The hot fluid spilled across his thighs.

"Ah, shit!"

"Sorry, Hemick," Frank said smiling. "Rookie mistake, though. Never take a sip when we're coming to a stop. We're the police; we always slam on our brakes."

Outside, freezing rain began to pelt the windshield. The Crescent occupants became distorted through the glass, as they looked back, praying the cop car wasn't there for another slaying.

"Look at them. They all look terrified," Hemick said, sipping his coffee again.

"Do you blame them? The only blood spilled around these parts is for drug money. Once you throw the words *serial* and *killer* together, it opens the door to a whole new world of darkness. They see us now and they're terrified of the possibilities."

"Makes sense."

"That's where you're wrong, son. And if you wanna be a detective always know this: we're on a rock, floating through space in an infinite universe. Nothing makes sense."

* * *

In the room of the dead, something inside him stirred. This was the life he intended to live, the dream he had never realized. He was being a detective, and a failed psych exam couldn't take that away from him now.

There's something here, he thought.

As he scanned the room and turned his head, his eyes met hers.

There were pictures hanging above the faux fireplace in the living room. In the center was a 4x6 picture within an 8x10 frame. The frame was tilted one way; the picture, crooked inside of it.

In it, a mother was smiling—her eldest son had just graduated, donning a red gown and cap. The father stood to the right, wearing his sheriff's uniform, clutching his *Stetson* hat to his side, and grinning from under his mustache. In the middle, shorter than the rest, was her. She looked the same as he remembered: red hair contrasting her luminous green eyes.

Ava?

He felt the same fear he did as a child—a nauseating, helpless fear.

Sanford rubbed at his face and eyes, hoping his mind was playing tricks on him. But when he looked again, she was still there, looking back at him. It reminded him of that Christmas Day, when he showed up at her house, seeking help. The way she looked at him; the jealousy he'd felt.

Her perfect fami—

His thought was cut off by the pounding of approaching footsteps, reverberating from down the hall. It could be the neighbors coming home, but a sixth sense told him otherwise and screamed at him to get moving. He grabbed the frame with Ava's photo and ran towards the bedroom. He could hear the footsteps getting louder, coming to a halt, the doorknob turning, metallic clicks as its internal mechanism spun, the clunk as it hit the lock.

"Who locked the door?" someone yelled from outside the apartment. "And where the fuck is the patrolman?"

Did I lock the door?

The sound of a key entering the knob was loud and unmistakable. Strangely, Sanford kept calm; he opened the bedroom closet.

* * *

Frank opened the door. An abrupt gust of wind hit him from the opened windows. Years on the job took over; he instinctually drew his gun. Someone was in here, or someone just left.

He scanned the room, letting the gun be his pointer.

"There's another picture frame missing," he said to Hemick.

Hemick, completely unaware of what was happening was in awe of Frank. He followed his lead and un-holstered his gun.

Sanford listened from the bedroom closet. In that moment he saw himself as someone he wasn't, like he was playing a role. He knew it was crazy, but for the first time in a long time, he felt alive.

The light to the bedroom switched on. Sanford's eyes bulged as his heartbeat quickened. He looked down at his scuffed up work boots, glowing from the light through the bottom of the closet door. They were perfectly in-line with a row of women's sandals, pumps, ankle-strap heels, and stilettos. The insane urge to howl with laughter screamed from within; he drew his hand to his mouth and bit down hard.

Frank gave the room a cursory look, his eyes stopped at the closet. With his gun leading the way he crept towards it. Each step was quiet and purposeful—light-footed for such a stocky man.

Inside, Sanford watched as the shadows shifted through the cracks of light; his breathing accelerated. He prepared himself to charge through the door and through the detective on the other side.

Frank's hand touched the doorknob.

Sanford heard the muted groan as the doorknob started to turn.

"Hey, Detective, it looks like whoever was in here went out the window."

Frank let go of the knob and backed away from the closet. A cold gust of wind blew through the open bedroom window behind him, throwing the curtains up in a wave. He went to the window and peeked outside. It was a fire escape, and sitting on the ledge was a dead potted plant kicked over, spilling snow and black soil through the grates.

"Looks like someone took the fire escape down," Hemick said, approaching Frank.

Frank looked down and saw the ladder extended to the ground.

"Looks like it," he said. "You'll be a detective in no time, Hemick."

Sanford stood in the closet coated in a thin layer of sweat.

"Call it in. We need to dust the place for prints again. Let's get down to the street, maybe we could find which way he went."

After the second the door shut, Sanford stumbled out of the closet. He pulled the sleeve of his jacket over his palm and began to wipe away any trace that he was there. The windowsills, the mantle, the closet door, everything he knew he touched, and things he thought he might have. This was no time to get sloppy.

Since we cannot change reality, let's change the eyes that see reality, Sanford thought to himself. Where had he heard that before? *Nikos Kazantzakis?*. No doubt another quote from the human part that was his father.

As he swept the apartment one last time, erasing himself, he knew where he had to go, who he had to find, and what he had to do. He walked out of the door and into the hall, wondering if he could.

Chapter 23

Lucy stood in front of him, defiant yet victorious. Half of her was in her house, with the door opened between them, leaving Sanford standing in the cold, speaking with plumes of air behind each word. The second he'd uttered the words, "*I can't,*" her animosity and love for her ex-husband went to war with each other. This was *her* weekend after all, not her's as in with Sadie, but her's as in her's and Richie's. They'd have the house to themselves, with every room at their disposal.

"What do you mean you can't take Sadie this weekend?"

"Look, Lucy, something's going on that's beyond my control and I need to fix it before it gets any worse. I need to go home, back to Sanford, Maine," he said.

Her mouth opened to speak but nothing came out besides a curious gasp.

She regrouped and venomously fired off questions. "What in the fuck are you talking about? You're not making any sense. Why in the fuck would you go back there? What, do you need to visit your old house with all those lovely memories?"

"No, well... maybe. What I need to do is see somebody I grew up with. She might be able to help me." He was being as vague as possible. He wouldn't dare mention Eric and toss Lucy into the world of his psychotic paranoia. Knowing her, she'd only think he was going mad, and that's not what he needed, no matter how close to the truth that may be.

"She, huh?" Lucy said with a crooked smile. "Is *she* the same one who scratched your face like that?"

He had forgotten all about the scratches. He hadn't even thought about them when he looked in the mirror. They'd become a sort of truth to him; his true self, defiled.

"I did this to myself. Dr. Wesley tried to hypnotize me."

Lucy hadn't wanted to feel it, but the sympathy came in droves. When it came to Sanford it always had, as if he were some bizarre caricature of Charlie Brown with a tortured past.

"That fucking quack," Lucy whispered. "I told you that you should find a new doctor. Besides, it's pretty obvious she wants to fuck you. But hey, you might be into that doctor/patient thing."

"Stop it, Luce. That's not what I'm here to talk about."

She sighed, thinking for a minute. "Well, it's your weekend with Sadie, and you know how important that is to her, and you know how important that is to me. So, you're going to have to take her with you."

A wave of nausea hit him.

"What? No, I can't do that! Are you crazy?"

"Why the hell not? Don't you think it's important for her to see where you came from?" Lucy said, hardly believing it herself.

"Are you joking? You know where I came from, and when we were together we agreed that she should never know about what happened to me!"

The cold winter air did nothing to cool the nervous heat radiating from him. He was mad—mad at the fact she didn't understand, nor could she, because he wouldn't tell her the full truth. Where he was standing—on the front stoop of their old house in twenty-degree weather—didn't help resolve his anger either. After all these years, she was still hesitant to let him inside when Sadie wasn't home.

At that moment, she opened the door and gestured him inside, as if she heard his thoughts and wanted to prove him wrong. *This woman must always be right,* he thought as he entered, shaking off the cold.

Lucy exhaled a tumultuous sigh, and took out a cigarette from her loose, exposing robe. She hadn't meant to do it, but her nipple popped out from the side of the silky cloth. Sanford couldn't help but notice it. Lucy took note of his reaction, adjusting her robe.

"I'm not saying you tell her what happened, but there's nothing wrong with taking her on a little tour," she said.

"I don't know, Luce," he responded, already half defeated.

"Please, San, I need this weekend, and you know how happy it will make her to go with you." She leaned back against the arm of the couch, the skirt of the robe across her naked thigh.

"Don't do that."

"Do what?" she said as her robe moved an inch higher.

She had him and he knew it.

"That..."

Lucy smirked as she put the cigarette to her mouth and lit it. She inhaled and let the smoke spill out of her mouth lazily.

The smell of the cigarette snapped him out of it.

"It's not gonna work," Sanford said, finding his confidence.

Lucy stood up straight and readjusted her robe, inhaling a harsh drag.

"Whatever," she said, tying her robe tight. "Look, Sanford, I'm done arguing with you about this. You have a lot to make up for, right? You don't want to be the absent father. Do you want Sadie growing up telling stories about the good times with you or the bad? Take her with you. You both need it."

Sanford sighed. To that, he had no response.

Chapter 24

Unbelievable.

But was it? All women are the same.

Goddamn women.

At least they were in Richie Kay's eyes. His ex-wife certainly was. She didn't like his drinking, so what did Richie do? He'd gotten clean for her. As clean as a whistle. And what'd she do? She cheated on him with his best friend, Dean. To be more exact, she gave mean Dean a mean blowjob.

Those thoughts of Dean bubbled to the surface of his mind as he watched his current girlfriend's ex-husband walk out of her house.

Her house, or our house?

Sanford Crow, *that fucking weirdo*; his cheeks were blushed as he walked to the car. Richie didn't have to guess what'd happened, in his mind he knew. He'd parked down the street when he saw that disheveled van of Sanford's in the driveway. His pulse raced when he got out of his car. Short, angry breaths escaped him as he approached the house on foot. The big bay window's curtains were drawn and he couldn't see inside.

Slowly he tip-toed back through the hard snow of the front yard. He'd lost his balance from the awkward footing and fell forward, catching himself with his hands in front of him in the snow. The cold, like piercing needles in his naked hands. He pushed himself back up to his feet. His socks were wet. His feet were cold. Walking through the snow in low-top sneakers wasn't his brightest of moves. It didn't matter. Nothing mattered anymore.

Un-fucking-believable.

The picturesque image he had of his life began to dissolve. He always wanted to be a family man; he knew he'd be a great dad, a great husband. It's what would give him purpose. He'd picture them living in the house. Lucy, cooking dinner as Richie helped Sadie with her math homework. "*Thanks, Dad,*" she'd whisper to him after he'd explain the formula for long division. Lucy, calling out, "*Dinner's ready!*" Richie, going into the kitchen with Sadie on his shoulders. Lucy, kissing him as he rubbed her protruding belly—their new baby on the way.

The cold in his hands turned to hot balls of hatred. Not for her; he knew Lucy wasn't like the rest. He loved her, and there had to be a reason for what was happening.

When it came to Sanford, Lucy hadn't told Richie much. But he was relentless. He had to know who he was competing with. Finally, after months of pestering, he'd broken her down. She'd told him the story of his past. In a way, Richie felt bad for him. In another way, he couldn't care less. But now, as he sat in his car and watched Sanford get back into his van, start it up, and fill the neighborhood with the clamor of a failing engine, he drew his attention back to the newspaper on the seat next to him.

The front-page story reminded him of what Lucy had told him about Sanford. She didn't give him much detail, but he didn't need them to connect the dots. Families murdered, the fathers as suspects, it sparked an idea in his mind. If Sanford was gone—gone for good—Lucy would be all his, their house would be his, Sadie might even call him *Dad*. The thought excited Richie in ways he hadn't deemed possible.

With Sanford gone, he'd finally become a family man.

CHAPTER 25

Every road, corner, and landmark came to him with total recall. Ever since they got off the main highway, Sadie watched her father as he'd point to a random building and give a tale of his adolescence. They were mostly fun and quirky, afterthoughts of a world gone bad.

He sought out his old elementary school and retold the story of a bully on the playground who tried to intimidate the wrong boy. "Just one good punch to the nose, and he never bullied me or anyone else again."

"Just like you told me to do, Daddy!" Sadie exclaimed.

"That's right, sweetheart. And those little girls never bothered you again, right?"

"Right! I made that Courtney girl run for the hills."

"You see, sometimes violence is the answer, just don't tell your mother I said that."

They both laughed. He hadn't known what to expect being back there, how he would take being home, where it all began.

Home, is that what this is?

What he knew is that his mind was a wildcard, erratic and overly sensitive, like an old used car, susceptible to breakdowns at any given moment. The fact that Sadie was with him was irresponsible enough, but he had hoped that since she was there, he'd be able to hold it together; she'd be able to hold him together.

Since Sanford left Sanford, both had gone in different directions. The town looked as if it were trying to keep up with the rest of the world but didn't know how. The old tire shop became a dollar store, the local pharmacy turned into a CVS; two Wal-marts were built on the opposite ends of the town. The movie theater—where he and Eric spent countless hours—still stood, but as an empty shell in a rundown building.

"What was once joyous, is joyous no more," Sanford said out loud, wishing he only thought it. When his father's words came out of his mouth, it left him with a nasty taste.

"What does that mean?" Sadie asked.

"What? Oh, just reminiscing is all."

Sadie drew her attention back to the window, having enough wherewithal to stop pursuing the question. Sanford loved that about her.

"Dad?" she called fragilely.

Her next question was one he was not prepared for, but one he expected.

"Yes, honey?"

"Um..." She took her time, trying to find the right words. Sanford could tell she was just as scared as he was about it. The light ahead turned red and they came to a stop. Sadie took a few breaths and continued, "How come you never... you know... tell me about your family?"

His foot turned heavy, frozen on the brake pedal. A car behind them honked its horn when the light turned green and they stayed put. He never wanted to lie to his daughter; he thought lies were the quickest way to lose her. Though lies and secrets were two entirely different things. He had always kept her in the dark, in a safe and empty room, where the truth couldn't touch her and couldn't hurt her. Never once had he thought to mention his father, much like Jonathan had never talked about his own. Now that the question was out, lying was not an option. He decided it was time for her to know.

They drove quietly for ten torturous minutes. Sanford's eyes led the way, concentrating, remembering how to get there, amazed at how easily it had all come back. When he turned on to the street, each house told its story. The neighbors that never knew until it was too late, and how they had made those cliché statements to the papers like "They were always such a nice family"; "He always seemed so normal"; "I never once suspected it."

He wondered how many of them still lived there, how many of them still looked out their windows at the house and remembered. But most of all he wondered if anyone lived in the house —*his* house. As his car approached, he saw that junk littered the front yard, windows were broken and spray-paint decorated most of the exterior.

"The Devil's House."

"666."

"Billy was here."

Sadie's eyes widened, as some small part of her father's story came to light without him having to say a word. They pulled into the driveway.

He put the car in park and could only stare. For a reason unbeknownst to him, his first thoughts of the house were those of happiness. Sanford and Eric playing tag in the yard, as their mother came out with a pitcher of lemonade, sweat beading on the glass. There was his father, smiling, throwing the baseball to his eldest son, and teaching him the correct mechanics to throw it back. But that all went away once he opened his mouth and started speaking to his daughter.

"This is where I come from. This is why I never told you about them. My father was a bad man, Sadie."

"What did Grandpa do?" Her voice was so innocent that a small part of him wished he could switch lives with her, as guilty as it made him feel.

"Don't call him that. To you, he's Jonathan."

"But you call him your father."

Sanford sighed. He wasn't looking forward to her teenage years, where every act would be one of defiance. "That's because he's a reminder of the kind of father I never want to be."

"What kind is that?"

It was in moments like these that Sanford wished he hadn't quit smoking.

"The worst kind; the kind that hurts their family," he said, knowing it wasn't enough, but Sadie seemed to grip what he was saying. "He's the reason I am the way I am. The things that you probably hear your mother saying about me."

Sadie nodded in quiet understanding, and Sanford buried the urge to ask what her mother had actually said.

* * *

All the windows were smashed in. From the outside, he could smell the black mold. Sadie stayed in the car, dumbfounded by the story she had just heard. Her father laid it out to her, re-edited, and distributed with a PG-13 rating. Nonetheless, it had still scared the living hell out of her.

Sanford steadied himself; he knew he had to go in, yet it was the last place on earth he wanted to be.

The window slid open with a shriek, warning him to turn around and go back where he came from. He stepped through the window; once he was fully inside, he half expected the window to slam shut behind him.

He didn't believe in ghosts, but he believed in memories. He could feel the malevolence seething in the walls. It was dark, even with daylight invading through the broken windows. He was in the den, as his father called it, but to him and Eric, it was just the room where old furniture came to die.

He could make out the shapes and mounds in the half-dark. The couch and chairs were now decomposing junk. Stepping forward, his foot kicked something, and he heard the unmistakable sound of a glass bottle rolling around. His eyes were readjusting and he could make out more of those bottles on the floor, alongside crushed cans and piles of stomped out cigarettes.

My house became the high school drinking spot, he laughed to himself. *If my father were alive...*

He meandered through the mounds of litter to the bottom of the stairs. He froze. It was there, the spot where he had made the greatest mistake of his life. He saw his child-sized boots, jacket, and snow-pants, dripping wet and carelessly filling the floor with water.

How could I have been so stupid? Even though he was only ten, he could never forgive himself for it. *If I was more careful, if only I went to the police, she'd still be alive, Eric would still be Eric, and my father would've been strapped to the chair a long time ago.*

Tears filled his eyes then ran in a rush down his face on both sides. He stepped away from the image of guilty wet clothes and ascended the steps, where far worse images awaited.

At the top of the stairs, with the kitchen straight ahead, he saw *her*. She was in front of the stove, wearing an apron with the pattern of sunflowers and making him blueberry pancakes because she knew it was his favorite. Her hips swayed back and forth as she poured the batter into the pan; the radio played another Motown classic.

"You want this one extra thick, Sanford? I know how you like it burned around the edges."

Sanford stepped into the kitchen as if he were stepping into a time machine. "Yes, Mom," he muttered to the empty black room, where any white paint had been smothered in dust and grime. He watched the mirage of his mother, being beyond motherly, the way she always was, as if she were trying to make up for their father. The tears continued to rush down Sanford's face as he watched her cook. When she turned around she had a pancake on the plate, ready to devour.

"You want some maple syrup, right?"

She held the plate under her stomach, as the blood rushed from her open stab wounds, filling the plate, covering the pancake. Sanford let out a cry and the image of his mother vanished as quickly as it came.

He stumbled out of the kitchen, into the living room. There, he could see some actual stains. The blood had turned black. Perennial—a long-lasting reminder of what had happened.

Crouching down in front of the stain, he sat Indian-style where he had a quarter of a century earlier. He imagined his father with the shotgun as if it were a profound act of courage.

To him it was, Sanford thought and shuddered.

Is this what he wanted? To change us into him?

So he could live on?

The thought of that turned his stomach sour. He felt the urge to vomit rising.

"Hey, what do you think you're doing here!"

It was a voice from outside. Sanford wasn't sure if the voice came from his own head or not. He got up and went to the bay window overlooking the front lawn and saw an older man standing outside of his car, holding a leash with a dog barking at the end of it.

The man was talking to Sadie.

Sadie! Sanford had forgotten she was even there. He ran outside, his fists balled up, ready to fight if he had to.

"Hey, get away from her!" Sanford yelled at the old man, who flinched and leaped back more spryly than expected. The old man clutched his chest.

"S-S-San... Sanford? Sanford Crow?"

Sanford froze and squinted.

"Sheriff Potter?"

"I haven't been the sheriff for a very long time."

Ava's father approached him, with one hand cupped over his mouth and the other still clasping the jacket above his heart. He was still a tall man but hunched in the way tall men age. His back had become an arch from horrendous posture. Sanford remembered he used to have the quintessential cop mustache. He'd grown it out to a full beard, much like Sanford's, but far more gray and grungy.

Sheriff Potter raised his arms and put them around the boy he once knew. The hug was awkward and confusing for both men, but so was the whole situation.

"You shouldn't be here," he said, looking around suspiciously. "The neighborhood isn't the same."

Sheriff Potter pulled away from the hug and looked at the man in front of him—a grown man, but with a face just as scared as it was the last time he'd seen it.

"They're all watching, Sanford" he whispered. Sanford looked at the houses surrounding him, catching a few rustling blinds.

"Meet me at my house around the corner. Do you remember where it is?"

Sanford nodded.

"Good, the missus would love to have a child in the house again too. She always has something in the oven. I think I smelled cookies baking before

I left," he said towards Sadie. His smile was warm and inviting. He turned and walked to the end of the driveway, his dog graciously led the way.

"We could give you a ride over, Sheriff," Sanford said.

"It's better you don't. These people would never understand. And don't call me sheriff, just call me Ed," he said and walked down the street towards his home, without looking at Sanford again.

"Daddy," Sadie said, "who was that man?"

"Someone that helped me a long time ago," he said. "So you want some cookies?"

Sadie's smile grew wide.

He walked around the car to get into the driver's side door. He could feel the eyes of the neighborhood upon him. *I wonder if they recognize me*, he thought, but already knew the answer. Before he got into his car, Sanford noticed it was quiet—there were no kids in the street; he wondered if there were even kids in the neighborhood anymore.

Chapter 26

The fat woman, Patty, dabbed the corner of her eye with the corner of the tissue. Her sob story was always the same: her kids, her husband, her job, her life, never-ending and never shifting course. She wasn't fulfilled, so she filled up on junk food.

Diane looked at her and couldn't help but be disgusted. She wrinkled her nose at the rolls of blubber overlapping each other, but otherwise, her face was a mask of sympathy.

"It's hard," Patty said, "being this big, it's hard to do anything. I treat the people around me—the people I love—like shit. I know I do, but I can't seem to help it. It's like I blame them for the way I look."

Diane nodded. She had to admit, the fat bitch did have a clear lens into her self, and it made her job that much easier. *But my God, is she disgusting.*

"Can you tell me what your parents were like, Patty?" Diane asked, wishing she didn't, but it was a good way to let the hour waste away.

"They were big... like me. Both are dead now."

Probably from heart failure.

"Heart complications," Patty said. "They would feed me whatever I wanted whenever I wanted, I guess the way I do with my children. They're big too... like me. Guess it's kind of like a vicious cycle, huh?"

"Kind of," Diane said, and coaxed her into delving deeper.

"It was all the time when I was younger. I'd get a bad grade, 'here's some cake.' I'd get a good grade, 'here's some ice cream.' There was this one time at school when the kids started chanting 'Fatty Patty' in the cafeteria because I walked in with a tray overflowing with food and I..."

Diane's mind floated away. She wondered where Sanford was, the one patient she actually deemed interesting. Knowing he went back *home*, she was surprised he hadn't called, and let her in on the details. Damn, she wanted those details. More than anything, she just wanted to know how it all would unfold.

Instead, there she was, with Fatty Patty. She was patient number two in a day of six, regurgitating one self-indulgent story after the next, with complaints and nagging and no real conviction to change themselves. They just wanted someone to unload their shit on.

And why not me?

But there it was too, the irony of complaining to herself with no real conviction of changing anything. A smile swept over her face amid a depressing anecdote of how cruel children could be. Patty stopped when she noticed.

"I'm sorry, is that funny?" she asked.

"What?" Diane said, confused. "No, of course not. Continue, please."

"Well, the other boy had my mashed potatoes and was flinging it from the plastic spoon, kind of like a catapult, into my face. A couple of the girls and two other boys were holding me still, laughing, betting with each other if I'd open my mouth and try to catch it..."

Diane drifted again. *I wonder what the weather in Maine's like right now. Cold, I'd imagine... colder than here.* Earlier, she was at the gun range, taking aim at past aggressions. The temperature was in the high twenties and Diane chose to keep her shooting gloves in the car. She wanted to feel the steel, cold against her skin. She wanted to imagine the worst-case scenario, being stranded in the wilderness, freezing, a bear with her scent in his nostrils. Would she be able to pull the trigger in time? To hit him where it counts? Or would she freeze when it really mattered?

Jake had been behind her, whispering the correct procedures.

"You sound like a broken record."

"It's better to be repetitive than dead."

She saw the bear, she saw the fraternity boy, smelled him, and she saw her father and thought about how he left. She saw her patients, all of them, including Fatty Patty. And she emptied the clip, each bullet, striking home.

Even now, sitting in her leather armchair, her trigger finger itched and curled into a loop. She imagined Sanford on the couch, in that state of his, hypnotized, yet out of her control. Her power, slipping; it was confusing. She had never seen anything like it before. If she hypnotized Fatty Patty, she could probably make her eat herself. The thought of that made her want to burst out laughing.

She looked over at her desk and noticed she'd left Sanford's file out. In the past week, it had been steadily growing thick. She had taken it upon herself to go into his past, finding newspaper articles about a serial killer in Maine, who'd murdered his wife and left behind two boys.

"He was such a nice man," one neighbor said. *"He seemed normal to me,"* the man across the street had said. *"He even let me borrow his lawnmower every weekend."* He was probably thrilled to have his name in the paper. Just once she'd like to read about when the neighbors had always known. How that man would give them the creeps, and they'd draw their shades every time he was outside. But that was never the case, was it? Especially with Jonathan Crow, who'd dedicated his life to blending in.

It's kind of admirable.

She wanted nothing more than to go down the street to the library and scroll through the past. She looked at the clock... ten more minutes until Fatty Patty was out. Ten minutes too long; an eternity in her mind. Plus, she had four more patients coming in, and the thought of that was pushing her to the brink of exhaustion.

"You know what the worst part was? When they were done, and I was left with a face full of dripping potatoes? I played into it and fed myself the food that was plastered on my face," Patty said, fully crying. The dainty tear wipes were no more.

Diane became more disgusted than ever.

"I'm sorry Patty, we're gonna have to cut this short."

"What? Why?" Patty panicked.

"There's an important phone call I'm expecting, and I have to turn the ringer back on to get it, which I turned off to not be rude to you. I'm sorry."

"Oh, okay. Well thank you, Dr. Wesley, this has been real helpful. Same time next week?" Patty asked.

"Same time next week," Diane repeated.

Watching Patty rock her body so she could stand was like watching a zoo animal. On the third body rock, she propelled herself to her feet, waddling like a penguin towards the door. When the door shut behind her, Diane sighed.

She didn't enjoy being mean. *Do I?* But she felt it best not to answer her own question. *I didn't lie anyway*, she told herself. Sanford was expected to call; it was only a matter of time. For now, she had an extra ten minutes to think, and she'd use every second of it to make sure she had the right thing to say when he did.

CHAPTER 27

Mrs. Potter had put on a courteous smile, but Sanford could see the fear hiding in her sunken eyes. She poured coffee into his mug. Her eyes caught his and she instantly looked away. Beyond the fear, Sanford could see her guilt—guilt for having fear in the first place.

The last time she saw him the blood of his family had been splattered across his face. Now, that same face was in her kitchen again.

"Me too, please," Sadie said, holding her cup out for coffee.

"No, not you too," Sanford laughed. "Milk will be fine for this one if you have any, Mrs. Potter."

She nodded and smiled. Sanford felt his heart pounding in his chest and the anxiety kicking like a baby in the womb.

Why should I care what she thinks? Why should I care what any of them think?

"I'm sorry, Mrs. Potter. We should go." Sanford said as Mrs. Potter turned away to put the coffee back on the counter. His apology left her frozen. Sanford could see her elderly body shuddering. She turned her head towards him, her eyes tearing.

"No," she said, trembling, "I'm the one who's sorry."

She slowly moved towards him. Sanford could hear her hip cracking as she did. When she got next to him she put her arms around his shoulders and hugged him. Sadie wanted to laugh when she saw her father's expression as Mrs. Potter cradled his head in her bosom.

"I'm sorry for being awkward like this, it's just seeing you... was like... reliving it all. But you're the one who's really reliving it, aren't you? Being back here, I can't even imagine what you're going through."

He didn't know what to tell her. The truth would be too upsetting. What would happen if he told her he thought it was all happening again, and how her own daughter's photo was found at a crime scene?

She'd probably go catatonic.

"For me, it's meant to be healing. It was my doctor's idea," he said, surprised with how easily the lie had come. "It's been pretty hard,"

"What has?" Ed asked in between sips of his coffee.

Sanford barely knew these people; all he knew was they were Ava's parents and they'd helped him when he needed it the most. Yet something about them made him calm. The house he was in wasn't only four walls and a roof; it wasn't just his place of refuge for when the *bad thing* happened. It was a home. He could feel that the moment he walked in. There was love there. It was the home he wished he'd had. Like the home he'd wanted for Sadie.

He figured his own father would've murdered these people.

They talked for several hours, mostly about what the town had become, what was new and what had stayed the same. His house, for one. It stood there, dormant and unused, except for the teenagers that would break in to drink and smoke. Ed told him that the realtors gave up on trying to sell it. Everyone knew what had happened there. They'd tear it down if it didn't create a chasmic hole in the neighborhood. Sadie was curled up in a ball on their flower-patterned couch in the living room, which was more of a museum filled with little trinkets and collectibles, ceramic figurines Sadie had wanted to play with but couldn't touch.

Sanford told the story of the first time he had met Ava, and how she could skip a rock better than he could. He brought her up on purpose, hoping they'd open up about where she was. They didn't. For the first time since they left home, Sanford realized he drove all the way up to Maine without even knowing if she still lived there.

"So, excuse me, but where is Ava?" he bluntly asked. He had tried to make it sound casual, but with his nerves so tightly wound it came off as anything but.

"To be honest, Sanford," Ed said, hesitantly, "we weren't sure if we should tell you."

"Really? May I ask why?"

"It's just... she's had a rough go at it. And we feel like seeing you, might make things worse... no offense."

"None taken, I'm used to causing that reaction," he forced a laugh to try and soften the mood. "Look, I'm not here to cause her any trouble, or even talk about what happened to me. It's just important for me to... see people, you know? To see the good parts of my childhood... instead of the despair. And truthfully, when I try to think about anything good from back then, it's usually Ava."

It was true.

There was a silent moment, lasting for what Sanford felt was an eon.

"It might be good for her, Ed," Mrs. Potter whispered to her husband, who stared back at her and nodded.

"She lives in Kennebunk now," Ed said. "It's important you know, Sanford, she just came out of a bad divorce... a violent one. She moved there to get away from it, to get away from him."

Ed got out of his chair, walked to the kitchen counter, and grabbed a pad and a pen. He began to write.

"Here's her address, number, and the name of the diner she works at. You could find her there most of the time. I suggest you go there first, instead of showing up at her front door."

"Thank you. Thank you for everything you did for me."

"Well, you're welcome, son. But I didn't do anything no one else wouldn't have done. Just don't make me regret giving you this," Ed said and handed Sanford her information.

"I won't," Sanford said with a smile. "I promise, I won't cause her any trouble."

Famous last words, he thought to himself. Even he had trouble believing them.

Chapter 28

"No!"

Another door slammed in his face.

He felt like a salesman, going door to door and annoying anyone who happened to be home. It was the same old thing: knock, flash his badge, watch their eyes roll, and ask, "Have you seen anything strange lately?"

Selling Avon must be easier than this.

After talking to the immediate neighbors a couple of days earlier—they had only described their screams—Frank hoped another resident in the building may have witnessed something, anything to help at all. A strange car maybe, or a strange man lurking around at the crime scene? But so far, as predicted, no such luck.

Someone was in there the other night; he knew it. The picture frame was missing, the fire-escape ladder was down, and his intuition was howling.

If I only opened that goddam closet! In his gut, he'd felt the perp was in there, watching him. *And probably now mocking me.*

Except the lab didn't come up with anything: no new fibers, no new fingerprints inside. It was as if a ghost swept through the place untouched.

Outside of the apartment was a different story. A partial palm and a few half-prints were discovered on the doorknob. The problem with that was it could be anybody. A curious child who walked down the hall could've let his curiosity get the best of him. But something told Frank that wasn't the case. The neighbors acted out of fear. They walked by this door every day, probably with a quickened gait. It was a game of patience now, waiting for forensics to make a match, but patience was a game Frank usually lost.

"Hemick, who do we have next to ruin our day?" Frank asked the officer assisting him.

Hemick smiled as he flipped the papers, given to him by the landlord, over his clipboard. "Let's see. We have... apartment 20B; the occupant's name is Crow."

"Crow? What kinda shit name is that? If I'm gonna be named after a bird, I'd rather it be an eagle or a hawk, or a..." Frank stopped talking and focused, his scalp raw from chewed up fingernails. "Did you say 20B?"

"Yeah, that's right."

"You do realize that's directly underneath the crime scene, don't you?" Frank asked on the verge of annoyance.

"Umm, yeah, I suppose it is. Oh and also, it's on record that Mr. Crow had logged a few complaints about the Serras above him. Noisy kids I guess."

Frank scratched at his head till he saw tiny flakes of skin falling down in front of his eyes.

"Let me ask you something, Officer Hemick," Frank said and took a deep breath, the way his wife suggested he do when he was feeling on the verge of combustion, "are you trying to piss me off, or are you just fucking retarded?"

"Umm, I don't... I'm not... are those my only two options?" Officer Hemick replied.

"Question answered," Frank sighed. "My point is we should've started with this one from the get-go, get it?"

"Yeah."

"Are you sure, cause it doesn't look like you do?"

“I get it, I get it, I just thought going in order might be more orderly,” Hemick said.

“Leave the thinking to me from now on,” Frank sighed, staring off down the hall, going through the Rolodex of his memories. “A subtle gift” he’d call it, nothing comic-bookish like a photographic memory, but an innate ability of his to remember the little things. In his line of work, the little things are what it usually came down to.

Crow, Crow, Crow; why do I know the name, Crow?

* * *

Richie sat sullenly in the kitchen. He was alone. And he felt more alone than ever. Lucy was at a meeting, he'd told her his stomach was feeling off and he was going to stay in and skip it. It took a few minutes after she drove off for him to go into the bathroom, open the back of the toilet tank, take out the bottle of vodka he'd hidden there and crack it open.

18 months sober and now this?

You fucking loser.

He ignored the self-ridicule and put the blame solely on Sanford Crow.

"He drove me to this," he said and took a swig.

It was hot going down his throat, sharp and biting.

Sadie was off with him in Maine. The thought of them together, sharing a memorable father-daughter road trip was driving him crazy.

"He's no father. I'm more of a father than him."

The bottle went back to his lips. Bubbles gurgled in the bottle as he gulped it. It went down like water.

Before he bought the vodka, he stood in the liquor store for twenty minutes, staring at the shelf of booze. Vodka was the way to go, it was harder to smell it on his breath. Or at least that's what he believed. He didn't know what was worse though, to fall off the horse, or to have planned it in advance.

He paced the kitchen. The newspaper article about the recent slayings lay on the table. He fixed his eyes on it. Richie already knew what he was going to do, he'd decided earlier. But building the courage to do so was another thing.

If the same thing happened to him as a kid, the police should know that, right?

Right. You'd be a good Samaritan is all. Hell, maybe it is him killing those people. Even if it's not, it might be enough for Lucy to see him for what he is, right?

Right. Make it an anonymous call. That way no one gets hurt but Sanford.

Right.

The bottle was upturned again, filling him like rocket fuel, giving him courage. He pressed his thumb against his right nostril and blew out a wet snot rocket into the kitchen sink. Then he walked down the hall, his head finally clear. He put his sneakers on, grabbed his keys, and opened the door. The bottle stayed in his free hand the whole time.

He drove into town. The first gas station he saw had a phone booth outside. He parked in front of it, took another big gulp, then put it down on the seat, where it would wait for him to get back and give him a congratulatory hug after a job well done.

The phone booth was confining as they all are, with four close glass walls and a tight ceiling. Richie felt it closing in on him. He wished he brought the bottle in with him, it was probably lonely in the car.

He picked up the phone, put in a quarter, and dialed the number to the local police station.

* * *

When Frank knocked again, he heard nothing but a stir of echoes. No one was home; it didn't take a detective to figure that out.

"Guess no one's home," Officer Hemick said. "Should we come back?"

Black crows spread their wings in Frank's mind. The name was somewhere in there. *Give it time,* Frank thought to himself, but his patience was as thin as he wished he was. His gloved hand wrapped around the doorknob and twisted, expecting some resistance but getting none. The door opened and the stale scent of an unused home wafted itself to Frank's nose.

"Sir, we don't have a warrant," Hemick nervously said.

Frank's radio went off on his belt.

"*Dispatch to Waters...*"

"This is Waters, go ahead."

"*We just got a tip in from an anonymous call. The sergeant said to call it in to you.*"

"Okay, I'm all ears."

"*The caller said to check in on a one Sanford Crow? Is that even a name? Regardless, the caller said this Sanford Crow might be your man.*"

Frank felt a certain warmth radiate from his gut, much like what the vodka had done to Richie. There he was, standing right in front of the open doorway to Sanford's apartment.

"Kismet," Frank responded. "Pure fucking kismet."

"*What was that, sir?*"

"Nothing, roger that." He put the radio back on his belt.

"They teach you anything in the academy, Hemick, or did you sleep through it? The door's opened, no one's home, and now we have an anonymous tip. It's just a matter of making sure everything's okay," Frank said, pushing the door open further, and drawing his flashlight along with his gun.

"Can't we just turn the lights on?" Hemick asked.

"The point is not to put attention on ourselves. If this Crow guy comes home and sees his light's on in the window... that could be a whole other problem, so we're not gonna ruin a potential suspect because your vision sucks. Just look around the place, and see what you see."

Even in the darkness, he could tell the life Sanford Crow led was a sad one. In such a small apartment, there was surprisingly no clutter, only the essential pieces of furniture any occupant would have—the bare essentials. There were no pictures on the walls, no art, no decorative pieces to make the place his own. The only thing that hung was a put-it-together-yourself bookshelf that stood on a slanted angle.

Not the world's greatest craftsman, Frank thought as he shined his light on the crooked shelf, which held only two books.

The first was a Stephen King novel, *The Stand.* Frank picked it up and let his thumb fan through the massive read. He placed it back down and grabbed the second of the two.

"*Wally Walnut Is Willing To Cope,*" Frank read the title aloud.

"Detective?" Hemick asked.

Frank stared at the children's book in his hand, his intuition barking at him again. It was wide and thin, colorful to capture a child's attention. There was a squirrel on the cover, surrounded by walnuts and acorns. The squirrel had a woeful look, forlorn, and was much grayer than the squirrels in the background.

"It's a children's picture book," Frank said as he opened it up and scanned through it. "It's a children's book about dealing with death."

Something is off here. This guy is off.

He put the book back in the same position he found it in, certain it was the most conflicting thing in the apartment, out of sync with the rest, like a game piece to a different board. *Or maybe it's not*, he thought to himself, eager to look around and see what else might fit.

Officer Hemick was in the kitchen trying to draw his own conclusions. Opening the cupboard, he felt bad for the man who lived there. One plate, one bowl, one glass—a single-serving life for a single lonely man. The place screamed of desperation, and the only conclusion he drew was that Sanford Crow was probably depressed. Hell, he was depressed just by being there.

In the living room, Frank noticed a stack of papers on the coffee table, handwritten. He picked them up and began to read from a random spot on the page.

The closer I got to the kitchen the more my senses started to gather. The smell of burnt bacon turned from appetizing to stomach-turning. My mother never overcooked bacon, but the smell of it was unmistakable, it was the smell of charred pig.

Frank wasn't much of a reader, aside from the occasional Tom Clancy or Robert Ludlum. After one paragraph he decided it was boring enough, and gave Sanford Crow's writing chops a *C* - at best. He put the papers down where they were, noting Sanford's handwriting was the neatest thing in this trash heap of an apartment.

Crow? It was a story, he remembered. *A story about what?* Frank scratched at his scalp trying to remember as he made his way into the bedroom. There was a tiny twin size bed in there, and Frank couldn't imagine how this Sanford Crow could ever bring a woman here.

Crow? Mr. Crow? Ron? Was it Ronald Crow?

He waved his light through the room, seeing the blankness of white walls. *Like an insane asylum*, he thought. As his flashlight washed over the room, it glared back and blinded him after catching a shiny object. He drew his light back to it, and the red flags that were waving in his mind shot upwards and exploded like booming flares.

The gold frame rested on top of the lone bureau in the room. The picture was gone.

"It's with the others," Frank whispered to himself. "It's with the rest of his trophies."

There was still some doubt left in Frank's mind. It could be a random frame, one bought from the store that looked similar.

No, this is it. I can feel it.

It's still not enough. Circumstantial as they say, or for this case, maybe just coincidental.

There's no such thing as coincidence in this line of work.

Maybe so, but a judge won't see it that way. Without a warrant, we can't even take this in as evidence. We need more. We need proof.

The proof will come. Once those fingerprints come back from the lab—I'll bet my wife on the fact that they're Sanford Crow's.

Nobody wants your wife!

Frank laughed to himself, staring into that empty frame. Officer Hemick came into the dark room and watched him.

"Is everything all right, detective?"

"Oh yes," Frank said, settling himself down. "I think we're gonna call it a night. Something tells me by tomorrow afternoon we'll have that warrant you were talking about."

"Okay great, I gotta get home anyway. My kid ain't feeling too great, think it's the flu."

Frank couldn't care less about his kid; he found all kids to be nothing but obnoxious. But as they walked out of the apartment, he felt a need to be polite, a need that rarely showed its ugly head.

"Hey. What's your kid's name, Hemick?"

"Johnny," he said, eyebrows slightly raised at the sudden interest. "Jonathan Daniel, but we call him JD for short. All of his friends also call him..."

Officer Hemick kept talking, but his words fell on deaf ears. Frank's attention was drawn to his son's name. In his mind, the Rolodex spun, stopped at *C*, spitting out a newspaper clipping dating as far back as the late sixties, or was it the early seventies? He couldn't tell, but that seemed irrelevant. It was the name that mattered, the one that was on the tip of his tongue. In Sanford's sad and quiet apartment, he satisfied that itch, startling himself and Officer Hemick as he screamed the name.

"Jonathan Crow!"

Chapter 29

They sat silently, bundled up from the chill of the outside which was still alive in their bodies. Sanford sipped his hot coffee as Sadie sipped her hot cocoa. She watched her father as he watched the waitress from a distance. She could see the struggle in his eyes; the overwhelming urge to quit behind them.

"She doesn't look the way I expected her to," Sadie said, trying to distract her father from his inner voice, who (she imagined) was telling him to hightail it out of there and jet back to New York.

Ava was working the other side of the diner. Sanford stared from over the rim of his coffee mug, hiding his face. The diner itself was typical. Red chairs and white tables, red and white booths. A long bar ran across the front of the kitchen. The floor underneath was gray and covered in mud and melting snow.

At twelve she was tiny, skinny, and frail. But this waitress with her name on her tag, Ava, was—to put it nicely—husky. Her hair was still fire red, and her skin was still peppered with brown freckles that Sanford still had the urge to connect with a pen. When he looked at her face he could still see that little girl inside of her, with the same green eyes, the same red hair, and that same radiant smile.

"Dad?" Sadie called out.

He jolted as his mind returned to his body. Hot coffee splashed down his neck and chest.

"Shit!" he screamed a little too loudly.

People looked over, Sadie couldn't help but laugh. The waitress across the diner looked as well and Sanford caught her eyes, holding them longer than he should have. Her mouth dropped, and she came close to dropping the coffee pot in her hand. He began raising his hand to wave in an awkward gesture of not knowing what else to do, but she turned her head before he could and walked to the back kitchen, hastily.

"Sadie, will you be okay by yourself for a minute?"

"Yeah, Dad, I'll be fine."

"Okay. You can order whatever you want when the waitress comes back."

Sadie rubbed her hands together in anticipation and opened the menu.

He inched his way towards the back of the diner. He pushed through the off-white double doors of the kitchen and saw Ava scurrying out the back with a cigarette in her mouth.

"Hey, you can't be back here," yelled someone with an apron, but Sanford paid no attention and followed the path toward Ava. "I'm gonna call the cops."

The snow turned to sleet, hampering Ava's attempt at lighting the cigarette shaking in her mouth. She brought her jacket over her head and created a canopy. This time the flame stood strong, and the first drag she took was deep, filling her lungs.

The fear of him was unjustified. After twenty-five years and the urban myths that never ended, it was like his legend grew to include the reason why it all happened. An innocent boy became the scapegoat for the lives his father had stolen.

The door behind her opened. She didn't turn around, only stared at his silhouette on the ground in front of her, black and twisted from the light.

"Please Ava, don't be afraid," the voice said from behind her, soft and sweet, just like the boy she used to know. "Don't be like the rest of them."

She turned and looked, instantly feeling the same guilt that her mother had felt earlier. But she stayed on guard; she learned the hard way to keep on her toes.

"What are you doing here Sanford?" she asked with a false bravado that stunned even herself.

"I'm surprised you recognized me."

"Surprised? I've seen your face in my mind every day for the past twenty-five years. You still have the same eyes. But you didn't answer my question, what the hell are you doing here?"

Sanford paused. He could tell that life for Ava had not been easy. Hell, she was a waitress at a diner in a vacation town, when vacation season had been over for four months. It was a far cry from what he envisioned for her.

"Your parents told me where to find you. Look, I don't mean to cause you any grief. I'll leave and you don't have to ever see me again."

The door opened again, and her boss loomed in the opening, ready for anything.

"Ava, you okay? Want me to call the cops?"

She looked at Sanford steadily, gauging the danger behind his eyes.

"No, Gus. We're good," she said. "He's just an old friend."

Gus stood a moment longer, then nodded and turned back inside.

"So, you saw my parents, huh?"

Sanford eased and raised his shoulders as sleet trickled down the back of his neck. "Yeah, I went back to the house for the first time, looking for... I guess, closure, you could call it. Your dad happened to be walking by and yelled at my daughter. That's my daughter inside, Sadie; she was waiting in the car and I guess he thought I was some kind of trouble-maker. Looks like there's been a lot of them over there."

Ava inhaled the last of her cigarette in a long pensive drag. Decisions of what to do next ran rapidly in her mind. She had to admit, it was nice seeing him with a daughter. She could otherwise only imagine him as a broken man, or one hell-bent with fury. But the man that stood in front of her seemed like neither of those. He seemed innocent, lost, and child-like, as if his body had grown but everything else was left behind.

"I wish he warned me," she finally said and flicked her butt into the soaking lot. "Come on, my shift just ended. I'll buy you a coffee."

The more he talked to her the more he could see the Ava he knew. She was vibrant and hysterical. Her laugh was a hearty, obnoxious cackle, and every time Sadie would make a joke Ava's laugh would fill the diner.

"She's got a quick wit this one. No way you got that from your father, huh?" Ava bellowed.

"Him?" Sadie said, thumbing towards Sanford. "He wouldn't know a joke if it farted in his face."

Coffee sprayed out of Ava's mouth and onto the table. Sadie laughed and covered her face.

"You did well, Sanford," Ava said, finally catching her breath. "I'm surprised."

"I surprised myself with this one," Sanford responded, smiling.

"So are you gonna tell me what you're doing here or what? Kennebunk isn't exactly the prime spot in the winter."

She was being polite, Sanford could tell. He knew that she knew something was wrong. How much could he tell her? And how much could he say in front of Sadie? There was nothing he could do but lie, at least for now.

"Well... I kinda—"

"Daddy's just visiting his past, and trying to make things right," Sadie interrupted, saving her father from another lie. He wondered if Sadie knew she was lying herself.

"Make things right?" Ava asked. "How are you supposed to do that? You can't go back and change who your father was."

"I know. It's more about making things right for me. It hasn't been easy," he said, finding the truth behind the lie.

"What hasn't?" Ava asked.

"Everything."

They talked for an hour, dissecting the last twenty-five years with as little detail as possible. Talking in front of Sadie was like having a cop in the room. The truth had its place, but it wasn't at that table, or at that time.

Ava mentioned her divorce, leaving out the long, sleepless nights of restlessly sitting in the dark and clutching a baseball bat, waiting for the sound of her ex-husband violating his restraining order.

Sanford was being oblique. He left out everything but the divorce and told his life story with holes the size of canyons. There was too much to fill in, needless facts of how his brain had trouble deciphering what was real and what was not. *Things are complicated enough*, he told himself, with an urge to laugh at how true that was.

"It's getting late," Ava said.

Sanford could see exhaustion in the puffy bags underneath her eyes.

"Yeah, I think it's long past bedtime for the little one. Do you know of a good motel? By good I mean cheap."

Ava laughed boisterously.

"I could point you to a good one that's cheap, close to the water too."

They stood from the table—stained with coffee mug rings—and said their goodbyes. Sanford knew he couldn't end it there. He had come all this way, and leaving without telling her anything would be unforgivable.

But he'd have to wait until later, until Sadie fell asleep, hopefully transfixed on the sounds of the ocean waves splashing her a lullaby.

* * *

It was a quarter past one when he pulled up to Ava's house. It was a single-story, canary-colored house, with a pointy triangular roof. The house was dark; all of the lights were turned off inside except for the unmistakable flickering blue light of a television from a small bedroom window. It was late, but it was the only time he'd have to say his piece before leaving Maine in the morning. This time for good.

Sadie was back at the hotel, sleeping like a stone. Before Sanford had left, he watched her and couldn't help but feel a twinge of jealousy about how restful it seemed. *She could sleep through the end of the world,* he had thought, and felt an eerie recollection of Eric.

He stood at Ava's front door, realizing for the first time that he had no idea what he was going to say. His closed fist froze, suspended in air as he waited for the courage to knock.

Tell the truth. That's all you can do.

No! Don't! She'll think you're cray. Tell her it's a copycat.

But is it? It might be. Do you even know what the truth is?

The jittering voices ping-ponged in his head. He gave up trying to think; before he knew it his fist crashed down on the door. He didn't know what he'd say, but standing out there freezing and pretending he did was a waste of time. Whatever came out of his mouth would have to do. Footsteps pattered down the hall and towards the door. Sanford brushed his hair to the side with his hand.

"Who is it?" Ava's voice called out, scared, tired, and tiny.

"Ava, it's Sanford."

"Sanford? What the hell are you doing here? How do you know where I live?"

"Your father gave me the address. Look, I'm sorry for showing up like this, and this late. But I need to tell you something without Sadie around to hear it."

"Tell me what?"

"Can you just open up, please? I promise I won't stay long."

He could hear a sigh from the other side. The metallic clatter of locks being turned.

The door inched open after the third lock came undone. He could only see half of her face but saw that it was uncomfortably un-trusting.

"It's late, Sanford. What do you want?"

Before he could even think of what he was going to say, he found himself reaching into his pocket and pulling out the picture of her when she was younger. He held it out in front of him so she could see it through the crack of the door.

"Where did you get that?" She sounded startled. "How did you get that?"

"That's what I need to talk to you about. Please, can you let me in? We really need to talk."

Through drawn shades, curtains, and blinds, nosey neighbors watched as the unknown man entered her house, noting the creepy van parked out front.

CHAPTER 30

The monitor was inches from his face. Frank pulled his eyes back and rubbed the blur away. Reading glasses were one of those things he was stubborn about. His vision was failing much like his body. Getting old was irreversible, but denial could last forever.

He'd been at it for the past two hours, rummaging through the microfiche, watching one newspaper article after the next whiz by in a dizzying flash. Mrs. Applebaum, the librarian, was a stout and quiet lady. She was at least as old as Frank, but she colored her perm jet black above a withering face. Nonetheless, she kept the coffee coming, and Frank was beyond grateful.

He'd made it to the summer of 1969, scrolling through the headlines from Maine and the greater New England area. The backlight from the monitor was not easy on his eyes, nor was the flashing black ink that would blur into faded lines as he'd discard another useless article.

Man Found Dead on Train Tracks, he read.

"No." He hit the button and the article vanished.

Patty's Diner: The New Diner of Maine.

"No."

A Nursing Home Fit For Queens.

"No."

Mother of Two Drives Her Family Off of Cliff.

"Fucking, no."

He looked at his watch, a bit loose around his wrist and dangling to the side, like it was bored to tears and had fallen asleep. He laughed at the thought with delirium.

"1:55," he said out loud to himself, in a poor attempt to kick his mind into gear. He thought about his wife laying in bed, with his side beckoning him to come home. She'd be snoring, loud and unpleasantly. But it wouldn't matter. The blankets would wrap around him like a cocoon, swaddling him to sleep.

His head dropped again, then popped back up as quickly as it fell.

A fresh cup of coffee was placed in front of him on cue, almost as if Mrs. Applebaum could read his mind.

Why is she here this late anyway?

* * *

Sanford had left almost an hour earlier, but he left behind the photo of her. He had told her about his brother and his apparent release from the hospital. Little Eric Crow; she remembered him as he was as a child, cute and harmless.

Her dog, Rambo, lay with her in bed. Having a Bullmastiff with her was the equivalent to a loaded gun. She hated feeling fear and all its attributes: the quickening pulse, the feel of being watched, the constant darting of her eyes across a dark room. Objects in her bedroom took on different, threatening forms. She put her arm around Rambo, and let her hand rest on his side. Calmness began to set in, with her hand feeling the air move in and out of his lungs.

This is stupid, she thought. *Why should I be scared?*

What happened to me? I used to be strong.

She picked up a cigarette and lit it. She lifted the picture Sanford had left her and kept the lighter lit to see it in her dark bedroom. It was of her brother's graduation. Her mother, father, and her, gathered around him with smiles. She looked into her youthful eyes.

If only she could jump into that photo and warn herself, she wondered where her life would be right now. But she couldn't.

She ripped the picture in half and began to cry.

Her thoughts raced, running laps around each other. She thought about the first day she'd met Sanford, skipping rocks. She thought about that Christmas morning when he showed up covered in blood. She thought about tonight. Then it started over, trailing back to skipping rocks with Sanford in the stream.

Her eyelids became heavy; she welcomed the feeling with open arms. Her sleep might come restless, but she'd take what she could get. Tomorrow, she decided, she'd go to her parents with Rambo. Nothing ever felt safer than your childhood home, even if it was closer to *their house.*

Her mind shifted to seeing her parents. A large cup of hot tea in front of her, served by her mother in that nightgown she'd worn every morning for the past twenty years while her dad yelled at the Patriots on the TV.

Her eyelids succumbed to the weight behind them. In a matter of seconds, she was soundly asleep, with Rambo snuggled against her, sleeping as well. If she had only stayed awake for another ninety seconds, she might have heard the muffled sound of glass breaking, followed by the creak of the front door as it slowly crept open.

* * *

He felt himself dozing off again, until a new article flashed by.

"This is it!" he screamed to the empty library. Mrs. Applebaum, as if operating on instinct, responded with a hearty "Shhhhh!"

Frank ignored her and re-glued himself to the screen.

There were a series of articles about it.

A Killer Amongst Us was the first.

A Town Left in Shock, the second.

The Maine Maimer, third.

It was the last title that did it. He remembered the idiotic name.

Frank began to read:

Local Sanford, Maine resident, Grace Crow, 30, has been found dead in her home at 631, Bleecker Street.

33-year-old husband, Jonathan Crow was also found dead.

Sheriff and neighbor, Edmond Potter discovered the bodies.

"Jonathan Crow's cause of death was self-inflicted," Sheriff Potter said. He added, "As of now, he is our lead suspect in the murder of his wife. Upon further evidence received, we also believe he may have been involved in other unsolved cases. I'll make an official statement by the end of the week."

Jonathan and Grace Crow are survived by their two children, 10-year-old Sanford Crow, and 6-year-old Eric Crow. Both children were unharmed but brought to the Fairweather Mental Institution for further evaluation.

As Frank sat in front of that prehistoric monitor, sifting through the back catalogs of the library's microfiche, his gut called out to him again. He read on about Jonathan Crow, but it wasn't the murderous father who interested him anymore, it was his eldest son, Sanford, the boy who made it to a sheriff's house after spending a whole Christmas Day barricaded inside with his dead parents and a shell-shocked little brother.

"Sanford Crow," he said out loud. "Where are you?"

* * *

Rambo jolted awake. On most nights his sudden movement under Ava's arms would surely wake her too, but tonight she was tired, worn out from anxiety.

Rambo didn't bark. It may have been the smell that hit him first.

Bacon!

Ava's trusted guard dog jumped out of bed, wagging his tail as he walked through the opened bedroom door. Sure enough, there was a small pile of lukewarm bacon waiting in the front walkway. His slobbering tongue inhaled the pool of grease that the bacon swam in and scooped the crispy meat into his mouth, clearing the floor as if it were his last meal.

A dark figure stood in the corner of the wall, his arms crossed over his chest, a shiny blade protruding from underneath, catching the dim reflection the streetlight cast through the adjacent window. The dog finished the bacon in a matter of seconds, then thankfully waddled over to the dark figure, wagging his tail as he did.

* * *

"You find what you need, Detective?" Mrs. Applebaum said, who seemed oddly peppy for so late in the night, or so early in the morning.

"I did. It would've been a lot easier if we had the microfiche down at the station. But thank you for putting up with me. You should go home, get some sleep too."

"Sleep is for the dead, or for those who can't read."

"Whatever floats your boat," Frank said, for a lack of anything better to say. "Goodnight, Mrs. Applebaum."

"Goodnight."

It has to be him, Frank thought as he walked out of the library into the cold and abandoned parking lot. He pulled his last cigarette of the day and lit it. Sanford Crow was the puzzle piece that fit perfectly. In fact, it fit so perfectly it was as if it were for a child's puzzle, where all the pieces were large and colorful with obvious borders.

He didn't like when something was that easy, or so blatantly obvious. Experience had taught him the ultimate lesson, if something seemed too good to be true, it probably was. But that didn't matter, and he knew it. This was his only lead, and he'd follow it to whatever may be on the other side of it. Because if Sanford Crow wasn't the killer, he was somehow involved, and to Frank that was a simple fact, as much as the grass is green and the sky is blue.

The road bobbed up and down like the ocean.

His mind drifted from Sanford to his pillow and back to Sanford. The road swayed in front of him. The double-yellow lines quadrupled. His lit cigarette dangled from his open mouth. He was getting too old for this and he knew it. But retirement scared him more than any perp could. He felt no lure to a fishing rod, like the other retired cops he knew, who went from chasing bad guys to striped bass. And he loved his Nancy. Whatever love meant to him now. It was just the idea of spending every waking minute with her that was horrible.

Where are you, Sanford? His brain felt impossibly heavy.

Where in the world is Sanford Crow?

Again, his head fell, and again he brought it back up with the force of a whiplash.

Where...

The third time his head dipped down was the last. The light switch turned off in his mind. His senses went dark. The cigarette fell from his mouth, as his hands fell from the wheel.

As Frank opened his eyes the tires had just run off of the road. He yanked the wheel to the left, barely avoiding a head-on crash into the tree line as he slammed on the brakes. The car miraculously slid between two trees that could have otherwise killed him.

He breathed heavily, wide-awake now. A burning sensation rose from this thigh. He looked down and saw the smoldering cigarette burning a hole in his pants. He picked it up and flicked it out the window.

The thought came in clear. In fact, it was the first time he took the thought seriously. He couldn't do this anymore, not at his age. The case of Sanford Crow would be his last. The finality of that thought was alarmingly certain, and he knew it was the clearest choice he had ever made. With his hands still trembling on the wheel, his face still pale from its proximity to death, he thought about how fishing might not be so bad after all.

* * *

The dark figure entered Ava's bedroom. A six-inch blade led the way. She tossed and turned in a restless sleep; she was having nightmares. The usual panic-fueled dreams of being back in school at the age she was, with a test looming but not knowing what it would be on.

The blue lights of the television ebbed and flowed on the wall. The neighborhood was quiet.

The dark figure fell upon her.

Chapter 31

There's still more to see...

Sanford's thoughts whispered to him as he lay awake, staring at the ceiling in bed. It was 4:30; he'd only slept a few hours. He was so tired when he came in from Ava's he didn't remember climbing in bed at all. Sadie was sound asleep in the bed next to his, chirping little snores like a chipmunk. He looked around. There was a small television and the bathroom didn't have a tub, only a single standing shower. The carpet was thin and torch-light red.

You have to go back one last time. This time we go into the woods.

It scared him when his thoughts came in the third-person, but he knew he had to go back to the house one more time. And this time he couldn't have Sadie with him. He looked at her. She was peacefully asleep.

You'll be back before she wakes. She won't even know you're gone.

Quietly, he slipped on his clothes, put on his boots, grabbed his keys, and was gone.

The drive over was mechanical, automatic; he let his subconscious take control and bring him back in time. He parked a block away to avoid suspicion. Walking the road was eerily quiet. The sun had yet to rise.

The house loomed ahead, dark and muted like it was barely there. He walked alongside it and into the backyard, his fingers gliding across the siding as he did.

The toolshed was on his left, on the verge of collapse. It was slumped, rotten through with holes in every wall.

Good, he thought. *Let it die slow.*

A silhouette appeared in the window, but he recognized the illusion. There was his father, naked and pleasuring himself.

"*Sanford*!" the voice called out from behind the window. The cold prodded him as he stood outside of the shed, just like it was twenty-five years before.

He moved along quickly. Wet leaves from the freezing rain the night before squished under his boots. Up ahead was his father's old chopping block. The innocent face of Eric appeared in the snow, terrified. Their father, towering over them, wielding the axe.

"Don't lie to me boy! What did you see!"

"Please, Dad, I can't!"

Sanford shook his head free of the memory, his childhood voice trailed off with an echo.

He turned toward the woods.

The walk brought him back to a simpler time, where the forest became the land of infinite possibilities. The imagination of a child would transform the dark green surroundings into a fantasyland, where the heroes wore capes and the monsters had fangs, ensuing no confusion.

The path carved through the woods was still there. If it were spring or summer he imagined the overgrowth would make it barely visible. Bare branches hung low along his path, causing him to duck and maneuver. Ahead, he heard the sound of babbling water.

He came upon the creek. Back as a child, it had seemed large enough to drown him. As he stared at it now, it seemed puny, something he could jump across with one leap. The bridge was to his right, or rather what was left of it. Jagged pieces of rotted wood protruded from the water like a sunken ship.

With the water low, half-frozen, and only five feet across, he was able to step on rocks and make it to the other side. The first day he met Ava came to mind.

The frigid air sent shivers through his core. He got to where the path opened up to the circle of stones. There was still no growth around the circle where the makeshift graves were made. He used to imagine his father coming at night, unseen, and trimming the trees around it to make sure nothing would grow past the border. A landscaper for the dead. But now—in the middle of the circle again—he felt it was death that kept life away, as if there were an invisible line killing any living thing that dared to cross it.

His eyes were drawn to the center. Two large mounds of dirt on the ground looked new and freshly packed, like something had just been buried. He felt nausea rise in his throat. The color rushed from his already pale skin. He looked around him, expecting to see Eric through the wintered trees, with a shovel in his hand and a grin on his face.

No one was there.

Slowly, he inched to the center and noticed that one plot was smaller than the other.

"No," he shouted out loud to the empty woods. "No, no, no!"

He jumped down to the ground, on the smaller grave, and clawed at clumps of dirt with his bare hands. He *knew* it wasn't her; Sadie was back at the motel, safe in bed. But that fact did nothing to stop the macabre thoughts.

The ground was cold, but the burial plots were softened from the fresh dig and rain. He wondered how someone could have shoveled through the frozen ground; it must've taken them all night.

He dug like mad with quick, violent thrusts of his hands, until a texture from the dirt and rocks was felt through the mud-stained tips of his fingers. It was soft, yet cold and wet; he recognized what it was right away.

Fur?

He continued to dig, confused. The deeper he dug, it became evident that what was buried was surely an animal.

The body was almost out but still covered with a thick layer of dirt and grime. It was a big dog, big enough to ward off intruders. Once the excavation was complete he wiped the dog's face with the sleeve of his coat and had a sick, tingling fear that at any moment the hound would leap up and chomp his arm. But no such thing would happen; the dog was dead. Sanford stared at it intently, and his blood froze.

It could be a different dog, he tried to tell himself, but as he did he noticed the collar around the dog's neck, with a tag dangling from the front. He leaned down and held the tag between his thumb and pointer finger. Sanford pressed his thumb down against the edge of the tag, and slowly wiped across.

RAMBO

Rambo's head was slick with muck and blood, but Sanford pet it anyway, and couldn't help but think how the same head was attached to a wagging tongue and tail only a few hours earlier. He turned toward the other grave.

The wet ground soaked through his jeans as he kneeled over the grave and dug at a zombified pace. He kept digging, until his fingers went from scraping through dirt and pebbles to running through strands of red, stringy hair. Through the black and white of snow and dirt, he could see the brilliance of Ava's autumn-colored scalp. He pulled his hands free from the ground with strings of her hair still attached to them. He refused to dig any further and stood up, looking down at the partially opened grave.

Thunder boomed as the sky above opened up; it began to rain.

My fault! It's all my fault!

Sanford fell to his knees and cried in long, moaning sobs. Tears tore from his eyes and were instantly washed away by the rain.

A branch snapped. Alarms buzzed. Sanford whipped his head up.

First, he saw the white tail bouncing up and down. Then he heard the sound of the deer's hooves trampling through the forest.

Sanford exhaled slowly, unaware he had held his breath in the first place. He breathed in again. *Smell the roses and blow out the candles,* he remembered how Lucy used to say that to Sadie to get her to calm down and...

Sadie!

Sanford had left her in the motel room. Alone.

He got up and ran.

By the time he made it to his van, he could feel prying eyes on him again. Voyeuristic neighbors beyond those drawn curtains. Sanford didn't care. He jumped into the van, started the engine, and threw the gear into drive, peeling out off of the street with a screech.

The drive to the motel was a blur. Stop signs and traffic lights became irrelevant, as did the horns and obscenities from other drivers. Sadie was all that mattered, and he'd run over any pedestrian who stood in his way.

But what about Ava?

"Shut the fuck up!" he screamed at the voice in his head.

What about her parents? They're going to think it was you.

There was no time for such realizations. He shoved them into the back of his mind.

The tires screamed to a halt in the motel parking lot. He parked diagonally across two spots and was out of the van before it made a complete stop. He ran to the room and pounded on the door, hollering Sadie's name.

He tried to pull the room key out of his jeans, but it clung unmercifully to a thread of fabric. She didn't answer. He ripped the key out of his pocket with excessive force and heard a tear. He fumbled it into the slot; with the first few attempts upside down and denying to turn. His breath was sporadic. The frustration was overwhelming.

"Fuck!"

Sanford burst through the door like dynamite.

"Sadie!" he hollered, but couldn't see her anywhere in the room.

She wasn't there.

A compulsion to rip out his hair rose. The television was still on. Loud, erratic voices from a cartoon, with comical *BINGS* and *BONGS*. With his heart thundering in his ears so loud he almost missed the sound of the toilet flushing from behind the closed bathroom door; the tiny figure of his daughter stepped out.

"Daddy? What's wrong?"

Her father stood across the room; his hair was a ratty mess, his clothes were muddy and disheveled. He looked insane.

He bolted towards her, almost tackling her. She was in his arms and being squeezed in a matter of seconds. It took her a moment to realize that he was hugging her. Her feet swung in the air as he spun her around the small motel room. Sadie held her breath to mask the grimy scent of her father.

"Pack your stuff right now!" he yelled as he put her down. "We have to go!"

"Daddy, you're scaring me!" She was on the verge of tears.

He ignored her and stuffed their clothes back into the suitcase, mixing her clothes with his. Sadie couldn't help but be afraid. The bags were packed before she had a chance to help. She was back in his arms, being hauled out of the room with bare feet.

They left in a flash, leaving the door opened behind them and the television on, the canned *Looney Tunes* theme song trailing behind them.

* * *

It was coming soon; she could feel it, because she was on the verge of coming as well. The phone was in her hand, though she wasn't using it to call anyone besides the dormant urge to orgasm. Her newly acquired cordless phone would do the job; she paid enough money for it and figured an invention as technologically sound as this could be used for more than just talking to people.

In her fantasy, the gun range was empty. It was still winter and snow blanketed the ground. Jake had just finished showing her the proper way to hold a shotgun. His big arms wrapped around hers; the cold air prickled against her skin. With the shotgun in her hands, she turned it around on him and cocked it. *Now take off your clothes,* she said; it was her turn now, and she was reclaiming her power.

She got sucked away into a world where she dominated. Jake's muscles were powerless against her. He was tied up and gagged, though he didn't seem to mind. She was in control, and no frat boy would take that from her again.

Diane bit her lip, trying to stifle her scream. But her orgasm would have none of it and echoed itself through the half-empty building. It was Sunday and she hoped most people stayed home. But she didn't care, not really. The orgasm was pure ecstasy, and she wanted to live in that moment forever. But of course, like everything else good in her life, it was fleeting and gone before she could even pack her bags.

She was back again, staring at her walls decorated by useless diplomas for a life she barely wanted.

Her legs were splayed in front of her. The left leg hung over her desk; her four-inch heel dangled from her toes. The right leg was tucked into her chest. The phone was still in her hand and pressed against herself as she stared at her own knee, inches from her face. Teeth marks were engrained with indentations, red, and almost bleeding. She didn't even remember biting herself.

She wiped off her phone and put it back in the receiver. A notepad sat to the side of the phone, with talking points written in a doctor's scrawl. She picked up the pad and reread what she wrote, wondering when Sanford would call.

Her computer was on. She opened the file titled: *S. Crow*.

It was the story of Sanford Crow, yet to be finished. She was on the verge of nudging it in the right direction, as if her words were defining the narrative.

She swirled her chair around and looked at the wall behind her. Diane's *Times* article hung in a bold, black frame. Natalie Gleeson's end had justified the means. For it was the ending that sold the story. It was the ending that mattered.

Where are you, Sanford? She thought to herself, staring into the frame and seeing her own reflection staring back from the glass. Her mirror image was darker—like a shadow of herself—unblinking. Her green eyes looked black, and the more she stared into it the more troubled it made her.

The phone rang, causing her to jump in her chair. She fumbled the phone and pressed it to her ear.

"Hello," she said in more of a sigh, "this is Dr. Wesley."

The line was almost quiet, except for the erratic breathing that was pushing its way into her ear. She could tell right away it was him.

"Sanford? Is that you?"

"Doc... I'm in... I'm in trouble," Sanford proclaimed.

And with that, Diane was excited once again.

* * *

"What? What kind of trouble?" Sanford heard her ask through the phone, but the question was deadened through the sounds of passing cars. Sweat stood out on his forehead as he stood inside the phone booth on the side of the road. Outside it was raining, with arctic gales blowing.

He looked out through the glass and into the window of his van. Sadie sat there, a frightened look fixed on her face. He had to get it together for Christ's sake, for Sadie's sake. Another blackout was looming, he felt it as dark clouds in his own personal sky, waiting to unleash a storm. Sadie stared back at him with large, unblinking eyes.

"What's happened, Sanford?" Diane asked again.

Should I tell her everything? That was the first question that came to mind. *Would she believe me? Would anybody?*

"I think he followed me," Sanford finally said.

"What? Who followed you?" Diane responded, and he could tell she was confused.

He! Who else but he? It has to be him.

"Eric!"

Saying it out loud eliminated all doubt in his mind.

"Eric? Your brother, Eric?"

"He came up here after us. He's following me—Ava! He killed Ava! Don't you understand? He killed her dog! He's not gonna stop. I thought..." Sanford rattled off the words without catching his breath.

Diane was quiet on the other end. At first, Sanford thought the connection was lost.

"...Sanford, I don't understand. That's simply... not possible."

It was the last thing he expected to hear. How could she say that? How could it not be possible? In his mind, it was the only possibility now. And Diane was the only one who knew about him.

"You don't understand? You're the only one who could understand! You're the one who called me and told me about his release!"

A long, droning silence took hold of the phone again, and Sanford felt the urge to demolish the phone booth into a million tiny pieces.

"I think you need to come back here as soon as possible," she said, and he could tell in her voice she was serious.

"What? Why? What's going on?"

"We shouldn't have this conversation on the phone, Sanford," she said. "You need to come to my office."

"Doc, tell me what the fuck is going on! I just saw my friend's dead body, okay? Tell me! Tell me now!"

Diane took another deep breath and exhaled slowly through the muzzle of the phone, letting Sanford hear every ounce of weight in her decision.

"Okay," she succumbed, "this is highly irregular and unprofessional, but... I guess it's right. I think you need help, Sanford. We need to get you back into a hospital."

The words were so confusing that he felt they were spoken in some bizarre alien tongue. The darkness in his mind began to gather.

"Me? No, not me. Eric—Eric's the one. Eric needs help!"

"No, he doesn't, Sanford." Her words hung in the air.

"Eric is dead."

What?

That's not possible.

She was mocking him; that was the only thing that made sense. But why would she? She's a professional—his doctor. Her whole purpose is to help.

With that thought, he asked his next question slowly.

"What do you mean Eric's dead?"

She sighed.

"I mean, Eric's been dead. His body was found over a year ago, Sanford. He was severely burned in a warehouse fire outside of the city. This warehouse was a common place where the homeless slept. Forensics was able to identify him through a dental match, along with a few other bodies. But he is dead, Sanford, I promise you."

"What? That's... it's just not..." The wheels of Sanford's mind spun at a delirious speed.

My brother's dead?

There was an image of a little boy on fire. He imagined that boy as he was when they grew up together. Sanford and Eric Crow, running through the woods and playing tag. But the younger of the Crow boys was fully engulfed in flames. The young Sanford still laughed boyishly as he tagged the boy on fire, patting the flames from his hand as he did.

"If Eric's dead... then...?" he began to whisper into the phone, thinking out loud, unaware of his own voice.

The phone booth began to shrink, encasing him. He had visions of being strapped to a bed with nothing around him but the color white.

Then came the *dripping.*

"You're... not right, Sanford, and I fear they made a big mistake when they released you."

The phone dropped from his hand and swung back and forth from the receiver. He stepped out of the phone booth and into the rain, letting it wash over him.

"*Time steals your memory, Sanford, slowly, but persistently,*" he heard his father's voice distantly in his mind, slipping through his own lips.

"Sanford?" He heard Diane's voice lowly echo from the swinging phone. "Sanford?"

He turned back towards the van and began walking slowly. Sadie had the strange feeling that she was looking at a man otherwise indistinguishable from her father, but somehow, fundamentally, different. His eyes were like two dull mirrors. Looking down he saw the few strands of red hair still clinging to his wet fingers. He brought his hands up to his face, staring as if it was the first time he'd seen them.

"It was me."

PART THREE

A MURDER OF CROWS

CHAPTER 32

The crow screamed a malevolent cry, filling Frank's morning's air with fury. He'd barely slept a wink. His mind was on the edge of complete and utter exhaustion. The window was cracked open, letting a cool winter breeze enter their muggy bedroom on the top floor. When he heard the squawk his eyes gave up on being heavy and flashed open.

Looking towards the window, he saw it land. Its eyes were black as beads; the beak, crooked and sharp. Images of Sanford Crow danced in Frank's head. He was his man, he had little doubt, but something crawled in his conscience. It's what kept him up all night. The simple fact was that he felt bad for him—the boy who witnessed it all, not the man who decided to reenact it.

"Fucking crows," Frank whispered from his bed. He felt tension through his whole body like a constant hiss, trembling his every nerve.

Don't they migrate south? Or did this one get left behind, like another little birdie I know?

"What's that dear?" Nancy asked, as she moaned back to life. Her sleeping pills were in a bottle next to her on the end-table. Frank felt the urge to swallow the bottle whole. While the birds migrated, maybe he could hibernate this winter, then wake up to sunshine and chirping from a less ominous bird.

But no, he had work to do.

"Nothing, Nance. Go back to sleep. I'm gonna start the coffee."

"Okay dear, sounds good—" her own snore cut off the sentence, as she entered back into the medicated land of empty dreams, where crows had no place to squawk.

As he slipped on his coffee-stained robe, which was so old he couldn't recall its natural color, Frank found his mind slipping to thoughts of his ex and her cold, dead body on the floor. Every time he pictured it he thought about the rules and laws of investigating, how they become nothing more than handcuffs on the good guys. He couldn't help but to see her in most places, for it was the moment that changed his life, as if the self that was him had been sucked out of his body, leaving it hollow, only to return with half of its humanity stripped away.

This would be his last case, that much he knew, just like he knew who the fingerprints belonged to on the doorknob to 20C. Today those results would come in. With that, along with the anonymous call about Sanford, he'd have his warrant. It was all irrelevant though, meaningless protocols adding up to nothing but a waste of time. He had a Crow to catch, and figuring out where that Crow might land wouldn't be hard to do. He had the address of the ex-wife after all. One thing he learned about having a wife (ex or present) was that they always knew where you were.

It was a morning for instant coffee; he would take its lead and be quick and decisive. The sound of Nancy's snores reverberated down the halls in gargling, restless breaths. It was the sound of her choking in her sleep. Frank had become calloused to it and to how she refused to see a specialist about it. He wondered what it would be like if she really did die in her sleep.

He wondered what he would feel.

On the kitchen floor, her head rose in a crackling twist.

"*It wouldn't be the same, Frank,*" she said in a hoarse whisper, "*no one will ever be the same as me.*"

He stared at the empty floor, agreeing wholeheartedly. His insomnia left him dazed, which he knew was probably not a good thing in his line of work, especially with the day he had planned ahead. But there he was, whispering out loud, "I'd trade her for you if I could."

* * *

"Daddy, you're scaring me!" Sadie yelled as the van careened in and out of lanes like they were in a police chase that wasn't happening. Sanford barely heard her, the only voices he heard were Diane's, telling him over and over again that Eric was dead, and his own voice, persistently calling himself a monster. But Sadie's voice remained there, behind everything, pushing through. Through the swamp between his ears, he heard her panic.

"Sorry, baby, Daddy's in a rush. I'll slow it down," he said and eased off the gas.

"What's going on, Dad? Did something happen?"

What could he even tell her?

Why, yes dear, apparently your loving father murdered his childhood sweetheart, along with her cuddly dog. And you know what? He doesn't even remember it!

No, that wouldn't fly, none of it would. What mattered now was her safety, and that meant protecting her from himself. He didn't understand the monster inside, he couldn't. It wasn't like the one that lived in his father, because that creature had fangs he could control. But this? What Sanford could feel growing inside himself was like a disease that had no cure. It came out in the dark while the good part of his brain slept. There were depths to it he couldn't reach or see, and all he knew was that he wanted Sadie as far away from it as possible.

"Nothing happened, sweetie. Your dad is just not feeling right."

"Are you sick, Daddy?"

He looked over at his daughter, and what he saw scared him more than anything ever had before. In Sadie's eyes lived a fear of her own father, and within that fear, he knew life had come full circle.

"Yes, sweetie... Daddy's sick."

* * *

The phone rang, dissolving the image of *her* sprawled out on the tiled floor and bringing Frank back to his tiny but tasteful kitchen, where Nancy had decorated the walls with the Norman Rockwell Collector Series Plates, and a large, out-of-place spice rack, displaying every spice from Adobo to Za'atar.

He picked up the phone.

"What?" he barked. It was all he could muster.

"Frank, it's Longobardi from forensics."

Longobardi was the only good man in the department, at least according to Frank.

"Longo, what you got?"

"You sound pretty worse for wear, Detective. Losing sleep on this one?"

"I lose sleep on all of them. Enough of the bullshit, just tell me what you got so I can close this godforsaken case and maybe sleep enough to have a dream."

"You got it, hoss..." As Longobardi spoke, Frank listened intently, with what felt like a smile growing on his face. It was an alien feeling, one he hadn't felt in quite some time.

His intuitions were correct, as usual, and he'd get his warrant. But after he hung up the phone he heard the faint whisper of doubt still lingering. Sanford Crow only had prints on the doorknob, but nowhere else inside. It was as if once he entered the apartment he ceased to exist. A lawyer would have a field day with that. But it was enough for now, it had to be.

The kind of atrocity he grew up in would whittle anyone into a madman. To Frank, if Sanford Crow hadn't become a freak like his father, it would be considered divine intervention.

* * *

I'm a fucking freak, is what he thought, wanting to scream it out loud, but instead he acted calm and cool for Sadie's sake.

It was his father in his mind that he felt. It was his father the whole time, waiting patiently, dormant like a splinter cell biding its time.

So here he was again, Jonathan Crow—the devil from Maine—standing front and center stage as those blood-red curtains parted wide. He'd been hiding in the shadows of Sanford's mind all along, awaking when his son slept or blacked out.

TA-DAAA!

It still didn't make sense to Sanford, none of it did. How could he not know about Eric, about himself, about his whole goddamn life?

There was only one answer to this, to the problem of himself, and it was one he had felt tugging at him for years. It would poke at him, taunt him, prod him—though never with such conviction, never with such just cause as now.

He looked over at his daughter; her concerned expression, with a furrowed brow and quivering lips, hadn't changed since he scooped her out of the motel like a piece of luggage. If he was going to do it, it would have to be nowhere near her. That Crow gene was waiting inside of her too, and he would never be the one to ignite its potential. He'd go away, take his creepy van, and park in the middle of the woods, where it would take an explorative hiker with plenty of gall to find it.

But how would he do it? That was the question that teethed in his mind for years.

Sadie was now asleep from exhaustion and worry in the passenger seat. Her head was supported by the seatbelt strap and dipped down every time he hit a bump. As he watched her calmly breathing, he knew. It was her only hope for normality.

For the first time in a long time, he felt total peace of mind.

The only way to save her life is to end my own.

Chapter 33

Her pointer finger arched in a loop as she lay in bed, becoming a trigger. She pulled it over and over again, always imagining the same frat boy as she did. John Coltrane played erratically from the living-room speakers down the hall. It made her think chaotically. It made her wonder how hard it would be to pull the trigger when the moment counted.

There was a man next to her in bed who was her, what, boyfriend?

No, no, no, no. Just a man who has his purpose.

He snored like a hog with a sinus infection, drowning the noise of Coltrane. It made her mad, and she pointed her imaginary gun at the ceiling, blowing it to kingdom come.

She looked over at him. His belly protruded from under the blankets like a bubble begging to be popped. He had thinning brown hair peppered with gray, standing up in a prickly mess. She was disgusted with herself.

Come on, Diane. Don't you have standards?

She did, but she also had needs. There's only so much a vibrator can do after all. This nameless chap was found at her local watering hole. It had been one of those days, long and lonesome. Whining patients had replaced her own nagging conscience. But that wasn't it; she had more on her mind than her insufferable Monday clientele. Sanford Crow loomed in her thoughts like an annoying, neighborhood brat, ringing her doorbell and leaving a flaming bag of shit to stomp out.

That's not fair, she thought to herself as she sat at the bar earlier in the evening with a tall, straight martini wavering in front of her.

Very unprofessional.

Who knew what course she'd set him on, or what could possibly unfold. It wasn't the right thing to do, she knew that. She should have at least waited for him to come home, and say what she had to say in a safe environment. But things had sped up faster than anticipated, and she was working on the fly.

At the bar, the schlub had approached her with undue confidence, inflamed by the scotch in his glass. At first, she wanted him to scram; she wasn't in the mood to play along tonight, to say all the things he wanted to hear, to act interested, to wear the smile. It all sounded so... tiring.

When she looked at him, it wasn't his looks that grabbed her attention, no. It was the wedding band on his ring finger, squeezing the life out of it, turning it blue.

"Hey, pretty lady," he slurred, "can I buy you a—"

"Martini, straight-up."

The smile on the drunkard's face went impossibly wide.

"You heard the gal," he said to the bartender. "Fill her up!"

The scene played over in her mind as she lay there in bed with him now, hoping, wishing, begging he'd go away. Was she so damaged that the only reason she fucked this man was because he was married? She tried not to ask herself such questions. With the way she'd been feeling, thoughts like that only fueled a growing fire. Besides, she didn't even come.

"Hey," she said to the hog snoring alongside of her again. "Hey!"

"Huh? What? I'm sleeping."

"Yeah, I know. So get out of here and sleep alongside your wife. This isn't a motel"

Wife brought pain to his eyes.

"Fuck, what time is it?" he asked.

"Time for you to go."

* * *

When he stalked his prey he felt alive. It was the only time he did. The curious part of him wondered if it really was his father in there, or some other monster with fangs, hollow and empty on the inside. Void of guilt. But for now, he'd given up thinking about it.

He watched her for a while, gaining answers to his favorite questions: what did her day consist of, what is her morning ritual, who else had access to the house, and of course the kicker, when is she alone?

There was no need to write down this information because it was the kind that stuck, clinging to his hippocampus as if it were a clipboard. Though, if you were to ask him what the date was or what the weather was like the day before, his brain would be a stormy fog rolling through a deserted street, obscuring anything deemed irrelevant.

She had gotten out of the car with the groceries in her hands. Bags upon bags of food, lady products, and toiletries. He could've asked her if she needed help, but he knew she was the kind of woman not to trust a stranger. In her eyes, he might not be one, but the person on the inside was sometimes a stranger to himself. He continued to watch from across the street, sitting in a bland family station wagon he'd boosted a few towns over. His loins throbbed and begged for him to take care of it, but he had already begun the process of evolving. Such needs would soon be beyond him; soon enough, everything else would be as well.

She was beautiful; he had always thought so. As if beauty had anything to do with it. She could have been the blue ribbon winner in the annual fugly pageant, and he'd still be doing what he was doing. This was his crescendo, the final curtain call, the only true ending he knew.

But not yet, he told himself, *there are still a few things to take care of.*

After walking down that path, half-eclipsed by overgrown grass, she entered her house. He turned the key in the ignition. The car sputtered to life, reminding him of the one they had when they were kids. He and his brother in the backseat, playing with toys and reading comics as their father drove to Ogunquit—not too far from Kennebunk, where he had just returned from.

He looked in the rearview mirror, seeing a brother who wasn't there—young, with a hopeful future. The boy looked up from whatever comic he was reading, his pupils dilated and his skin as pale as liquid paper. It looked as if he was dying.

"Soon," he said to the mirror. "We'll be together again soon."

* * *

Diane was alone now—a state of being she was quite familiar with. When alone, she could let her true self shine, instead of acting with the false civility of a doctor to her patient.

She strolled through her home, practically naked with a silk robe untied and opened, fluttering behind her as she walked with her perky breasts and wine glass leading the way. Music played from the record player. CDs were still the craze, but she couldn't bring herself to restart her collection of rare jazz in a different format. Besides, it sounded better on vinyl; it sounded authentic. In a world where authenticity was rare, she'd cling to her record collection as a reminder of what being human meant.

Her wine was as rare as her jazz; both were from the 1940s. She imagined herself alive back then as she moved around her living room, pretending to be the only woman with a prestigious career in a ballroom filled with housewives and maids. They were all in black and white. Gentlemen smoked cigarettes out of long, thin holders, as thin as their mustaches.

She hadn't noticed the curtains were opened. Her nipples were hard again. The eyes of the man outside noticed; he hypnotically walked closer to the window. As she danced and spun around with her eyes closed, a splash of red wine spilled across the sleeve of her silk robe. She raised her eyes to the window in front of her and saw the portly man standing, awestruck, gazing into her opened robe.

She screamed and dropped her wine glass.

It crashed onto the hardwood floor, shattering. Quickly, she shut her robe.

The man outside was mortified. He held his hands up apologetically and slowly walked towards the front door. She watched his every move, almost frozen, and jumped when she heard the doorbell ring. She crept against the door and hid, hoping the man would think she vanished.

He knocked on the door; she jumped again.

Why are you so afraid? She thought, and couldn't find an answer.

"Dr. Wesley?" the voice called out from the other side of the door. "I'm so sorry to have startled you."

"Who the fuck are you?" she asked, giving more force to her question than she thought she could muster.

"I'm with the police. I just have a few questions for you if you don't mind."

"Questions about what? I need to see some identification."

"Okay, do you want to open up and I'll show you?"

"No! Press your ID against the window you were just jerking off in!"

"Mam, I wasn't jerking—"

"Just show me the ID."

He walked back over to the window and pressed his wallet against it. Diane put her face near the badge and read, *Detective Frank Waters.* She recognized his bloated features from the newspaper. She turned around a little less frightened. A strange excitement of the unknown had taken its place.

She opened the door.

* * *

His needs weren't going to be satisfied tonight. Patience. Killing for sport was something he didn't really believe in, at least not anymore. But after seeing her...

Maybe one more will do it, he thought as he cruised the streets in the station wagon, reminiscent of his father's.

The thought of breaking the cycle was rather thrilling. Maybe this time he'd discard his father's M.O., leave it to a random act of violence. But who?

Anybody, he thought, *anybody at all.*

"*No*!" the voice cried out from behind some wall in his mind, as if there weren't enough voices in there already. "*Purpose is needed—purpose is always needed.*" It was his father's voice. For once, he didn't mind it. In fact, he found it somewhat comforting.

"Okay, Daddy, but who has purpose?" he asked out loud, looking into the rearview mirror, seeing the eyes of his father staring back from behind those horn-rimmed glasses.

"Oh, come on now, son, there're plenty of them."

"Yeah? Like who, for fuck's sake?"

"Well, let's think of everyone we've seen and heard. We have that prissy psychiatrist to get rid of. But... no, we may still need her around... for you know what." He winked through the mirror.

"Then of course there's that man." Jonathan pointed at the half-read newspaper crumpled on the front seat.

"That man is nothing but trouble, son."

"It's true, he is, but he's also a cop."

"How does that come close to mattering? People say that like it's some kind of superpower, like he was constructed from the pages of those comics you and your brother would always gobble up. A cop is nothing but a man, son, and you know what a man does, right?"

"A man bleeds. I know. But it's not the right time, at least now."

"Yeah, you're probably right. It may cause some problems for our grand finale. There's Sadie's teacher, remember her?"

He thought about it, she did have a pathetic air—she almost begged to be taken out of this world. But no, Sadie was going to need another woman figure in her life soon. The one thing that Sanford and he would agree on would be the safety of their Sadie.

"No, not her."

"Well, son, we're running out of options here. Unless..."

His father's eyes went wild with sudden excitement. He didn't have to say it out loud, because they were of the same mind, living in the same space, now laughing at the same twisted thought.

Chapter 34

The kids always called him Panda in school. With his pale skin, baggy eyes, and all-around bulk, the name stuck to him like flypaper. He didn't mind, not really. It brought him a certain type of notoriety that his birth-given name, Kevin, could never do. Only his mother called him Kevin, and he would listen to her use it relentlessly as she'd extrapolate on the meaningless day-to-day details of her life on the phone.

When the phone rang, his heart sank. He knew it was her; it was always her. The woman lived less than ten minutes away, yet she felt compelled to call him at the same time every day, the way only an overbearing mother can.

"What?" is how he answered the phone.

She'd go on in her Queens accent. *"That's no way to answer the phone!"* He was already having a terrible day amongst a horrible week. As he heard her motherly voice, he felt the urge to wring the phone like a dish towel and cover the floor with its tiny bits of plastic.

"Sorry, Ma."

A detective visited him earlier, and the questions he'd asked about his friend were troubling, to say the least. Though he wasn't sure what was more troubling, the questioning or the answering. He cooperated hesitantly, describing the steady demise of Sanford's state of mind. He'd talked about his blackouts at work, his eerie passion for the job, and the ever-growing creepiness that Sanford seemed to exude daily.

He felt like a rat. But the fact that Sanford was the lead suspect was far from surprising. What worried Panda the most was that they didn't know where Sanford was. They confirmed he had been in Maine with his daughter and dropped her off at home safe and soundly. It was all news to Panda. He'd just been sitting around and waiting for Sanford to come calling with another job. *Why would anyone go to Maine in the winter anyway?*

Sanford hadn't been home when they showed up with their warrant. Panda gathered that much, and wondered the mess they must've made of his apartment.

If it wasn't a mess already.

"Are you even listening to me, Kevin?" his mother said and didn't wait for a response. She went on, babbling about her sister and the way she talked to her before, how it ruined her day.

Panda pressed his bong to his mouth with the phone pressed to his ear. He lit it, inhaled, and let the bubbling sounds soothe him. His lungs filled with smoke that he let pour gracefully out of his mouth.

"What was that, Kevin?" his mother asked.

"Nothin', Ma."

"Can you imagine that, sweetie? The nerve of her to say such a rude thing to me, after everything I've done for her!" Panda had no idea what the *rude thing* even was, and wouldn't dare ask. That would create another twenty-five-minute ear battering. He'd let her say what she had to say until there was nothing else, then he could go on with his night of indulgence.

"Are you even listening to me, Kevin?" she asked again, momentarily pausing from her breathless chatter.

"Yeah, Ma."

The coffee table in front of him was covered with the cliché trash of a single man. Empty Chinese food cartons stuck to the table in hardened pools of soy sauce. An ashtray, filled to the brim with menthol cigarettes, dusted the table with ash. There was a porn mag with the pages stuck together and a bottle of hand lotion next to it—the only sanitizing item, used for unsanitary purposes.

"Okay, well it's time for me to go. My show's about to start. Thanks for listening, sweetie. I love you."

"Okay, Ma."

They both hung up the line at the same time, and Panda felt relief wash over as he pressed the bong to his mouth for another round.

His eyes drifted to his own midsection. The white tank top he wore emphasized his cartoonish gut, making him laugh at his own sluggish body. As the last of the weed smoke slipped from his lips, he reached for his pack of menthols and lit a cigarette.

The TV blared, as did the stereo. In his high frame of mind, he couldn't decide which form of entertainment he wanted more, so he let them duel it out in a mishmash of sound. There was an old western on the screen, and the shot was of a young Clint Eastwood in a grisly close-up. His five o'clock shadow emphasizing his intimidating glare.

On the stereo, music blasted. It was always hip-hop in his apartment, in his headphones, and in his car. He'd never call it rap music if it was done exceptionally well. When it was, it was called *hip-hop* in his mind, and *A Tribe Called Quest* was his paragon of perfection. Q-Tip rapped above a smooth beat, providing an unorthodox soundtrack as Clint Eastwood faced another duel.

The noise hindered his ability to hear anything else. For example, he couldn't hear the percussive smash of a window from an intruder. As he lay on the couch and admired the fearless Clint over the horizon of his own gut, that same intruder touched his boot down on the hardwood floor of Panda's apartment.

The oblivious Panda grazed on the couch, shoveling handfuls of microwave popcorn down his gullet and barely chewing. The CD in the stereo was on its last track, nearing its final minute, masking the man's steady breath, a knife being pulled from its wooden block on the kitchen counter.

Twenty-seconds left in the song, and as the beat began to fade, the sound of boots began to soften, as their owner tiptoed closer towards the couch. Clint Eastwood was about to draw his gun. A cigar rested in the corner of his mouth, smoke rising. Panda tried to impersonate it with the cigarette he held, but he knew looking *cool* was something he had forfeited at least twenty pounds ago.

Ten seconds left in the song and the intruder stood behind the couch, watching the duel along with Panda. Good Ol' Clint saw the flinch first and drew, laying down his enemy in the dusty streets. Both Panda and the intruder behind him smiled.

Two seconds left in the song, and the last thing Panda saw was glimmering steel swiftly passing in front of his eyes. It startled him, but he still hadn't moved away, he had only looked above his head to see a faceless man, masked in his own fear. The song ended, and the blade swiped across Panda's neck. He wished the music was still playing so he could listen to something else, anything else, besides the sound of his own blood gurgling out of his opened throat.

He slid deeper into the couch—dark brown suede, now splattered with his own blood, forming abstract russet stains. He was thankful to be high. It made the act of dying intense and frightening, yet somehow easier. After what he had done to Sanford, it seemed somewhat appropriate. Where he came from you didn't rat, and as he lay there—drowning in himself—he felt more like a rodent than ever.

CHAPTER 35

There was a jackhammer in his head. Sanford couldn't remember much about the night before, but after learning about himself, he realized he didn't want to. He remembered dropping Sadie off at home. Him not getting out of the car. Her looking back at him with concern. Then he came to where he was sitting outside of now: *The Peekskill Pub.*

He had gotten drunk—he'd known that much—in an attempt to paralyze his father, or whoever the killer was inside of him.

It could be Eric.

He had passed out in his van and realized how stupid that was. The police knew who he was by now, and they must've known his address, his license plate, and certainly his creepy van, which was a rolling billboard for who he was. The last thing he remembered was a shaky walk towards it, after stumbling off the wagon and out of the bar he was in.

Memories from the night fused in small meaningless chunks. First, it was the bar, dimly lit and poorly decorated with sports memorabilia. A football jersey from the New York Giants hung over the bar like a flag. The jukebox sat in the front by the kitchen door and spun *Summertime* by Janis Joplin. Sanford remembered sitting tucked away in the far corner of the rectangle bar; a fake potted plant sat next to him. Its plastic leaves dangled over his drink. Whiskey was on the menu, he remembered that as well; Whiskey and...?

Tequila.

The taste in his mouth made him want to vomit.

He'd been clean for six months, carrying around a chip for each milestone like a blue ribbon.

The barstools around him were filled with sweaty, overweight slobs. Fat hung over their seats. The air was warm like stale breath.

Why did I come here? That was the question he asked himself as he sat in that bar with his whiskey, barely aged a year.

The news on the TV in the corner of the bar had chimed in with a breaking report from the local world. Sanford heard his name and then saw his face plastered across the eighteen-inch screen. The anchorwoman, with her hair in a foot-tall perm, announced the lead suspect in the case that had a small city on edge.

And surprise, surprise, guess who?

He sat with his baseball cap on and pulled it down to his eyebrows, hoping the bartender—being the only one who actually looked him in the face—wouldn't notice the comparison to the madman that flashed on the screen. But he was preoccupied, as was the rest of his clientele on that gloomy Monday night.

"Sanford Crow," said one of the drunkards, barely able to sit on the stool. "What a dumb fuckin' name!"

The other drunks around him laughed and agreed. Even Sanford laughed. It was a dumb fucking name—a name his father bestowed on him, along with a few other unfavorable traits.

As he sat there, with his barely aged whiskey, he had a thought, or a fantasy more like. He pictured it as his last drink as a free man. It made perfect sense, only he wished it would've been a better whiskey; he bought what he could afford. Suicide was always his answer, but maybe getting caught on purpose was the best way for this to end. At least then he could still have a relationship with Sadie, through long, handwritten letters, and visitations through plexiglass. There's no death penalty in New York. He'd be locked away and left alone.

To do what, though?

I could write.

The daydream of sitting in a cell and writing his story slowly became intoxicating, morphing into another pipe dream. Without thinking any further, he took his hat off, brushed his hair back, and let his wild eyes shine.

The reaction wasn't as expected, mainly because there was none. The last of his whiskey went down as he stood up and walked to the broader side of the bar, where the more down and out drinkers sat.

"Tequila," Sanford said to the bartender and looked him dead in the eyes. The man nodded his head and poured, not a hint of interest on his face.

"That guy looked crazy, huh?" Sanford said to an overly drunk man sitting next to him. The man wore clothes covered in dirt and grease; the strain of physical labor smothered his exhausted face. Most of the men in the bar were from the local Highway Department; once their timecards were punched out, their booze cards were punched in, and they'd drink until their eyelids became weighted down beyond rising, then wake up to do it all over again.

"What guy you talkin' about, guy?" the man responded, unaware of most of his surroundings besides for the bar in front of him, which he was planning to rest his head on momentarily.

"Never mind," Sanford said, got his drink, and moved on.

He stood next to two men at the bar who were watching the TV, one of whom made the comment about Sanford Crow being *a dumb fuckin' name.*

Sanford said, "How you guys doing?" and shoved his face between the two of them.

Both reacted with an equal measure of confusion and bitter annoyance.

"Fine, chief. You?" one of them responded—the fatter of the two.

"Good, I'm good, a little drunk, but good. See I quit drinking months ago for my wife. Well, my ex-wife. Had a kid and all of that, so I kind of had to get my shit together, ya know? But shit always seems to fall apart no matter how hard you try to hold it together anyway. Am I right?"

"Listen, pal," the skinnier (but still fat) of the drunks said, "if you want a therapy session you talk to the bartender, otherwise keep your whiney shit to yourself."

Sanford laughed, "Nah, I already got a therapist for my whiney shit, I'm just trying to talk about life. But hey, I don't wanna bother you guys. You look like good guys. That comment you made before was pretty funny too, about that dope's name on the news."

"What the fuck are you talking about, chief?" the fatter man said.

"The guy on the news, with the name Sanford Crow, you're right, it's a dumb fuckin' name," Sanford said.

"You're goddamn right I'm right, I'm always right. Except for the day I asked my wife to marry me," the fat man said and gave a hearty laugh joined by his skinnier counterpart.

"Ha-ha, well I hear you on that," Sanford said. "You don't remember what the guy looked like?"

"What guy?" the skinnier man said.

"The guy with the dumb fuckin' name. The lead suspect for the murders around here."

Both of their faces went dark.

"We don't talk about that in here, chief," fat man said.

"About what? The murders? But you just commented about the killer's name."

"Yeah, the murders, asshole. The name is just a name, we don't pay no respect to it," the skinny man responded, followed by a burp.

"You see Reggie over there?" the fat man said and pointed to a man sitting at a high-top table by himself. "His brother was one of the victims, along with his sister-in-law, niece, and nephew."

"Oh... Jesus..." Sanford whispered. "You fellas have a nice night," he said and walked away.

Sanford watched Reggie and could see hurt in every inch of the man, as if he were painted in a thick coat of it. The idea that Sanford was the one who caused him such pain was unfathomable. He started walking towards him without thinking.

Reggie, sitting hunched over with his black and red flannel tightly hugging his shoulders, saw Sanford coming and prepared himself for another parasitic conversation. Talking about his loss seemed to be the only thing that anyone cared to talk about. Even the ones that didn't bring it up, brought it up in the way they looked at him, with sorrowful eyes and pouty lips. The man he saw approaching didn't possess those features. There was something off about him. It was in the eyes. To Reggie, everything was in the eyes.

"Hey, can I buy you a drink?" Sanford asked.

"Sorry pal," Reggie said as he sipped his own drink, keeping the glass by his mouth, and shadowing his face. "I'm not gay."

Again, this wasn't the reaction Sanford expected. He figured once Reggie saw his face, he'd see the same face that was on the evening news—the face that killed his family.

"Neither am I. To be honest with you, those guys at the bar over there told me about what happened, and I thought—"

"You thought you'd come over here, buy me a drink, and wax poetically about life and the meaning of it? Or no, better yet, you're a reporter, looking for another juicy angle to what happened to my family? Listen here you fucking vampire, I need your sympathy like I need an asshole right here..." Reggie pointed to the center of his forehead. "The fact of the matter is you can't relate to my loss, no one can."

"Actually, I can," Sanford said, surprising himself. "I lost my family when I was ten-years-old, they were murdered right in front of me."

Sanford couldn't believe he opened such a private door to a complete stranger. But he felt like he owed him that much, and a hell of a lot more.

"Shit, I'm sorry to hear that," Reggie apologetically. "But I still don't want to be bothered. I come here because everyone knows me, and they know enough to let me drink in peace."

"Why don't you drink at home?" Sanford asked, genuinely interested.

"Because they're home with me."

"Your brother?"

Reggie slammed his drink back with authority, then brought the empty glass down just as hard.

"Let me ask you something... what'd you say your name was?"

"I didn't, it's Mike," Sanford lied, momentarily forgetting his need to confess.

"Well, Mike, did you have a brother in that family of yours?"

"I did, his name was Eric. He was six." Sanford had to admit, it felt good to talk honestly.

"Then you know. A brother is a different thing. They say blood runs thicker than water, right?"

"Yeah."

"Well, not sure what those bozos told you over there, but Ronnie was my twin brother. He meant more to me than my parents ever did," Reggie said, then motioned to the bartender for two more of whatever Sanford was drinking.

He went on, "I never had a family of my own. The wife, the kids, the house with the white picket fence—it all seemed stupid. Until Ronnie got married. He had the perfect wife, the greatest kids, the job to afford the house they deserved. You see? He was the better of the two of us..." He stopped talking as the bartender came over with two tequilas, and stayed silent after throwing back the shot, looking more tired than ever. "But we always had the same face..." He trailed off, staring into the distance with an air of finality.

Sanford put a hand to his own face, feeling the subtle creases from the self-induced scratches he'd made. His bloodshot eyes lit up with recognition. Knowing what he had to do, Sanford stood up and put down a ball of crinkled cash on the table.

"I'm truly sorry for your loss," Sanford said and left.

Outside, Sanford breathed in the cool air, as he stumbled towards his van. He opened the door and sank deep into the beat-up seat. Before he blacked out he saw a parked car in his rearview mirror. A station wagon with wood paneling along its sides, just like the one his dad used to drive.

CHAPTER 36

It doesn't fit his M.O. Frank thought as he stood over the body of a lifeless Panda. His throat was slit open like a peering eye. Frank looked into it, waiting for it to blink. Panda was leaned against the couch. His dead eyes staring at the ceiling.

Why kill his friend? It seems sporadic.

"Because he's a sick fuck," Frank said out loud, but still something about it didn't jive. The motive was clear, especially if Sanford Crow found out Panda had talked to Frank. It was the emotion of it that was all wrong.

Frank wondered what the world would look like through the eyes of a psychopath. If there was no emotional connection to anything, did they see people as a collection of shapes and colors—things that can simply walk and talk?

It hit him hard, on a personal level. He had seen this before; the random kill outside of the killer's norm. It was when *she* died, the love of his life.

"He had an itch that needed to be scratched," Frank said out loud, completing his thought. The forensics team was in the room, snapping off photos and collecting evidence. Not like it mattered. He knew where the evidence pointed no matter how tired he was. Officer Hemick stood alongside him, also looking half dead while the other half was being slowly kicked along by coffee.

"What's that, detective?" Hemick said in the midst of a yawn.

"He was bored. He didn't want to kill his friend; he needed to."

"You say this like you're surprised that a psychopath is acting like a psycho."

"I'm not surprised, but I'm worried. He's almost done, you see? There's probably one more killing he needs to do. His crescendo. And if there's a family he's after, there's only one family left that makes sense."

"Makes sense? What about any of this makes sense to you?"

It was a fair question.

* * *

The kids were jovial and rowdy. Being the day before Christmas Eve meant it was the day before Christmas break. There was no school until the new year rang in, and when the last bell of school rang out, the little beasts were released into the wild, bursting out of the schoolhouse doors like a stampede.

The bus drove its usual route, with the usual passengers. In the front were always the nerds, not like Sadie cared about such things. She knew that nerds liked to study and do their homework on time. They were always the first ones to raise their hands in class. Something about them seemed cool to her. For as much as they got ragged on by the jocks and bullies—who always sat in the back of the bus, causing a ruckus and the bus driver's blood to boil—they never seemed to care what anyone else thought. They were themselves, tried and true.

She wasn't a nerd and she wasn't a jock; at eight-years-old such tags were already stapled to most of the kids at school. That is until high school rears its ugly head, and those two divine groups get divided into their tinier subdivisions; groups of groups where kids find their niche and where they belong. Then real life comes along and such groups become as meaningless as where they were currently sitting on the bus. This was all according to her father's advice, who she couldn't seem to get off of her mind.

As the bus made the turn onto Sadie's street, she could see the police cruiser parked outside of her home, and an unmarked car in the driveway. Tiny beads of sweat trickled down her limbs as her heart puttered along faster.

"Daddy," she whispered out loud with worry.

The other kids saw the police as well. Collective "Ooo's" and "Ahh's" filled the bus like the studio audience of a sitcom.

"What'd you do Sadie?" Jesse Blackmore said, one of the worst bullies in Sadie's class.

"I didn't do anything!" she barked.

"Sure! Tell it to the judge! You'll be going to jail, or maybe the same nuthouse your fucked-up father came from."

"What?" Sadie asked.

"Oh, what, you didn't know? Well, let me be the one to tell you. Your father is crazy! Nutso! My dad said he's the one killing people. It's on the TV news. They said he was in a nuthouse since he was a kid. Just like you're gonna be!" Jesse said, laughing. Then he started the chant, "Crazy Sadie! Crazy Sadie! Crazy Sadie!"

Before she understood what was happening, the whole bus was chanting it, even those sweet nerds in the front couldn't help but join in. She had wondered why the kids were acting so strange around her, and why they ignored her and whispered behind her back. There was only one thing left to do.

She cried.

The bus stopped in front of her driveway. The door opened and the chant of "Crazy Sadie!" was released out into the neighborhood. She put on her book bag and wiped away the tears. Each face she passed was laughing.

Sadie stood at the top of the stairs and saw a man she'd never seen waiting in the driveway for her—a plump man, who looked tired and frustrated.

"Crazy Sadie! Crazy Sadie! Crazy Sadie!"

The man extended a hand and helped her off of the bus, only to go up the stairs after and face the barbarous crowd of children.

"Hey, listen up!" Frank shouted, showing his badge and gun on his waist. The kids quieted.

"I don't know what you kids think you know, or what your stupid parents told you. But Sadie Crow is not crazy—she's a hero! She's our detective in training, and we're only here to get her advice on our latest case. So, if any of you ever chant that name again, she'll have the whole department's permission to arrest you on the spot. Do you understand?"

He was met with wide-eyed stares and dropped jaws in response.

"Okay, good! Now go home and do your homework or something," Frank said and got off of the bus. Sadie was standing there, smiling at him.

He gestured for her to go inside and Sadie led the way down the front path, covered in a light blanket of snow.

Lucy was standing at the doorway, smoking a cigarette in a cloud of worry. Richie was looming behind her. Sadie had never seen such a look on her mother before, full of fear, dread, and disbelief.

She looked lost.

"Lucy," Frank said as they approached the door, "you mind putting on some more coffee?" Lucy nodded and pulled from her cigarette until there was nothing left but the filter, then flicked it out into the snow-covered yard. They followed her into the kitchen and sat down at the table. The seriousness of the situation gave Sadie tightness in her chest. She didn't like the feeling at all.

"Is what those kids are saying true?" she asked in a soft voice.

"Of course not, Sadie. This has nothing to do with you. There's nothing about this that makes you crazy." Frank said.

"I know that, I'm not stupid; I meant about my dad."

Richie sat at the table next to Sadie, putting his hand on top of hers. He had a smirk on his face.

"Oh," Frank said. Sadie's maturity surprised him. He looked to Lucy for help, but she was lost in her own little world.

How long has it been since my last drink? The question seemed to scream at Lucy like an interrogation. She fingered the sobriety chip on her neck.

"They think your daddy is sick is all, honey. They wanna get him some help," Richie chimed in. Frank was grateful for the effort.

"Don't patronize me, Richie," the eight-year-old girl responded. It almost made Frank laugh.

She looked towards Frank and said, "I know my dad is... off. But he's also a good person too, and he would never hurt someone else, not in a billion years."

"You're a very wise little girl, you know that?" Frank said.

"So are you."

This time Frank did laugh. He liked this little girl a lot.

"Look, Sadie, sometimes somebody can be sick, and at times become someone else, who is far removed from the person they are."

Sadie was silent.

"Can you help us help him?"

She took a deep breath before responding.

"I'm not gonna help you get my dad, because he didn't do what you say he did."

"Sadie," Lucy said, crawling out of her daydream. "Listen to the detective, we need to help your dad, and this is how we do it."

"No!" Sadie snapped. "If you think he did this, then you don't know him either!"

Lucy's sigh was loud. "They just want him to come over here, and then he can explain it for himself is all. Right, Detective?"

"That's right," Frank said, realizing that talking to children was not one of his strong suits. In fact, it was a suit that didn't fit at all. "Your daddy's the only one who can clear this mess up. If it's all one big misunderstanding, then your daddy and I can figure it out together. But listen, Sadie, there are other police officers out there that won't give him that chance. They think he's hurt a lot of people, and that he's dangerous. There's a chance they might shoot first and ask questions later. You understand?"

Sadie began to cry. "They're gonna shoot my dad?"

"No, sweetie, not if we help him first," Richie said, shooting a look at Frank. "Detective? Can I have a word with you?" He motioned his head to the adjacent living room. Frank got up and followed.

When Richie walked to the living room with the detective following behind, he did so rigidly. Tension ran through his limbs like slow-churning wet cement. Richie only wanted Sanford out of his way; he'd never thought he was dangerous.

"Should we be worried here?" Richie asked, his voice low and trembling.

Frank inspected him before he answered. He scratched his scalp as he tried to figure Richie out.

A coward, maybe?

"Worried how?"

"How? Is that a joke? That a fucking maniac is after me... I mean them... us."

Frank could tell right away he didn't like this man. Something about him seemed artificial.

Self-serving.

"Well, yeah. You should stick around and protect them. We're going to have patrolmen in unmarked cars outside, just to be safe. I don't know much about Sanford except for what I've read. I haven't even questioned him yet. But from what I can tell that little girl loves her dad. So we use that."

Richie's erratic breath came uneasily.

"Ease up, son. It'll be all right," Frank said.

"Fuck no it won't. This is not the way it's supposed to be. You were supposed to have him arrested already!" His whisper was getting louder.

It didn't take Frank long to realize what was happening. His fingernails ran through his scalp for a couple of swipes.

"Ah, so it was you," Frank said, smiling.

"What? What was me?"

"The anonymous caller. I figured it had to be someone who knew him."

Richie became quiet. His breathing seemed to cease completely.

"It's okay. We would've gotten to him anyway. The evidence is glaring."

"Well, maybe you assholes would've had him already if you didn't put his goddam face in the news," Richie said and took a breath. "I'm sorry, I'm just... I don't know, fucking scared I guess. I got a bar to run, you know? I can't just stick around here all the time."

"I understand. Do you have protection? Something you could leave with Lucy and Sadie?"

"I don't, but she does. A Luger 9-millimeter. Sanford got it for her on one of her birthdays." He nervously laughed. "Kind of ironic I guess, huh? He bought her a gun for protection, that she'll use to protect herself from him."

The irony wasn't beyond him; Frank ignored it anyway.

"Just make sure she keeps it handy in the house. Away from Sadie of course."

"Of course," Richie agreed, nodding eagerly.

Frank could see the weasel inside of him. He could tell Richie was itching to get out of there. Just to be safe, he'd tell Lucy to hide the gun himself.

CHAPTER 37

Diane wasn't often afraid. Or at least that's what she told herself. The incident at Berkley College had dulled her, quieting fear to a forgetful murmur.

Yet, as Diane sat in her office she found herself experiencing fear on a level equal to the manics and phobics she'd consulted. But Diane's fear was simpler; she was afraid of Sanford Crow. Since her chat with Detective Waters, Diane had been in a constant state of flux. He'd come for her. She'd been toying around with the emotions of a fragile mind. Why? For literature? Money? Fame?

Things had gotten out of control though, hadn't they? She never thought in a million years that sweet Sanford could turn to murder. The other deaths—before his trip to Maine—she only saw as coincidental; a bizarre throwback to his past. But after Sanford called her and told her what he did to Ava, she passed that news on to Detective Waters. He'd told her about Panda. Now, sitting alone, she held on to her own gun for comfort. The sweat from her palm slicked the handle.

She was next. She felt that, down in her bones.

But if she wasn't....

The manuscript she had almost finished had bestseller written all over it. It could be award-winning.

Her office was cold. The heat blared but it couldn't seem to vanquish the chill in her body. She sipped her coffee, systematically, refilling the cup every time it passed halfway. The gun never leaving her hand. Christmas carols jingled and jangled outside. It was the time of year that cheer radiated. The sound of it made her sick.

She stepped towards the window and looked out. A station wagon pulled up, the older kind with wood paneling on the sides.

She watched through drawn blinds in an open slit as big as her eyes. The nozzle of the gun held the slit open. The wagon pulled around and into the parking lot. She backed away from the window, nervously filled up her coffee again.

The clock read 1:40. She had twenty minutes until her next appointment, which she was greatly looking forward to. She'd sit at her desk with the gun tucked in the top drawer, waiting to be pulled at a moment's notice. As much as she hated her patients, she'd be grateful to not be alone. Her next patient was a beast of a man, one who visited the gym far more than the therapy office.

Maybe I should get back into the gym. The treadmill at home can only do so much. Maybe I'll hire a personal trainer. A young guy, with muscles, in shape. A guy who knows exactly how to—

"What's up, Doc?" a voice called out from behind her. She froze.

She knew who it was before she turned around. The gun stayed in her hand, pressed against her thigh, as if she'd forgotten it was there at all.

"I saw you through the window. Do you like my new car? I stole it. It's kinda fitting, right? My dad drove the same thing."

Diane tried to speak but found that her tongue refused to cooperate.

"Don't be rude, Doc, I believe a hello is in order," Sanford said. "Or is that too much to ask for a patient whose life you ruined?"

"I didn't... how would I... I never meant to..." No sentence seemed to fit or wanted to complete itself. Sanford pushed forward. He charged at her, not even acknowledging the gun in her hand. She retreated quickly behind the desk.

"None of this would've happened if it wasn't for you and your shit psychiatry!" Sanford said as he tried to close the gap around the side of the desk. Diane moved away just as fast, keeping the desk between them. Then she felt it. The metal in her hand.

Oh my god...

She raised the gun, pointing it across the desk at Sanford's face. He seemed not to care.

"I never hurt anyone before!"

"Not that you know of!" Diane screamed back. The gun trembled in the air.

"That's right, cause I'm so fucked up I don't know anything, right? Tell me, Dr. Diane, if I'm so goddamn crazy, how come I don't remember any of it but I can remember everything else?"

"Self-fulfilled fantasies," she yelled, panicked. "You were in the hospital for three years, Sanford, and you made up a world in your own mind of what you wanted your life to be while you were there. But you were just a boy, and life was controlled there. Out here it's not! You're killing the ones you love and care about. Ava, and now Panda!"

"Panda?" he said, the news of his death hit him like a punch to the gut. It stopped the chase around the desk.

The gun stayed focused on Sanford's forehead.

"And now you're here to kill me too!" Diane yelled.

Is that why I'm here? Sanford thought.

"If I kill you it would be the only one I can remember." He tried to laugh but it sounded desperate. "Tell me, if I made up a world in my mind, how come I can't do that now, when I'm living out a fucking nightmare?"

"Self-realization?"

"Are you asking me, Doc? And how about a little bit of your own? Realize what you did to me!" Sanford jumped on top of the desk and was about to fling himself forward. It was then Diane was done aiming. She let her training take over. Her finger fell on the trigger.

Squeeze, don't pull.

The gun made a loud click. Her heart sank. It sounded like the noise of her own death. She'd forgotten the safety was on. After all those hours of training and shooting, she'd forgotten all about the safety.

Sanford, who had barely flinched at all, jumped. Diane turned to run but he tackled her to the ground. The gun fell from her hand and tumbled across the floor. Her face was in the rough carpet, which muffled her scream as she tried to squirm free.

"Help!" she managed to yell, forgetting her receptionist was still at lunch. She grabbed ahold of a leg to the couch and was able to pull herself up enough to turn around and kick her heel forward. She felt her foot crunch into his crotch. She got to her feet, but with one of his hands fastened around her left ankle. She saw the gun peeking from under the couch.

"Ava is your fault! You told me to go up there!"

He surged forward again and took her down with ease. They fell on top of the couch. His hands wound tightly around her throat. The squeeze was firm and satisfying.

Diane made groans and gargles in an attempt to make the words come out. She was on her back and staring into his eyes. While he was choking the life out of her, she couldn't help picturing what would happen when she died. Who would be affected by her death? Who would care? Would anyone even shed a tear? She saw a funeral service with empty chairs. A priest, preaching to nobody.

"I-I-I'm sor-r-r-ry," she pushed out of her mouth with fleeting gasps of air.

Sanford found himself outside of his own body, watching as if it were a movie, hating the villain committing the crime. He looked at the end of his strangling hands, to Diane's eyes—wretched and bulging. Streams of tears ran down her strained and purple face. This wasn't him; even the joy he felt while choking her seemed artificial, as if it were a role he was trying to play. He loosened his grip and jumped off of her.

Diane croaked like a frog and desperately inhaled heaves of air.

"What am I doing?" Sanford asked, staring at his open palms. He had never felt such darkness in himself.

He went to the floor and tucked his knees into his chest and wrapped his arms around them. His face dug into his sharp bones.

The cry came unexpected, hard, and deep.

In all her years of psychology, Diane never had a case like Sanford Crow's. At that moment—no matter what the degrees said, hanging now lopsided on her office walls—she was clueless. She did the only thing she could think to do. Kneeling beside him, she put an arm around him.

"It's okay," she said. "It's okay, it's okay," over and over again.

His cry became loud and childish. Wet snot leaked from his face as he wailed and moaned.

"How?" he managed to form the word.

"How, what?"

After getting himself together somewhat, he dried his face with his shirt and said, "How is it okay? I murdered people: Ava, Panda, and those... families... those children? I just tried to kill you!"

She thought about what to say next.

"Cause you're sick, Sanford, you can't help it. There's only one way to help yourself, and the people around you, and I think you know what that is."

He steadied himself and rose to his knees.

"Yes," he said, gaining more purpose in his voice, "I do."

He stood up, went to the couch and grabbed the gun, then tucked it into the back of his waistband.

"Sanford, no! You can't take that!" Diane pleaded. But he didn't listen, nor did he look back. He walked out of her office.

Diane stayed on the floor, watching him go. The contents of her previously pristine desk scattered around her.

Chapter 38

Work was slow, as it always was on Christmas Eve. But Richie was drunk, which was good. He liked being drunk. *I have control over it*, he told himself, conveniently forgetting about all the years he hadn't.

In the back office of his bar, Richie was alone, contemplating. It was a confining room, small like a walk-in closet. There were no windows and the desk he sat at ran the length of the wall. A small, oscillating fan blew hot air across the room in waves. In front of him was the paperwork of a business owner, most of which consisted of unpaid bills. The fan blew loose sheets of paper on the floor, where he'd let them stay. In his hand was a Christmas coffee mug. Large green and red lettering read *BAH HUM MUG*. He brought it to his lips and inhaled the aroma of scotch, then warmed his gut with a splash of it.

He felt cowardly. It's what drove him to drink. What kind of protector was he?

The kind that stays alive.

Emptying the mug down his throat, he got up from the desk and walked out of his office and into the bar to get a refill. Decorations hung in his way like dangling webs. He drunkenly swatted down the lettering of *Feliz Navidad* as it grazed his scalp.

"Take it easy, Scrooge," Lizzy, the bartender, said. She was wearing a Santa hat. She was the one who'd decorated the bar, climbing ladders and hanging cliché gimmicks up with corny Christmas sayings. She'd even worn elf shoes that came to an upward point and bells on the tips that jingled every time she moved. The merry sound of it drove Richie nuts. He grunted as he walked past her behind the bar and went for the bottle of scotch. Lizzy shrugged.

The bar itself was empty, besides for a few stragglers of the lonesome kind. A fat Mexican man sat at the far end, drinking Jack Daniels straight.

Richie told Lucy it would be a busy night and the place would need him. It was a craven act and he felt like the gutless wonder he was. Drinking helped to bury it.

Lizzy had a pack of Camels by the register. Richie picked it up and pulled one out. He'd never smoked before, but the habit felt perfectly fitting for the moment. Lucy always smoked when she was nervous and swore it helped.

"Going out back for a smoke," he declared to Lizzy.

"Since when do you smoke? And sure you can have one," she sardonically said.

"It's my New Year's resolution to try new things." His smile evaporated once he turned around.

Outside it was snowing at a steady pace. The weather was supposed to turn for the worse. Richie wasn't looking forward to the rain, but the snow he loved to watch. It reminded him of being a child and imagining what it would be like inside of a snow globe. He stayed underneath the canopy, sipping out of his mug and admiring the snow. Above him was the sign to the bar, *The Eastside.*

The parking lot ahead of him was empty. Snow covered the black concrete. The Camel was in his lips. He liked the taste of it. The lighter sparked a flame. Richie inhaled. His lungs caught fire; his hands went to his knees as he bent over and coughed them out—his *BAH HUM MUG* cup tipped, almost spilling out his precious scotch.

To the left and behind him, the alley stood, between his bar and the dollar store next to it. While Richie was hunched over, he noticed there were footprints in the snow, leading from the parking lot straight into the alley.

He straightened himself. The cold seemed to hit him all at once. But it wasn't just the weather, it was from the eerie sense of being watched. He sipped his scotch to warm himself and fuel his courage, what little he had left. The footprints were large, seemingly belonging to a clown. He followed them as he took another sip, then followed that with another drag from the cigarette. This time he didn't cough. Slowly, he moved, creeping to the end of the building, around the corner to the alley, to where the footprints traveled. The cigarette stayed in his mouth and the smoke rose from the cherry into his eyes, stinging them and causing him to squint. The wind blew, howling in his ears. He rounded the corner, holding his mug up as a weapon.

A black cat hissed. It jumped from the ground, up on a box, then onto the dumpster. Richie couldn't help but laugh. He took another long drag from the cigarette and flicked the butt of it at the cat, who merely hissed again, dodged it, and limberly scurried down the alley in flash.

Richie missed the remaining footprints, which led all the way down the alley, around the building, and back to the front.

As he laughed, snow crunched behind him. By the time he registered the crunch as boots, it was too late. The *BAH HUM MUG* fell from his hand to the snow. It rolled under the dumpster. It would stay there until after the holidays, when the garbage man came and rolled the dumpster out. He'd wipe the mug clean from the mounting grime and claim it as his own.

CHAPTER 39

Diane sat at her desk, rubbing the red lines on her neck where Sanford's fingers had been, envisioning the horrid scene that occurred not too long ago. She had cancelled all of her appointments, being Christmas Eve there had been plenty of them.

A newly opened wine bottle was rapidly diminishing on her desk. The switch from caffeine to alcohol was seamless. Every time she replayed what happened, the glass would be empty by the end of it. Luckily, her patients knew what she liked, and behind her desk was a growing stockpile of cabernet wrapped in shiny silver, red, green, or gold paper.

Something nagged at the back of her mind; an annoying little voice, one that normally was never heard. It spoke up in soft whispers at first.

"What you did was wrong... what you did was dangerous...what you did..."

She drank a full glass of wine in a few gulps and poured the following just as fast. The wine cascaded over the glass and sloshed on her desk, splattering red marks on her perfectly white calendar schedule. Was it really that bad, tugging the strings to her puppet? It stirred something in her, a feeling she hadn't felt in years, not since her dissertation of Natalie Gleeson.

The room became hot and stuffy. Anxiety was pounding at the door of her heart, causing the blood to flush her skin.

She breathed slowly through her nose and exhaled slowly out her mouth. Training people to survive panic attacks was her forte, but she never had to implement those tricks on herself, until now. They were stupid; she was stupid, or at least she felt that way.

Paper bag, the thought came like an epiphany. She had stacks of them in her desk drawer for moments like these for her patients.

Inside the drawer, she grabbed the whole pile. A flurry of brown paper bags flew out of her hand and scattered to the floor. She grabbed for one, struggling with her fingers to open it. Soon enough the earthly scent of the brown paper filled her nose, she took large forceful breaths to slow down the helpless feeling.

As she calmed herself, she reached for the wine bottle with one shaky hand. A file caught the corner of her eye as she reached over, peeking out from the opened drawer. *Sanford Crow.* She pulled it over and flipped through it.

He came after me once, who's to stop him from coming again?

She closed the mammoth file and grabbed a pen from her desk. Her hands had stopped shaking and the decision came clearly. She wrote his name in all caps: *DETECTIVE FRANK WATERS.*

There had to be a limit to the doctor-patient confidentiality, when lives are at stake, no? She emptied the last of the wine down her throat. Serenity took hold. Sure, she lied, she manipulated, she had been the creator of her own Frankenstein. But now she would do the right thing.

Maybe he choked the apathy out of me.

It could've been a fool's errand, but she wouldn't run from it. The thought pressed her dimples into a smirk. She put on her jacket and picked up the file with the detective's name scribbled on it. It would be his now. She felt the weight of guilt lift from her shoulders as she walked out of her office, out of the building, and into her car, warming it for a moment before driving off in the direction of the police station.

Chapter 40

Sanford's head throbbed unmercifully. It felt like he had awoken from another session of binge drinking, but he had only passed out in the car.

Passed out or blacked out? It was a question he was terrified to ask himself. But he'd rationalize, it was just the time of year. It was always the holidays when he was at his worst.

Christmas Eve usually fell upon Sanford without warning. This year was different; it steadily crawled up to him. After twenty-five years of struggling, it was almost time to quit. He found himself more and more enthused by the idea. There'd be no more disturbing thoughts and no more voices; no more death.

Well, there'd be one more death.

To think, if he had only done it earlier... the lives he would have saved.

Shoulda, coulda, woulda.

And how would he do it?

He considered blowing his brains out before, never with much conviction, but nonetheless it was there. Messy, but efficient.

He'd parked the station wagon across the street from Lucy's, where he had slept. As he sat inside of it he watched and prepared his speech. All he wanted to do was say goodbye, and to tell Sadie that none of this was her fault. He'd give her the chance to hear what he had done from his own lips instead of the gossip nightly news and the teasing by kids at school. Also, he wanted to say goodbye to Lucy. He would tell her that after everything they'd been through he'd never once stopped loving her. And he would die doing so.

But only Lucy was home, Sanford could see her stalking in the window, wearing the robe that always seemed to fall open at the appropriate moment. She was smoking a cigarette, shaking fiendishly. Maybe he should go in now, have his words with her before their daughter came home from wherever she was.

Who knows, he thought, *maybe those words can turn into something else... for one last time.*

As he was about to exit the car his fingers froze on the door handle. He hadn't registered the odd, out-of-place cars on the street—he'd seen this street countless times, with the same cars parked in the same spots. These cars were different. He'd seen enough movies to know what an unmarked police cruiser looked like, and he saw two of them parked on opposite sides. A conventional work van was parked half a block away, facing Lucy's. It was in front of a wooded area instead of a house. Sanford's hand went from the door handle back to the wheel.

He drove around the block to the backside of Lucy's. It seemed simple enough to get around them—the back of the house was separated by a dense cluster of trees connected to a neighbor's yard. The road was empty on the other side. Sanford parked the wagon in front of the house behind Lucy's. His head was on a constant swivel as he parked the car. If they came he would not go quietly. He had his own way out; it was tucked into the back of his waistband. The metal pressed against his bare back was a constant reminder.

He exited the car and moved through the dark as if he was part of it. The snow settled on to his winter coat, which was a dark enough blue to be black at night. He ran around the side of the house and through the backyard. There was a doghouse and a child's playground covered in snow. He entered the woods and moved through the trees with an agility he'd forgotten he possessed, carving out his own path through the untouched woods. Suddenly, it was Christmas Eve in 1969. There Sanford was, moving through the trees, escaping the monsters behind him.

The back of Lucy's house looked quiet, besides a handful of asymmetrical snowmen Sadie had tried to build, standing guard. It made him sad to see. He wished he'd been there to show her how to make them; he wished he'd been there for most of her life.

He snuck through the yard, trying to muffle the sound of snow under his feet. With every step he looked around, expecting to see guns drawn. But there was nothing. He quieted his thoughts the best he could as he reached the back porch, where he hoped Lucy hadn't locked the door.

When he put his hand on the knob, he noticed the door was ajar. He barely gave it a nudge as the wind creaked it open the rest of the way. His heart hammered in his chest.

Was I here before?

When he slept the monster awoke, like the *Wolfman* movie that frightened him as a child. But no, it wasn't possible. He'd seen Lucy in the window, smoking her cigarette. He hadn't seen Sadie. It was Christmas Eve; she shouldn't be anywhere else but home. Where would she be?

I didn't...

I couldn't...

Sanford rushed through the basement door. It was dark, but he remembered the layout and expertly made his way to the stairs, which he climbed in leaps and bounds, three steps at a time.

At the top of the staircase he exploded out of the door and called out, "Sadie!" in a hoarse whisper.

Lucy was across the hall in the kitchen. Fear froze her in place. She breathed in, filled her lungs, and prepared to empty them with a blood-curdling scream.

Sanford saw. He lunged forward and sealed his hand over her mouth, suffocating the scream as it squealed out. Lucy's arm stretched out, reaching for the kitchen cabinet above her. Leaning back, Sanford tripped out her leg and brought her down to the cold kitchen floor, where he held her as gently as he could.

"Shhhhhh... It's me, Sanford..."

He could feel her breath coming fast and hard against his hand and struggled to find a way to steady it.

"Where's Sadie?" he asked. The question made her body spasm. "Shhhh... I just need to know, is she okay?"

Lucy detected genuine concern in his voice. She moaned behind his hand, hoping he'd ease his grip over her face enough to let a scream escape. The cops outside would be able to hear if they weren't asleep, or dead.

"I'm gonna take my hand off," he whispered into her ear. "If you scream... I'll make you scream louder." The threat almost brought tears to his eyes. It wasn't him saying it; he was only playing the role. As far as Lucy was concerned he was a serial killer, a psychopath, a man with no grip on reality.

Slowly, he removed his hand. Her body was a ball of tension in his arms. He could feel fear radiating from it like a furnace. It was sickening to think she was petrified of *him.* He'd never thought in a million years they would end this way.

Somewhere down the line, the past caught up to him.

"Who the fuck are you?" Lucy asked in a whisper. Sanford backed away from her and released her body on the linoleum floor.

"I don't know," he said and leaned his back against the cabinet.

“All the things they say I’ve done, I don’t remember doing. But I did them. That scares me more than anything in my life... scares me more than my father ever could,” he said. “I’m not here to hurt you; I never wanted to hurt anybody.”

There was a time Lucy loved this man. Even for all of his faults, at one time he was a man worth loving.

“There are cops outside you know?” Lucy sighed.

“Yeah, I know.”

She could hear the defeat in his tone and see it in his posture. His shoulders sank, and his head dropped with them, falling into his chest.

“Coffee?” she asked.

The pot was half full, with the bottom of it charred from constant usage.

Sanford nodded.

“So, what do you want?” She asked as she poured them both a cup, watching the scene unfold as if she were outside herself.

“Just a goodbye,” Sanford said and sipped his burnt coffee.

“Don’t be so dramatic. You say that like we’re in a goddamn movie.”

“Where is she?”

Lucy’s face darkened.

“I’m not...” she began to say but realized she needed to tread carefully. “She’s gone for the night, sleeping at a friend’s house. I thought it was best for her to be somewhere else.”

“Somewhere else? It’s Christmas Eve, she needs to be with family.”

“Family? Is that what you are now? You haven’t been here for years, Sanford. And you’ve never been here on Christmas. And now look what you’ve done. You’ve killed children. Children, Sanford. And you expect to be a father to my daughter!” Her voice was rising.

“If you came here to kill me, Sanford, just do it already! But I will never let you hurt her!”

“Hurt her?” Sanford said, getting up from the chair with a jump. “You really think I would do that? Do you not know me at all?”

Lucy stared blankly and then fell into a fit of delirious laughter.

“Is that a joke? How could I know you, how the fuck could anyone know you? You don’t even know yourself!”

Sanford had no response; he agreed whole-heartedly. He didn’t know himself at all. The things he’d done were things done by a stranger, a maniac, a wandering drifter he had never met and never wanted to. He could feel that part lurking in his mind, laying footprints in his father’s shoes. Biding its time.

“You’re right, I shouldn’t be here at all.” He spoke carefully. “I would never hurt you or Sadie in a million years, but there’s something inside of me. I think it’s Eric.”

“Eric? As in your brother, Eric?”

“Yeah, Diane thinks I conjured him up out of some kind of guilt. And he’s in me, fueled by anger and hate, the culmination of my father’s legacy. I have no control over him... I have no control over myself. There’s only one solution here. I think there was always only one solution.”

Sanford reached behind his back and under his shirt. He gripped the gun’s handle and pulled it out. In that moment he felt the clearest he’d felt in a long time. There was no more waiting, it was going to happen here and now, and he was happy that Sadie wasn’t around.

Lucy saw the gun drop to the side of his hip. She wanted to scream but couldn’t. Thoughts raced at Olympic speed and fear froze all other motor skills. Her eyes went back to the cabinet above her.

Sanford squinted looking at it. He lurched over and opened the cabinet door, hearing Lucy panting.

Her gun was on the bottom shelf. The gun Sanford had bought for her.

He grabbed it and looked at it confused.

"What were you gonna do with this?"

She didn't answer. She watched as he pulled out the cartridge to check the ammo, and popped it back in.

"I told you, Lucy, I'm not here to hurt *you.*"

With both guns in his hands, he lifted her's and turned it towards himself, pressing the nose of it against the side of his own skull.

"Sanford, no!" Lucy managed to yell, breaking out of her petrified state.

"It's okay, Luce. This is the only way. I see that now. I won't be a coward like my father. It'll just be me that goes. None of you are coming with me."

Time slowed. He smelled the burnt bacon his mother had cooked that fateful morning. The chill in the air from the power outage. He saw his mother, dead on the floor. The butcher knife. Eric huddled on his knees in the corner, blank and lost. His father, Jonathan, sitting in his favorite armchair, whistling *Silent Night* with a shotgun to his side. Sanford took a deep breath and closed his eyes.

The doorbell rang.

Sanford spun around. He instinctively aimed both guns at the door, ready to shoot through it.

"Expecting company?" Sanford asked with a growl.

Lucy tightened.

"Richie," she confessed. "He's supposed to come over after work."

"Well, shit. Go on," he said, waving the gun towards the door, "answer it."

Lucy swallowed what bit of courage she had left, along with the turnip-sized lump in her throat.

She heard each raindrop pattering the house as a plea to run, and her pulse began to quicken with them.

She had no love for Richie. The truth was she did love Sanford; he gave her Sadie. But that didn't mean she wanted Richie dead.

A metal click sounded as Sanford cocked the killing machine in his hand.

"Open it," Sanford demanded. He tucked Lucy's gun into the back of his jeans. Better to aim with one.

Her sweat-filled palm wrapped around the doorknob, hoping he'd change his mind before she turned it.

She hesitated.

"Do it!" he shouted and pointed the gun at her head.

There were no thoughts now, only reaction. She turned the knob like there was never a choice. The door swung open, letting in a gust of furious wind and pelting sleet. They both stared out and saw no one standing there. Confusion swarmed for a brief second, until they looked towards the ground.

Lucy screamed. She fell towards the door and crashed into it. It held her up. Sanford stared blankly at what was in front of him, bewildered.

It was Richie, sitting on the concrete of the walkway. He was soaking wet and hunched over; his chin was to his chest. He looked like a drunk who'd passed out where he'd fallen.

Sanford inched closer to him, slowly, expecting him to leap up at any moment.

"Rich?" he whispered. He nudged his feet with his own; Richie didn't budge.

The rain was coming down harder, soaking Sanford from head to toe. He kneeled down, bringing his face in closer to Richie's shadowed features. "You alright, man?" he asked and gave him a little push on his shoulder. Richie limply collapsed on his back. His eyes rolled to the back of his head. Lucy screamed again as she saw the knife sticking out of his sternum.

"No, no, no! What'd you do, Sanford? What the fuck'd you do?" Lucy turned her attention towards the street where one of the cop cars was parked. "Help! He's here! He killed Richie!"

"Lucy... how could I? I was with you..."

She could barely see the car through the rain and rolling fog, but the silhouette was unmistakable. The policeman's car was parked right in front of the house, where a streetlight shone behind it. In a small break in the fog, she saw the officer, leaning against the opened window, unresponsive. He was dead, even through the darkness she could tell.

"Sanford... how could you—" She turned around and gasped. Her face turned white. Someone was standing behind Sanford—a man, tall, skinny and expressionless. She couldn't move. The rain turned to snow.

Sanford watched her, mystified himself. Her hair and white nightgown were wet, accentuating her curves. Too many emotions gathered in him.

"Sanford, behind you!" she finally screamed.

As he started to turn around he felt a sharp pain in his head, erasing those scattered thoughts. His legs gave out from under him and he fell to the cold, wet pavement. He saw nothing but the night sky. The clouds were a deep mass, smothering the moon and the Earth's shadow across it.

What have I done? It was the last coherent thought he made.

He heard Lucy scream.

His vision faded to gray, then everything went black.

CHAPTER 41

Sweat stains pooled in Frank's armpits and down his back. The police station's heat was cranked up enough to thaw an iceman. The bright lights above him made it worse. He was in the Interrogation Room, being the room with the biggest table, and the least distractions. The large two-way mirror reflected his frustration. Frank scratched at his scalp while reading file after file, hoping to dig out a decent thought that would weave it all together.

It was already a long night. The coffee tasted as stale as the air around him, but he gulped it down relentlessly. In front of him, the table was covered with photos and files. Some were of a warehouse fire not so long ago, where Eric's body had turned up. Others were of Jonathan Crow and Sanford.

"Merry Christmas, Frank, or is it Ebenezer now?"

"Huh?" Frank responded, annoyed, and looked up to see Detective Cohen, the only other detective in the department worth a damn—in Frank's eyes.

"It's past midnight, it's Christmas. Don't you have a wife to get home to?" Cohen said, happy to have struck a nerve.

"What? Oh, she's sleeping now anyway. This is urgent. Why are you here? It's Christmas, don't you have a family to annoy instead of me?"

“I do, but we’re Jewish, so fuck Christmas,” he said and laughed. “Look, I just got in to wrap up a few things, but I saw this on my desk.” He waved a file in his hand. “It must’ve gotten mixed up, cause someone left it for you.”

Frank finally gave his full attention.

“What’s that? Give it here.”

“A please wouldn’t hurt.”

“I could make it hurt.”

Cohen chuckled and threw the thick file onto the table. It made an audible thump. Frank saw his stenciled name and tore into it like a starving dog.

“Does Sergeant Arrogant know you’re here?”

“Pssh,” Frank responded, “He wouldn’t know if he was here.”

“Good point,” Cohen laughed. “Hey, seriously, merry Christmas. Don’t ruin the holiday by being here too long, huh? Give Nance my best.”

“Yeah,” Frank said, flipping through the pages, barely paying attention. “Same to you.”

What he came across stole his breath. There were two stacks of files within the folder, and he had put them side-by-side in comparison. They were detailed medical records conducted for a research paper; it all stemmed from the Fairweather Mental Institution outside of Portland, Maine. The information was concerned with two subjects, both unidentified by name, but brothers, deeply affected by the same traumatic event.

Each sentence he read opened a new tunnel in which he found himself burrowing deeper, expecting some form of light to emerge on the other side. But the files were too massive; he couldn’t risk skipping a syllable. He got up and poured himself his sixth cup of coffee; his hands shook as he poured.

The end was near.

He could feel it.

He kept on reading.

* * *

"Deck the hall with boughs of holly. Fa la la la la la la la la! 'Tis the season to be jolly. Fa la la la la la la la la!"

The family sang along joyfully. Even Joy sang, who had been Sadie's neighborhood friend for as long as she could remember. The father wore a sweater too ugly for words. The mother kept her wine glass full with the sweetest of white wines, puckering her cheeks every time she sipped, and she sipped it often. The younger brother clapped along off tempo, decked out in his Christmas pajamas. Even the family dog, Charlie, sat there with antlers over his ears and a miserable look on his face.

Sadie felt like a shadow in the room, something beneath and behind the lights glistening off the Christmas tree. All she wanted was to go home and enjoy Christmas Eve with her mother the way they always had.

Sadie thought about past Christmases and the traditions that clung to her and her mother like static. They'd watch *A Christmas Story* to begin the day, sitting on the floor in front of the television. Halfway through they'd get up and leave the rest playing in the background as they decorated their tree, bought the day before by mutual agreement.

Her mother would put on music—all the Christmas classics, and a few lesser of the known besides to them, giving them the feeling of it being their own. The fact that they didn't get to decorate the tree this year made her sad to think about. It stood barren in their living room, like a lost tree had wandered in from the woods.

What Sadie loved the most were the smells. Baked cookies, pine, and that crisp scent in the cold winter air mixed together to form the unmistakable smell of Christmas.

The one thing she didn't like was the continuous absence of her father. This time of year always came along with her father's disappearance. There wasn't a time she could remember—even when they were together as a family—when he was around. It was almost as if he turned into Santa, and vanished every year to do his job. That was the lie her mother told her once when she was five, and it stuck, for a while. She even told her friends how her daddy was Santa. "*That's why their names are similar,*" Lucy had told her. "*Santa and Sanford, Sanford and Santa, they're two of the same.*" The truth came around the same time as the divorce.

There was something in her telling her to go home. Whispering that at this very moment her mother and father were at the house, together, waiting for her to decorate the tree. She envisioned herself atop her father's shoulders, placing the star on top. She saw the perfect Christmas, no matter how crazy the concept seemed.

Yet, there she was, engulfed in a bizarro *Disney* depiction of a Christmas gone wrong. The family was gathered around the stereo, swaying back and forth and singing. She had put on the fake smile and moved her lips along with the words, but not a lyric slipped out. She felt like crying.

As dorky as they were, they were dorky *together*.

"I gotta go to the bathroom," she whispered to Joy in the middle of their Rudolph rendition.

"Okay, hurry up," Joy said. "Frosty's up next."

She nodded her head in fake glee and backed out of the circle, creating a gap that instantly closed in on itself, as if the Christmas spirit had consumed the empty space.

However, before Sadie could escape to the bathroom, she heard the record scratch to a halt. The family cheered, hollering over the timid chimes of the clock.

"Merry Christmas!" they shouted in unison. Smiles and rosy cheeks surrounded her. As Sadie tried to back away and get to the bathroom—which she didn't *need* to use—they flanked her, suffocating her with love through hugs and kisses.

It was a nightmare.

"This must be so hard for you," the drunk mother said. "We're gonna make this the best Christmas you can possibly have, we pro-*umh*-mise." She hiccuped.

"Thank you," Sadie said. Her politeness was welcomed by another hug. Christ, how she missed being home.

"Well, it's Christmas now, so you know what that means, Joy," the father said.

"Santa's coming!" Joy responded and her baby brother began to cry.

"Danny's a little scared of Santa," the father said. "Doesn't understand the concept yet."

"He should be scared. A strange man like that, breaking into your home in the middle of the night to eat cookies. Can you say Amber alert?" Sadie laughed at her own joke.

The family quieted and looked at her.

"Sorry, it was just a bad joke. I can't wait for Santa!" She beamed her best false smile.

"Well," the father went on, "it's time for bed then. You know he won't leave presents if you're still awake."

"Oh no! Come on, Sadie! Hurry up!" Joy shouted and scurried quickly down the hall. Sadie could only sigh, hoping it was indiscrete.

They got into her room and Joy was under the covers before Sadie could blink.

"Really? I thought you were joking," Sadie said.

"Joking about what?" Joy's voice came muffled from under the covers.

"Getting into bed before Santa comes. You were saying that for your brother's sake, weren't you?"

"What? What are you talking about?"

"You do know Santa's not real, right?" Sadie said as a matter of fact before realizing she couldn't take it back.

"He's real! You're a liar!" Joy shouted in a whisper.

Sadie sighed again.

"You really think some fat magic man flying through the sky with a bunch of deer? Deer can't fly, Joy, they can barely walk without crapping everywhere."

"Stop it!"

"Stop what? Being honest with you when no one else will? You should be thanking me. I bet you still believe in the Tooth Fairy, and the Easter Bunny too, right?" Sadie felt a surge of pleasure. Hurting Joy wasn't really the goal, but something had to change; maybe if she offended Joy enough, she'd be kicked out and forced to go back home—the only place she desired to be.

"Tell me, what does a big furry bunny hiding pastel-painted, hard-boiled eggs have to do with Jesus? If I woke up and saw a creature like that, I'd beg my dad to shoot it."

"Yeah? And your crazy dad would love to!" This time Joy's shout was far from a whisper.

Sadie fell silent. Tears flooded her face.

Pure blistering rage erupted like a shook-up bottle of soda suddenly uncapped. Sadie was on top of Joy, crying uncontrollably and raining down weak but meaningful slaps. Each strike only connected with blankets, delivering little to no force, but it was enough to make Joy scream.

"Take it back!" Sadie shouted.

Joy's father charged into the room and pulled her off of Joy.

"Santa's real!"

"My dad is not a killer!"

The parents had no idea what was going on. It was Christmas after all, such behavior was a far cry from what their traditions allowed.

"Mom, she's lying, right?" Joy asked.

Her mother was too drunk for such questions.

"It's not that he's not real... it's that he's... I don't... um."

It was all Joy needed before she slipped into hysterics. Sadie had calmed but was still in the grip of Joy's father. Maybe now she could go home. She had, in fact, ruined their Christmas.

They calmed Joy down the best they could and brought Sadie out into the living room. Going home was not allowed, nor was sleeping in Joy's bedroom. The parents set up blankets on the living-room couch and pleaded with her to just go to sleep.

Guilt seeped in.

Laying there, emerged in the corona of Christmas lights, she thought about her dad, where he was, and what he was doing. Sleep would not come tonight, but she had an inkling that her father might. This Christmas, maybe he was finally coming home.

— • —

Chapter 42

Sirens rang in his ears. It wasn't from a police car or ambulance; it was just ringing—a distorted high-pitched nuisance. Sanford was slowly awakening from a deep slumber, his head pounding.

He ran his fingers through his hair, lying on his side. His palm pressed against his skull, trying to suppress the incessant throbbing. He felt a sticky wetness on the back of his head; it ran down his neck in a warm stream.

It was time to breathe. He inhaled deeply, slowly filling his lungs to capacity, then letting the air wheeze out like a leaking tire. All he wanted to do was sleep.

Sanford rolled onto his back and opened his eyes in the dimly lit room. He stared up at the ceiling. There was the ugly brown watermark from a leak in the upstairs bathroom. It reminded him of long ago. A period so detached from his life now that he felt it belonged to another person.

Maybe it did.

His hand stretched out from his side, slowly and awkwardly. He thought for sure he had a concussion.

Bare skin touched his reaching hand. Unresponsive. He didn't dare look. Tears streamed from his eyes as he ran his hand up further and felt her hair. It was wet and tangled. He turned his head and was met with her blank, lifeless eyes.

Lucy...

He rolled himself up and kneeled over her body. He used his hands to try and cover up the puncture wounds in her chest and stomach, as if he could stop the bleeding by pushing the blood back from where it came. He couldn't peel his eyes away from hers.

Why'd you kill me, Sanford?

I thought you loved me.

Why would you take me away from Sadie?

Why are you just like your father?

"Shut up!" he screamed into her still face.

He wanted to pick her up and hold her but he was too afraid. He could only kneel in her blood and hold her hand. The same knife that was sticking out of Richie's sternum was now sticking out of her. And then it hit him.

Sadie.

What if she came home? What if she saw it? What would that turn her into?

Me.

Sadie deserved better than that; she deserved better than him.

I have to leave something behind... an explanation. An apology.

That's when he thought about his sessions with Diane. The writing seemed to help. The writing cleared his mind, helped him cope, gave him the chance to see the situation from outside of himself. Maybe...

He went into the kitchen and grabbed a legal pad and pencil from the junk drawer, bringing it back into the living room. When he saw Lucy again the hairs on the back of his neck stood up. It was the way she was laid out.

"*Is mommy sleeping?*" he heard Eric asking him. It was a voice so tiny and distant he barely heard it at all.

It was the same: the stab wounds, the configuration of her body, it was the same as his mother.

The clock on the wall read 1:25 A.M. It was Christmas morning after all, and he felt like that scared little boy from twenty-five-years ago, only taller.

Before he realized what he was doing, he grabbed the knife by the handle and pulled it free from her stomach. A spout of blood spat up like a weak geyser.

He was about to wipe off his fingerprints on the knife but thought, *what's the difference?* It was obvious who'd killed her.

He sat down and placed the knife on the coffee table next to his pad. He picked up the pencil. Nearing its end, everything became clear. He put pencil to paper.

By the time I came to, my palms were caked in her blood...

A good start. It was a decent way to capture the reader's attention, but would that reader be a little girl or a stocky detective?

He couldn't know; the only thing he knew was he needed to write it down.

He needed to write it all down.

CHAPTER 43

Frank put down the file and rubbed his eyes.

"You look like shit, Frank," Sergeant Harrigan said, stepping into the room.

Frank's back felt like a hunchback's, with large black bags hanging under his eyes.

What the fuck's he doing here?

"Forgot my wife's present. Had it wrapped up in my desk drawer... Rachel wrapped it for me," Harrigan answered the question that wasn't asked aloud.

"Okay," was all Frank could say, his head buried in the papers.

"What you doing here so late, Frank? It's Christmas."

"Look, just let me do my job. I'm having a breakthrough here."

"Breakthrough to what? The Crow case? What's there to breakthrough to? Once we get this Sanford Crow, the case will be closed. If you think you can just sit here and put in overtime for a case that's already solved, you're sadly fuckin' mistaken."

"That's not what—"

"I know what you and the men think of me," Harrigan said. The vulnerability behind his words made Frank cringe. "Sergeant Arrogant, right? Well, I may be arrogant, but I'm not all that dumb. You're trying to get those overtime Christmas hours! Fuck that! Now, I'm no Scrooge, so I'm telling you to go home to your wife on Christmas!"

Frank fell somewhat speechless.

"Sir… if you'd just look at what I found here. There's a chance that Sanford Crow isn't—"

"This discussion is over, Frank. There's no more taxpayer money going into this one. Case is solved, and like I said, once that sick fuck is in chains, the case is closed. Now, if you wanna entertain yourself with some of your bullshit theories, that's your business, and you do your business on your time, not ours. You understand me, Frank? So go home; that's an order."

Lava began to boil in Frank's gut. He closed his eyes and breathed in. There's no reasoning with the unreasonable, he knew that, and he knew it would be a waste of time—time which he didn't have to waste.

"Fine," Frank said, "I'll go home, I'm just gonna make a stop at Lucy Crow's house on the way to check on our guys. Is that all right?" Frank spoke at an even keel. Calm, as he seethed and roiled on the inside.

"Yeah, in fact, I'd prefer it. Consider that an order as well."

Frank knew the game; he was trying to test him, trying to break him. But he wouldn't bite, not tonight. There were far more pressing issues at hand.

"Sure."

The Sergeant studied him for a moment and turned out of the room, whistling *Jingle Bells* as he walked down the hall.

Frank sighed and brought his attention back to the files, gathering them up in a pile to clear out. One piece of paper fell free from the disarray of the table, gracefully floating to the floor and landing on top of Frank's foot. He bent low to pick it up and realized he had not yet read it. It was the doctor's recommendation from the Fairweather Institution. It was written in barely legible script, but just clear enough for Frank to read. Chicken-scratch, in fact, was his second language.

The doctor had quoted his patients, along with detailed anecdotes of their behavior. He thumbed back to where the directory was—a list of orderlies, nurses, and doctors, some with numbers attached.

What the hell, Frank thought; *good things tend to come in bunches.*

Frank picked up the phone and dialed a number at random. He didn't care about the time, or the fact it was Christmas. He'd wake the dead to get answers.

On the third ring, a female's voice answered.

"Hello?" the woman asked, groggy and confused.

"Hello, ma'am, I'm sorry if I woke you. My name is Frank Waters, I'm with the police department in Peekskill, New York."

"Huh? What? What time is it?"

"Uhh, it's early, or late, depending on how you look at it. This is Evelyn Amato, correct?"

She cleared her throat.

"Yes. Who is this again?"

"I'm sorry to have disturbed you Mrs. Amato, but I'm a homicide detective out of New York, and I wouldn't have called if it wasn't for the utmost urgency. If you don't mind I have a couple of questions for you about your time working at the Fairweather Mental Institution," Frank said and waited for a response.

"Homicide, you said?" Evelyn asked. Her voice now alert.

"Yes, ma'am."

There was silence for a while, the long droning kind, as if this call has been expected for quite some time.

Frank held the phone pressed against his ear. Finally, he heard her sigh.

"I think I know what this is about," she said.

"You do?" Frank said and leaned back in his chair. "How about you tell me then?"

She did, and Frank listened. He could tell she'd been wanting to tell somebody for a while.

The moment he hung up the phone he urgently gathered the papers in the file, hoping there was still time. The clock on the wall screamed at him, 2:44. His gun slapped against his protruding love handles as he swung his trench coat around his arms. What he'd uncovered was nothing concrete in the eyes of the law. But to Frank, it was the truth, solid as titanium.

Running out into the storm, pellets of ice stung his face like buckshot. He tried to shield it with his arm across his forehead and walked blindly through the iced parking lot. Frank slipped and fell to his knees, planting his hands in front of him and feeling the cold burn of ice as they slid against the slick gravel.

Carefully, he got up and walked to his car, methodically, as if he were on a tightrope, sliding until he gripped the door handle to his car. He got in, fired the engine, surprised that it kicked over on the first try, and threw the car into drive.

He weaved around the few cars on the road. Last-minute Christmas shoppers clogged the streets hours before in hopes of getting that perfect gift. Mostly men, he suspected, heading to the mall to buy something shiny for their wives. But now it was too late for any stores to be open.

What about Nancy? I didn't get anything for her.

There was no guilt in the revelation. After so many years of marriage, he figured she'd grown to expect such things. Their anniversary was a month before the murders began. The date passed with no more than an overcooked dinner he had shown up late for.

He brought his attention back to the task at hand and hoped he wasn't too late. But he had a sneaking suspicion that no matter how quickly he got there, it wouldn't be quick enough.

CHAPTER 44

The numbers on the digital clock flashed red. It was 2:50 and Sadie had given up on sleep a while ago. Something inside of her was pounding through her hollow gut, echoes of an inner turmoil warning her that something wasn't right.

She was on the living room couch, close enough to the front door that she could sneak out. Pellets of icy rain shattered against the bay window hanging above her. The weather was the only obstacle, but she knew she'd rather be out there than in here. She got up on her feet and tip-toed to the edge of the stairs. The front door was down on the landing; she could hear the volatile storm pressing against the door. The coat rack was to the left of the door with her blue and pink jacket. Before descending, she stared down the dark hallway; shadows danced off the Christmas tree lights in the shape of leering elves and crooked candy canes. Keeping an eye on the closed bedroom doors, she took each creaking step down slowly. She made it to the landing, strapped on her boots, and zipped up her jacket.

Her gloved hand reached out and turned the knob. The force of wind blew open the door the rest of the way. She caught it before it crashed against the wall. Ice stung her ears. The wind blew sideways, spraying streaks of white through the air in zig-zags.

Her house was a block away. Black ice stretched treacherously across the pavement; she treaded slowly. The wind howled in her face, gunning shards of ice. Her pink and blue jacket was zipped to the top; she wished it could keep going all the way over her face. She pulled her hood over her head and tucked her chin down, only her eyes peeked out from behind the pink hood.

Sadie was going home. Ghosts, the Christmas Spirit, or even God himself would fail to stop her. Her father needed her, and that was all the motivation she needed.

CHAPTER 45

Sanford wrote fluidly, through the errors and through the next word to come. He had to admit, in such a short span of time it was the best of his writing, and with that, it was the best writing he would ever do.

There was only one more sentence to write—his closing statement—to wrap up the twisted tale of his life, which had been condensed to seven pages. He couldn't help but think: *What would my father say?* A ghastly thought, but a fitting one nonetheless.

Sanford looked around the room from where he sat. He saw ceramic figurines on the shelves—a long-forgotten hobby. They were of dolphins, zebras and monkeys, unicorns, centaurs, and other mythological creatures. He pictured Lucy and Sadie going to yard sales and flea markets, finding the perfect not-so-perfect figure. There were paintings on the walls. Hotel art. Above a church painting was a cross, slightly askew on the wall. Sanford never knew Lucy to be the religious type. He thought of Jesus momentarily. How heavy it must've been, lugging that around on his back, heckled and taunted by an angry mob.

His attention fell back to Lucy, sprawled out and dead on the floor like a taxidermy rug. Sanford's fingerprints pointing out his guilt.

How heavy it must have been...

He started to write again.

When he finished his last goodbye on paper he put the pen down, got up from the couch, and grabbed his gun from the floor in the foyer. The steel was extra cold from the melting ice that gathered over it.

I must've dropped it dragging Lucy inside.

The living room floor was hard on his knees; he fell to them next to the lifeless Lucy. It was time to join her, and the rest of them. He hoped they'd have him. Maybe, if there was an afterlife, he'd see his mother and his little brother again, grown up but wearing the same Christmas pajamas he had worn all those years ago.

Who was he kidding? There was nothing good coming. If there was a place for him to go he figured the only person he'd see was his father, burning alongside him.

There was a picture of Sadie on the bookshelf, alongside Lucy's copy of *Jane Eyre* and a scented candle, which read *Christmas Morning* on it. He let his eyes linger on the photo, Sadie from first grade, a smile, all teeth. Sanford smiled despite himself, then exhaled deeply and evenly. He closed his eyes.

The barrel of the gun entered smoothly, as if his mouth were designed for it, fitting like a holster.

It wasn't so bad—having death in your mouth, in some ways it was comforting. The cold, black steel with its hollowed barrel was ready, willing, and able to end his nightmare with no more than a simple squeeze.

Thank Christ.

Air wheezed into his lungs as the last gasp he'd ever take.

"I mub yuh, Adie," he said, his words mumbled by the steel.

No more killing, no more struggle.

"Sanford, don't!" an unfamiliar voice shouted from in front of him. The jolt of surprise almost caused him to pull the trigger on instinct. He opened his eyes. Ahead of him was a man he'd seen before, but only in papers and on the nightly news. He was a plump man, with heavy bags under his eyes.

"Don't do it, son."

It was too late not to do it. He knew what he was. He shut his eyes again.

"Listen to me, what's happening here is not what you think," Frank said, his eyes were fixed on Lucy, then came back to Sanford, who thought he looked as tired as he was.

"Don't do this. There's things going on that you don't understand. And I believe you're innocent."

"Innocent?" Sanford shouted, pulling the gun out of his mouth. "Look what I've done!"

"I don't know what happened here. But I can tell you one thing, I can tell you about my instincts. They've gotten me through all kinds of tough times on the job, and when I've ignored them is when I paid the greatest price of all. My instincts are telling me now that you're being manipulated, son. Here, let me show you."

Frank reached into his trench coat slowly, like any sudden movements may cause the troubled man to shoot. Sanford tightened his grip on the gun, settling it against his head.

"Easy, Sanford, easy," Frank calmly said as he pulled the file out from his jacket. He held it out in front of him like some sort of peace offering. Sanford was deeply confused. The file looked thick.

Frank took a step forward with it.

"Stay there!" Sanford shouted.

"Okay, okay… I'll stay here, but it's imperative you see what's in here, because what's in here is about you, Sanford. It's about your time at Fairweather. Do you remember Fairweather?"

"Fairweather?"

The name left an aftertaste of dirty water in his mouth.

"Yes, Sanford, the Fairweather Mental Institution, in Portland, Maine."

Frank squatted down on his knees as slowly as his weight would allow. The file was opened to a certain page, two scrawny boys looked up, pale and malnourished. He slid the file over.

Once Sanford saw the photo, his grip on the gun loosened.

* * *

The Crows were the famous case of Fairweather. The main attraction: the sons of the Maine Maimer A doctor could make a name for himself in treating them, in *curing* them.

At first, they were kept together, mainly because Eric wouldn't move an inch unless his older brother did. Sanford was his security blanket. In the beginning that's how they saw it, but after a few months of one step forward with three steps back, they saw Sanford as a blockade to Eric's progression.

The day they were separated coincided with their first trial of electric shock therapy. Sanford could still feel it now as he looked at the picture of Eric and himself. He rubbed the side of his temple.

They were in their room, in their separate beds, the same way they would have done months earlier, in their home, reading each other's comics. This room wasn't home; it was far from it. There were no posters on the walls. It was hollow. Empty. There was nothing but white.

Sanford was talking to Eric; he was talking much more now, but Eric was yet to talk back.

"If you were the Incredible Hulk, do you think you could control it? You know, turning green, and becoming a monster? In the comic, Bruce Banner is always trying not to turn, but when he turns he saves the day. I think it would be better if he wanted to turn. Maybe when he turns into the monster, that's who he really is, you know, like on the inside? Kinda like Dad." He was rambling, and the look in Eric's eyes remained dormant and medicated.

The lock on the door turned with a loud clicking sound they'd grown to fear. The door pushed open, revealing new monsters draped in white, with needles in their hands instead of claws.

Dr. Clyde Kelley emerged from the lesser orderlies—the Dracula of the low-end vampires. He wore miniature spectacles that perfectly circled his eyes, making them not look like eyes at all. He was a short man. But his authority made him towering.

"Today's a special day, boys," he said wolfishly. "Today you go your separate ways."

Eric's look of vacancy became alive with worry, as if he finally realized where he was.

"We need to try something new. The problem with something new is that you can't have anything old holding you back. You see, that's what you are to each other; you're the past. And we're trying to look forward, so there can be no rearview mirror in sight."

Sanford remembered the way Eric looked at him then. He mouthed one word, *no.* Sanford could hear it, echoing loud through his skull and bouncing off his cranium, back and forth.

The bright fluorescent lights in the room buzzed with a hum that seemed to get louder and louder.

"We have different rooms for you on separate sides of the hospital, one you'll get very familiar with, and pretty soon the two of you will barely remember each other. Because today," Dr. Kelley pointed up to the light as it flickered again, "you meet Doctor Shock."

Kelley opened his palms towards the boys, the orderlies rushed in on them like vultures. Sanford fought back with what he could, which wasn't much. His body had turned frail from the trauma and an almost terminal lack of appetite. He swung wildly at the first orderly, who swatted his limp fist away. He felt a sharp prick in his ass; a wave of sedation settled over him in seconds.

Eric didn't fight. He couldn't. Terror lived in his eyes and embodied his whole being.

Sanford felt paralyzed but aware as he lay in bed. His listless eyes watched as they gathered Eric—his little brother, the last of his family—and carried him towards the door.

Their eyes connected for the last time. Sanford tried to scream, to plea, to bargain, to say anything to keep them together, but the chemical that coursed its way through his body wouldn't allow it.

Then came the only words Eric had spoken since that Christmas morning. He shouted gravelly but clearly to his older brother, his protector, his last of kin: "Don't let them! Stay with me! Stay with me! Stay with me!"

The needle went into Eric's flesh, his words trailed off. Sanford watched as Eric was hauled away, dragged into the abyss of white. He had a feeling about it then, a premonition: it would be the last time he'd see his little brother again.

* * *

"Turn the page, Sanford," Frank said as he moved his hand to the butt of his gun. Sanford was too immersed to notice. Even if he had, the desire to care would be minimal at best. He did as he was told and turned the page.

Dr. Clyde Kelley's signature marked the bottom, in large swooping letters.

Something inside of Sanford didn't want him to read it, it didn't want him to peer through the periscope above the murky waters of his mind.

But he had to.

Sanford Crow, the older of the two, has demonstrated a positive response to therapy.

Sanford read on as Dr. Kelley described how electric shock therapy is what unlocked his emotions. How afterwards he grieved, crying randomly throughout the day, and cried himself to sleep at night. Soon enough, Sanford had become the prototypical patient: taking his pills when given, talking through therapy, and building his social skills with the other children.

It hadn't taken long for him to get through the system. And when he finished with one he was on to the next. Until foster-care was the final system he'd entered.

He went on and found his brother's name.

Eric Crow has demonstrated the opposite attributes of his brother. Eric has regressed. He remains mute, and we fear he's suffering from psychosis.

Sanford's breath quickened as he read about Eric. How the last words he'd spoken were shouted at him as they got separated.

"Stay with me! Stay with me! Stay with me!" Sanford could still hear Eric's voice in his head, bouncing through an echo chamber.

He read how Eric had grown violent, how he'd lunge at nurses and doctors, all while remaining perfectly quiet.

One event, in particular, was unsettling.

Eric had been put in the general population, with the hope that being around other children his age would help progress his treatment. The children were at *free play*. Some were playing hide-and-seek, some were banging on the instruments, while the rest sat quietly and colored at the table in the center of the room.

They'd made a mistake by putting Eric in there with his restraints off. He listlessly stared at the other children around him, until he focused on one child drawing with a colored pencil. Something in him snapped and Eric sprinted at him. He'd grabbed the red pencil out of the boy's hand and held it up in a stabbing motion. Before he brought it down, the orderlies swarmed and tackled him. The needle went into his backside. Eric went to sleep.

"Jesus," Sanford whispered to himself.

It was in the last paragraph that Sanford seemed to grasp what Frank was getting at. He'd even circled it for Sanford to see. Kelley had let go of the professional doctor lingo; the fear in him bled through.

As his doctor, it is my concern that Eric may never be released. Tragedy was the trigger, but I believe insanity may just run in his family. I've never been afraid of a patient before, but this boy is different. Eric Crow is hopeless.

Sanford brought his head up from the file.

"I... I don't understand," he said, continuously thumbing through the massive file. "But he's... dead..."

Frank exhaled heavily.

"There was a fire in an old, abandoned warehouse. Eight bodies were found: five men, two women, and one child. One of the men was identified as your brother through his dental records. But that was the only thing identifiable. The burns were too severe, and the iris were noted to be hazel."

"But Eric had blue eyes," Sanford spoke in a whisper.

Frank nodded.

"It didn't settle right with me. I made some calls and spoke to one of the nurses, Evelyn Amato. Do you remember her?"

Her name brought it on immediately. She was the kind one, also with placid blue eyes, a kind face amongst a mass of menacing men.

"Fairweather Hospital was closed down just over fifteen years ago," Frank explained. "Allegations of experimental procedures, cruelty. You were discharged long before then, but Eric never was. They kept him there, locked up. After all of their tests, experiments, medicine and therapy failed on him, they essentially gave up, and left him in a padded cell alone; his only human contact was this Dr. Kelley. But what's not in that file in front of you is the fact that Eric escaped."

Sanford was silent and still, his eyes fixed on the detective.

Frank went on, "The hospital covered it up, you see? With all the allegations against them, Eric's escape would bury the place. This Dr. Kelley was found dead in his home soon after, blunt force trauma to the head, and no one ever caught who did it. Evelyn told me she knew it was Eric, because it had to be. But she didn't say anything; a feeling isn't evidence, and the hospital had its own interest in keeping her quiet. But I'm not sure we have that much more time here, Sanford."

Sanford could only remain still, struggling to comprehend. None of it made sense to him.

"But..." Sanford began to speak, laboring to find the words, "then, where is he?"

The floorboard in the hallway creaked. Frank had heard it first and drew his weapon.

A shot rang out, shattering the silence of Christmas morning.

Frank's gun hit the floor. Sanford watched him as he grabbed his stomach with both hands. He crashed onto his knees with a deep grunt, then fell to the ground in a curled up ball. Frank was always told a gut shot was the worst. Goddamn, they were right.

Sanford was frozen, lost in himself.

Behind him, footsteps became louder. A figure appeared amid the glow of Christmas lights, tall, with a face carved from stone. It's cheeks were sunken into its face, along with its eyes. His thin chest protruded jaggedly, skeletal.

“Hello, older brother. How’s it going?” Eric said with a severe lisp and smiled, revealing a mouth half full of teeth. Strings of saliva hung like spiderwebs when he spoke. With what seemed like inhuman speed Eric grabbed Sanford’s gun and tucked it into the back of his waist.

“You didn’t think I would actually let you shoot yourself, did you? We have a lot of catching up to do!”

Eric made his way to a dying Frank.

“Well done, detective,” he said, raising the gun to Frank’s head, and almost absentmindedly pulling the trigger.

“Well done, indeed.”

Chapter 46

Sadie, with her head hunkered into her jacket, stopped at the top of the walkway to her house and heard the loud bang ring out from inside of it. At first, she thought it was fireworks. Big kids from down the block maybe. But it was too close to home.

She crept to the living room window. The blinds were drawn and all she could see was the inside light along the window's edges. She was strangely thankful that she couldn't see anything else. Something inside told her she would hate the sight.

There was one way to get in her house besides busting through the doors. Her instinct told her she'd have to be quiet. She'd always kept her bedroom window unlocked for moments like these—the moments she needed to sneak in and out.

It was on the clear nights that she'd wake in the middle of the night to see the moon like a spotlight through her open window. She was drawn to it. Her blankets would peel away and she'd be up and at the window, stepping out onto the overhang with tiny bare feet. She'd climb down. She'd remember her father telling her how those stars burned away millions of years ago and it's only the last of the light from the blinked-out stars they were seeing. He'd tell her how it's like seeing into the past while standing in the future. Those nights were hers. The rest of the world slept quietly as Sadie Crow owned the moon.

This night was not like those.

The tree next to her window had thick limbs like the arms of a giant, which any eight-year-old could easily climb. The storm had left the branches frozen over, slick with ice. Icicles dangled off like massive fangs.

But Sadie had sure feet. From limb to limb, she pulled herself up in record timing. She stepped onto the canopy under her window, unsuspectingly onto a patch of black ice.

There was no time to think as her body flailed forward. Her chin made contact first, walloping against the roof. Her hand instinctively reached out, desperately grasping for anything to stop the fall. Her fingers reached for the gutter.

She remained cool. The cut on her chin blazed with pain, keeping her alert. Adrenaline coursed through her veins as she pulled herself up over the edge of the weakened gutter.

She rolled onto her back and exhaled a tremendous breath of relief, staring into the black of the night sky. There were no stars; the moon was hiding. The snow and sleet continued to fall as she stared up. It was somewhat peaceful. Then she heard it again, an ear-blasting explosion from the living room.

What's happening? She crawled towards her window.

She found it slightly ajar.

She stepped inside and landed in a puddle of freezing water. She noticed a trail of muddy footprints leading out of her door and into her hallway.

Her heart fluttered in waves.

Smell the roses, and blow out the candles, she thought in her mother's voice, the way her mom would always tell her how to breathe in moments of panic. The last time was at a soccer game, when she had a chance to win it in a shootout. "Smell the roses, and blow out the candles, sweetie," her mother said on the sidelines after she ran over to her before her kick.

She crept out of her room slowly, avoiding the spots on the hardwood floor that creaked. The sounds of a man sobbing drifted up the stairs and into her ears. The descending staircase seemed long and ominous.

Her courage pushed her forward, taking her down one step at a time.

The cries became louder, clearer, and a new sound trailed behind them. It was a different kind of sobbing, one that was muffled, as if it came from behind a door. She was halfway down the steps when she forgot her footing and stepped on the one spot in the staircase that wailed. She froze for a whole minute, waiting for whatever doom awaited.

Nothing came.

Smell the roses, and blow out the candles.

She kept going.

Her eyes were clenched shut when she poked her tiny head around the wall and slowly opened them. When she finally forced them open she saw a tall, sickly man. She'd seen him before, *but where?*

Then she remembered it, *the movie theater.* It was his face. He looked like her father.

The man was blocking the rest of the room off from her sight. But she could see the floor, and she could see the growing mass of red. Sadie squeezed her eyes closed and reopened them. There was someone lying on the floor, still and lifeless—a woman.

The tall man inched over; he was saying something that Sadie couldn't hear. That's when her father came into view. He was on his knees, his hands were covered in blood; his face was as white as the snow outside, with tears streaming down his cheeks.

It was the scariest sight she had ever seen.

"I'm gonna give you a choice, older brother," she heard the tall man say with a lisp. "Consider it your rite of passage."

"You stay right there," the tall man demanded, then walked out of her line of sight. The source of that muffled sound of horror emerged as he came back into view, dragging another person, bound and gagged.

Sadie pleaded with herself to wake up. This had to be a dream; the real world could never be so crazy. Especially on Christmas.

"Now, older brother, I want you to kill her."

CHAPTER 47

The gag in Diane's mouth suppressed her scream. She was writhing on the floor trying to kick free, but the zip ties around her ankles and wrists prevented it. Mascara ran from her eyes in deep streaks of charcoal. Under her bare feet, she could feel the surface changing from hardwood to a shaggy rug. Her bloodshot eyes caught Sanford's as Eric dragged her past him. The way Sanford was crying had scared her more than anything.

Eric tossed her next to the body of Frank Waters. Her squeals of pure horror satisfied him immensely, as she squirmed to get free in the ever-growing swamp of Frank's blood.

"Now, older brother," Sanford heard Eric say, "I want you to kill her."

With that, Sanford's sobbing ceased. His eyes widened, his mouth gaped open.

"Ha-ha, you should see your face right now! You look like someone killed the woman you love right in front of you. Whoops, silly me!"

How Sanford imagined this moment was nothing like it was. It'd been over two decades since they'd last seen each other. In his mind, their reunion would come with mighty hugs, tears, and joy.

"Did you hear what I said?" Eric yelled and put the gun inches in front of Sanford's face, the barrel down between his eyes. "Kill her!"

"Bu-bu-bu-but. Wh-Whyyy" Sanford stuttered out.

"Are you kidding me? Wh-Whyyy? Because, Sanny, it's your destiny."

He threw his head back and laughed.

"This is what the Crow legacy is, you see? This is what Daddy wanted for us. Too many people live life under the rule of law; made up rules that hold no weight. Men thought up these rules for other men to obey, to make them their slaves. That's what your whole life is, Sanny... slavery! You go to work, clean up another man's blood, which by the way is a pretty fucked up job to have, and that's coming from me." Eric laughed his fake laugh again and continued on. "You do that, collect your money, pay your taxes, buy useless shit, when inside you know you're something more, you're something better. Inside, you're like me, because it runs in our blood. We are our daddy's children after all, and twenty-five years ago he bestowed on us our birthright. Can't you see that? Are you that blind? Can't you see the Christmas present he gave us that day? He was trying to set us free!"

"No! You're out of your fucking mind," Sanford said, now crying.

"No, older brother, you are! The whole world is. But all it takes is one moment to change that. Like me, prying out my own teeth." Eric smiled, revealing his cracked gums. "Once you kill her you'll be changed, you'll be free, and we can be together again, doing anything we want to do, because when you're free anything's possible. Consider it a rebirth, and where there's birth, there's blood; it's as simple as that."

"I don't want that!"

"Yes, you do! I've been naughty, Sanny, and I've been spying. I bugged your home, I bugged her office; I've been watching you, hearing you. I know everything about you. You almost killed this bitch once. She deserves it, you know she does after what she did, after all her dirty lies! She told you I was dead, she even suggested you kill yourself! Why? I'll tell you why, older brother, you were never her patient at all, you were her subject. And the only thing she cared about was your story. Look..."

Eric revealed a small stack of papers, folded in his inner jacket pocket. They were loose and untethered. He wound up as if he were about to throw a frisbee, then let the papers fly from his hand towards Sanford. They fell like confetti, swarming the living room with their terrible truth.

The cover page landed on top of the file Frank had given Sanford. *Sanford Crow: A Father's Creation. By Dr. Diane Wesley.*

The words assaulted him. Betrayed him. He looked towards Diane. Her eyes glued to his with a guilty indignation and deep sorrow that Sanford had known far too well.

Eric turned and booted Diane in the stomach with all his force. Sanford could see the pain as it overrode her fear. Her hair was slick with the snow and rain from outside, mixed with tears that flooded sideways from her eyes; her makeup like warpaint.

Sanford wanted to help her, but at the same time, from somewhere deep down, he felt the darkness for a moment. After all, if she didn't lie for her own benefit, perhaps none of them would be in such a predicament. Perhaps Lucy would still be alive. But that's all that it was: a moment. He caught her eyes among her constant struggle. *I won't*, he mouthed the words to her, hoping she'd understand.

"So what's it gonna be, older brother?" Eric said. "Either you do it, or I do it. But if I do it... it won't be pretty."

Sanford tried to play out the possibilities to himself. First, he imagined charging him. Eric was sickly thin after all; he could barrel into him and let his closed fist hammer down until there was nothing left.

No, that won't work. At that point, Eric was across the room, with Diane and Frank in between them. There was too much ground to cover, too many obstacles. And Eric had a gun.

Then he imagined turning around, high-tailing it out the back door. He could leave Diane to die by the hands of his brother; she may even deserve it. He could find Sadie, escape, go to the police.

But... no. He couldn't have that on his conscience; not another death.

It hit him, it was the only real option he had, it was the only one that made any sense.

"I'll do it," Sanford said, and he watched Diane's face turn as gray as a tombstone.

"You will?" Eric said calmly. "Hot damn! Now we're talkin'."

Eric went over to the coffee table, where Sanford had earlier placed the knife down. He picked it up, his hand gripped around the handle loosely. In front of Diane's eyes, he limply swayed it back and forth.

"My brother's gonna penetrate you, sweetheart."

Eric handed the knife to Sanford, still pointing the gun at him. It felt foreign in Sanford's hand. A knife like that was only used to cut through meat—juicy tenderloins and T-bone steaks. He had never cut through anything living.

"Eric, no," Sanford said. "Not with this, I'm not ready for this."

"Not ready? What are you talking about?"

"My gun; just let me use my gun."

A shit-eating grin split Eric's face.

"You must think I'm dumb as shit, older brother. What? You want the gun, so you could turn it on me? Is that your grand scheme?"

"I'm not gonna do that, Eric. I just can't use a knife, you gotta understand that. If you want me to do this it'll only be with a gun. It's the only way I can. You can even hold your gun to my head as I do it."

He could see Eric mulling it over, just as he could see Diane trying to come to grips with her own demise.

"Okay, okay, you win, Sanny. I'll let you use a gun. But I have a better idea." Eric's smile widened.

Eric walked behind him. A few seconds later Sanford heard a shriek that pierced through his heart and straight to his soul. Dread fell upon him like an avalanche.

"No! Let go of me!" Sadie screamed.

Eric had grabbed her from around the corner of the stairs.

"No! Eric, no! Sadie!" Sanford exploded from his knees with the knife still in his hand. But Eric had his gun out, firmly against Sadie's head.

"No, no, no!" Eric said, climbing an octave with each word. Sanford could see it was all a joke to him, a mighty good time, and immediately fell back down to his knees with his hands in the air, pleading for mercy.

"Please, Eric! I'm begging you..."

"You're pathetic. If only Daddy could see you now. I was gonna let her witness it from over there, maybe that would transform her too. Two birds, one stone. But no, this is better. This is more fun!" Eric lisped, dragging Sadie past him to the other side of the room, stepping over Frank's body.

It didn't take long for Sadie to notice the identity of the dead. First, she saw Frank; a twinge of sorrow swam through her. It lasted mere seconds until she recognized the other body.

"Mom?" her inquisitive voice asked. "Mom!" Her shout echoed through the house, the neighborhood, the town. "*MOM!*"

Sanford had never felt such remorse in all his life. It far exceeded that Christmas morning when he found his own mother dead; when he witnessed his father end it all. This was worse. This was the light of his life turning dark.

"Stop it," Eric demanded, but Sadie continued to cry.

"I said stop it!"

Sadie seemed to cry louder.

"STOP IT!" he screamed, pressing the gun harder against her skull. Sadie stopped, robotically, as if he had found a switch that flicked it off.

"You son of a bitch!" Sanford bellowed in agony.

"Considering we both had the same mother, you shouldn't be calling her names," Eric laughed.

"Listen, older brother, it's quite simple. Either you shoot your therapist..." he walked over to Diane, dragging Sadie, and gave her another boot to the gut. Her groan was abrupt like a cough. "Or, I shoot precious Sadie. You decide."

The barrel of his gun was pointed just above Sadie's ear. With his other hand, he reached behind his waist, drawing Sanford's gun, quick like a cowboy, then slid it across the floor, where it stopped in front of Sanford's knees.

Sanford remained still, staring at the gun on the floor, then looked to Diane, then to Sadie.

"It's about evolution, Sanford. You pull that trigger, and you evolve into something better, something without restrictions, no strings attached. Just complete and utter freedom. Join me, older brother. Come and join your family."

All Sanford wanted to do was to pick up the gun, take aim at Eric, and end this nightmare forever. But Sadie was too close; the risk was too real. The gun remained on the floor in front of him, mocking him, challenging him to make the impossible choice. But anyway he sliced it, he couldn't save her. That thought became clearer and clearer.

"Make a choice!"

With the knife still in one hand, he picked up the gun with the other and stood to his feet. As he stood up, he felt something under his shirt, brushing against him. Amongst the mayhem and the bashing of his head, he must've forgotten it was there. Lucy's gun, so tiny it was hard to feel.

Sanford walked over to Diane.

"Daddy, no!" Sadie shouted, still crying. Still in disbelief.

"Daddy, yes!" Eric slurred back and laughed hysterically.

"It's okay, sweetheart. It's the only way."

He stood over Diane. She made a muffled gasp and tried to slither away. Sanford jumped behind her, grabbing her by the arms to keep her still. Her hands painfully spasmed behind her back.

"Where are you going?" Sanford said menacingly in her ear. His eyes, wild and animal-like, made her believe it.

"Ooo, now we're having fun. I like the spirit, older brother!" Eric cheered. But during the commotion, he failed to notice Sanford slipping the knife into Diane's bound hands.

As the knife fell into them, Diane looked up at Sanford through hopeful, teary eyes. But he barely noticed; he just begged whatever God there might be to keep Eric distracted.

"It's time, older brother. Enough delaying the inevitable," Eric said from behind Sadie, squatted down with his head just above her shoulder.

Sanford looked down and saw Diane carving through her bindings in a steady, indiscrete manner.

Good.

He needed to buy some time.

"Eric, no one else has to die. You've made your point, okay? We can leave together. Just you and I, the way it was always meant to be."

"Oh, we will, older brother. And it will be you and I, just not the *you* I see now. You must go through the transformation. If you don't, I can't trust this *you*."

Sanford heard a moan and glanced down; he saw blood in Diane's palm. It looked as if she'd cut right through it.

He thought for a moment, then asked, "Remember when we were kids and how I used to take you with me to explore the woods?"

"This isn't the time to take a jog down memory lane!" Eric said, as his grip squeezed harder around the handle of the gun.

"Just humor me for a second, will ya? I mean I haven't seen you in twenty-five years, what's another minute? Do you remember the woods?"

Eric sighed.

"I remember something, but that boy wasn't me. I was born on Christmas morning, 1969."

"No, you're wrong! You were born thirty-one years ago, in May, you were a sweet and innocent little boy. We took a walk through the woods, pretending to be foreigners in a native land. We'd explore and look for arrowheads. Then there was that one time that we came across a wounded bird, do you remember?"

"Vaguely," Eric said, growing short of patience.

"It was a bluejay with a broken wing, and it was just laying in the leaves, flapping its one good wing and squawking for help to no one. I stepped right over it without a second thought. But not you, Eric, you bent down with such care and you cradled the bluejay in your arms. 'What are you doing?' I asked, 'we have to keep moving, just leave it there.' And do you remember what you said to me?"

Eric stared. Sanford held his gaze.

Eric finally said: "It's alive, and I'm gonna keep it that way." His voice was steady but softer than before.

"That's right, and you did keep it alive! That vet in town, Dr. Roberts, we brought it to him, and he mended its wing. Then you kept it out back so Dad wouldn't know, and you fed it every day until it was strong enough to fly away on its own."

Eric lowered the gun slightly from Sadie's head, his jaw slackening.

Sanford breathed in quickly, eyes wide, hoping against hope. Eric raised his eyes, doughy and almost pleadingly to Sanford.

Then came the laughter. Sanford saw it was all a joke; he was just trying to toy with him.

"Jesus, Sanny, you really think that would work? Now put that gun to Dr. Cunt's head and pull the fuckin' trigger! Cause if you don't, I will follow you wherever you go in this life like a fuckin' shadow. And as long as you're alive, I will rob you of everything that matters. Because it's me now, older brother, I'm the only one that matters now."

As long as you're alive...

Sanford's eyes widened with an epiphany. He glanced down to Diane's hands. The rope around her wrists began to cake with blood. Despite her bleeding palm, she still carved away, until finally, the knife cut through, freeing her hands and giving Sanford the one chance they had.

It's now or never...

Staring back at his younger brother, Sanford put the gun to his own head and savored the look of shock in Eric's eyes.

"What are you doing?" Eric shouted. "Put it back on her!"

"No, little brother, I will not die a monster."

Eric pulled the gun away from Sadie, stood up, and aimed it at Sanford, confused by the sudden loss of control.

Almost. Not yet. Sanford looked into Sadie's fear-stricken eyes. She was still in the way. It was too risky to take the shot.

"I'm sorry, baby. I love you so much, but this is the only way."

"Daddy, no!" Sadie screamed and jolted forward. Eric lost his grip on her and lunged to regain it, taking his eyes away from Sanford.

Sadie was still in the line of fire, but Sanford saw an opportunity.

He reached behind his back. Lucy's gun rested coldly against it. He pulled it out and placed the handle into Diane's opened palm. If he missed his shot, it might all rely on her.

Eric caught Sadie by the shirt and yanked her back against his chest. He looked at Sanford, who was now pressing the gun under his chin, much like the way their father had done all those Christmases ago.

"No! Put it down!" Eric commanded, flustered. The image of his father blowing his face off flashed in his mind.

"I love you, Sadie. You have to shut your eyes now, honey." Sanford looked down at Diane who was staring up at him, lost in the same miasma of confusion and fear.

Movement flickered in the corner of Sanford's eye. He glanced towards the detective's body, laying stomach down in the lake of blood between them. It was Frank's hand at his side, which had slowly curled into a fist.

Is he still alive? Sanford thought he might be. Eric stood with Sadie directly above Frank's body. The glimmer of hope Sanford had was shining.

"Sanford!" Eric shouted. The desperation in his voice evident.

"No more," Sanford said, occupying the intensity of Eric's attention.

Sadie shut her eyes, squeezing them as tightly as she possibly could. Spittle from Eric's screams rained above her head.

Sanford looked at his daughter, standing there helplessly. The poor girl had already lost her mother, he would do all he could to make sure he would stick around.

Please, God, let this work...

He pulled the gun out from under chin and aimed it at his brother.

"Get down!" Sanford shouted, startling everyone in the room.

Sadie's eyes popped open, to see her father pointing the gun towards her. She wanted to move, to get down, like her father instructed, but fear kept her paralyzed.

A bloody hand then reached up from below her. Frank's hand. With what little strength he had left, he turned and clutched Sadie by the wrist, pulling her down to the floor with him.

Amid the confusion, Eric's grip wained. Sadie slipped from his grasp. He saw the cop on the floor covering her with his body, then going limp, dying in his last heroic act.

Eric's eyes went wide. He looked back to his brother and aimed his gun at him.

Their eye contact was brief. They didn't say a word. Both brothers pulled the trigger at the same time.

Chapter 48

Both guns blazed. Everything else was a blur.

The shots were so loud that Diane's ears rang. She sat still in a moment of disbelief. Sanford collapsed alongside her, his chest irregularly spurting blood in her direction. She knew he was either dead or on his way to it.

She heard Eric gasp. Then he screamed, "Nooooo!" His free hand cradled his stomach, where Sanford's bullet tunneled in and stayed.

Diane looked at her hand and saw the gun. Comprehension took hold.

Eric was still on his feet, screaming. These plans—twenty-five years in the making—were now derailed and gunning it off the edge of the cliff.

Diane heard the deadened screams of Sadie, and saw the lifeless body of Frank Waters budging from her underneath him.

Sadie had squirmed free, covered in his blood from head to toe. Her eyes were on her father's. Diane knew she would go to him.

Eric knew as well. In his dying frustration, he raised his gun with a trembling arm towards his niece.

Now! Diane thought.

She felt a surge of adrenaline. She lifted the gun, saw the safety was off, and let her training take control. She felt the cold breeze of the gun range, Jake Hardy behind her, whispering.

"Lift your arms, bend your elbows, bring the barrel to eye level, squeeze the trigger, don't pull it."

"You sound like a broken record," she had said.

"Better to be repetitive than dead."

Eric turned to Diane as she drew, his own gun rising instinctively towards her and away from Sadie. He tried to take aim, but Diane's quick-twitch was far too fast. She pulled the trigger three times before he could pull his once. There was no recoil.

Two plummeted into his chest, one into his shoulder. He clutched his sternum with a gurgled moan and toppled over.

Sadie barely blinked through the stream of bullets that whizzed above her head as she crawled towards Sanford. She felt like she was a million miles away, in another dimension, where the only thing that made sense was the fact that her father needed her.

Diane stood up, still gripping the gun and pointing it at Eric, who lay motionless on the floor.

"Sadie?" she asked.

Sadie was at her father's side. His head was in her lap.

Blood gurgled from the corner of Sanford's mouth.

"Daddy," Sadie cried. "Daddy, please don't..."

His breathing was erratic. Short gasps of air heaved in and out, as he desperately tried to cling to them. He tried to speak, but choked on the blood in his lungs.

All Sanford could do was look at his little girl. What he saw, made everything else okay. Her open eyes, her beating heart—the fact that she was still alive. Even though he was leaving her as an orphan, he knew she'd be all right. Because she was better than he was, and he was better than his father.

As Sanford looked at Sadie, he realized that bringing her into this world was the whole reason for his existence, and with that knowledge, he could die peacefully.

Her little hand fell into his. It took all the strength he had left to give it a tiny squeeze.

"I love you, Daddy!" Sadie pleaded, then looked at her father through the tears of her eyes, and saw that he was smiling at her. In some bizarre way, he'd looked more alive than he ever had before.

Sanford's hand went limp on top of hers. His eyes shut and never opened again.

"Daddy—" she started to say and then stopped. Tears burned from the back of her eyes. Her breathing ceased in her chest. It had all caught up to her; this gross portrayal of Christmas. Sadie fell into shock.

Diane slowly walked over, scared, letting the gun take charge and lead the way, still aiming it at Eric.

"Sadie?" she called her name again. But Sadie remained silent.

Diane stood tall over Eric's body. She kicked his foot with hers. It flopped to the side limply. She couldn't trust his death. Like they do in the movies, she waited for him to remerge, drenched in blood and riddled with bullets for one last scare.

But Eric didn't rise. He didn't spasm. Eric Crow was dead, twenty-five years too late.

Blue and red lights flashed through the window, and sirens wailed a sweet song in her ears. The police cars came to screeching halts outside.

Diane went over to Sadie, who was on her knees, immobile alongside her dead father.

"Sadie?" Diane asked again. She put the gun down and lowered herself to her knees. She was face to face with her. Sadie's eyes were drawn to both her parents, dead on the floor of her once innocuous living room. The same room where her father taught her how to walk, where her mother had painted her nails for the first time, where Christmas mornings would start with her racing into the room and ransacking all the presents scattered under the tree for a loved and spoiled little girl.

Sadie's eyes finally blinked, air rushed back into her lungs, as the standing tears erupted down her face like water out of a cracked dam.

Diane breathed a sigh of relief as Sadie turned her head towards her and let her cries be heard. They collapsed into each other's arms, Diane whispering softly and reassuring, "I got you. You're safe, you're safe" gripping her tightly.

The police swarmed the house with guns drawn.

"Freeze!" and "Put your hands up!"

Diane and Sadie remained embraced, ignoring their demands. They were secure in their hug. Outside of it, the world existed, a world too big at the moment for either of them to face.

"You're safe," Diane said, but couldn't help wondering if Sadie would ever feel safe again.

— • —

Epilogue

The little girl—not so little anymore—waved goodbye to kids on the bus as she stepped off it and entered the warm Florida sun. No one waved back. It was a far cry from the winters up north that Sadie was used to, but she'd grown to loathe the Florida summers. Sadie would swim through the humidity into the air-conditioned house that was her Aunt Ellen and Uncle Peter's.

After her Aunt Ellen learned of what happened to Lucy, her own sister, she and Peter had taken Sadie in. Of course, it wasn't immediate. Sadie had spent some time in the hospital, trying to mend the wounds in her mind. Claremont Medical Facilities offered consultations and programs specifically geared towards children who'd experienced tragedy.

Diane Wesley had come to visit a number of times. Not as a doctor, but as a friend, doing what she could.

"How are you doing today, Sadie?" Diane had asked her. It was a week into her stay.

"I'm okay. Annie and I have been taking music lessons. We're gonna try to start a band."

"That's cool. What kind of music are you gonna play?"

"Whatever kind gets me out of here," Sadie said with a sardonic smile.

"Ha-ha, that's a swell kind to play. And don't worry, you won't be here much longer. I've spoken to your Aunt Ellen. Once you get the okay from the doctor you'll be going to live with her. They live down in Tampa, Florida, on a huge golf course, not too far from the beach."

"I know, I remember being there when I was younger. That was my first and only time on a beach."

"Well, you'll become a beach bum before you know it," Diane said. "They'll be driving up here to pick you—"

"I don't blame you, you know?" Sadie interrupted, cutting off the formidable chit-chat.

Diane was taken aback by the child's blunt candor.

"You don't?"

"If it wasn't for you I'd be dead," Sadie said. Diane was left speechless. She often wondered how much Sadie remembered from that day, what she knew, what she processed.

"You're a very special little girl, do you know that?" Diane said and meant it.

"Duh," Sadie responded and giggled. Diane smiled.

"And if you ever need anything from me, I mean anything at all, I'm always just a phone call away."

"Thank you," Sadie said and lowered her head in thought. "Well, now that you mention it, there's one thing I would like from you. It would really mean a lot."

"Of course, anything at all."

Sadie told her what she wanted; Diane's face darkened. She stared at Sadie for a long while, wondering if it was even possible.

"Are you sure that's what you want?"

"One-hundred percent."

"Okay, Sadie. I'll see what I can do. It just might take some time."

"Well," Sadie said, "I have plenty of that to go around."

Two and a half years had passed through the season-less haze of Florida. Sadie was an eleven-year-old girl when she stepped off the bus and waved goodbye to no one. She entered her gated community of lush and lavish houses, most with personalized golf carts parked in their driveways with license plates like *HoleIn1*, *EagleEye*, *Par4Course*, and *Swinger*. Some had fuzzy dice tied around the rearview mirror.

She got to her home and opened the mailbox. First, she sifted through the useless junk: clothing magazines, *Golf Digest*, coupon catalogs, and a few ads and bills she pushed aside. Then she saw a large, vanilla envelope addressed to her, the return address signed, *Dr. Diane Wesley*.

Sadie tore it open before she set foot in the driveway. There were multiple pages folded over each other, on the verge of bursting out of the envelope. She unfolded and flipped over the first page.

Dear Sadie,

The following is what you had asked for. It took some time, some favors, and some overall luck for me to get my hands on it. But considering I was his therapist, it wasn't impossible. It isn't the best of quality; his handwriting is a step below chicken scratch, and they're only photocopies, so that will explain the fading. Though it's the best I can do.

If I'm to be honest with you, which I vow to be, I should tell you that I've had this for quite some time. For two years to be exact. It may have been wrong of me to hold on to it, and for that I'm sorry. I feared that reading it might set you back after how far you've come. There's a lot in here, Sadie, a lot of sadness and a lot of truth.

He had written a lot in a short period of time, and after reading it, I understand why you wanted it. But please understand before you do read it, it's going to be difficult to get through. He loved you more than you will ever know, Sadie. And that's why he did what he did. Just remember, he wrote this believing he was the villain, before he died the hero.

Call me after you read it if you need someone to talk to. I'm here for you. Always.

Your friend,

Diane

Sadie stuffed the letter into her book bag, then rushed through the front door, eager to read more. She couldn't help but be frustrated when she saw her Aunt Ellen in the kitchen, preparing to cook. All she wanted to do was go into her room, slam the door, and read about the life her father had lived.

"Hi, Sadie baby! How was school?" her Aunt Ellen asked.

"You know, same old same old."

Ellen's eyes were a light gray, with silver sparkling when the sun caught them just right. She looked a lot like her sister, if a bit more rough around the edges. It replaced a piece of Sadie's mom in her mind. When she looks back at her mother now, all she could see is her with gray eyes. The green was gone.

"Is everything okay? You look... flustered," Ellen said, treading lightly in a world she was still getting used to. She and Peter never had children. Sadie wasn't sure if they were capable of it or not, but she was thankful for their willingness to try. They weren't quite sure what to do with her, how to act. They more or less raised her as a friend, which gave Sadie the freedom she craved.

"Yes, Aunt Ellen, everything is fine. Just have to get a jumpstart on my homework is all."

Ellen's face beamed.

Sadie smiled at the ease at which she prompted this response.

"That's great, Sadie baby! You're such a good student. Go ahead, sweetie, and get started. Maybe when you're done you can help me finish up dinner? I'm making your favorite tonight."

"Veal parmigiana?" Sadie asked, enthused.

"Veal? I thought it was always chicken?"

Sadie saw the disappointment on her aunt's face.

"Of course it's chicken!" Sadie quickly laughed. "I was just joshin' ya, Aunt El. You should see your face though."

Ellen smiled. She hadn't quite got used to Sadie's brand of humor, but she always laughed anyway.

"Well, I'm off to the coal mines!" Sadie cheerily said and excused herself.

She ascended the stairs in leaps and bounds, jumping three at a time. Her father's words burning her through her backpack. She rushed into her room, shut the door, and belly-flopped onto her bed. Among the mass of blankets, pillows, and stuffed animals, she ripped her bag open and pulled out her father's confession and began to read:

By the time I came to, my palms were caked in her blood.

It was that first sentence that resonated with her. Images of that shaggy rug drenched in blood. Her mother's head lolled to the side; her eyes open and lifeless.

Sadie breathed in deep and tried to continue.

It was the same, only twenty-five years earlier. The exact same.

Sadie was still on the first page when she brought her head up and stopped. This was more than a declaration of guilt, more than a suicide note. These were his memoirs, broken down into seven pages. This was the saga of Sanford Crow.

Diane was right, he had written a lot in such a short period of time. It was as if his story was begging to come out of him. Sadie only hoped that it helped. Maybe rehashing all of this is what helped prepare him for what he had done. Maybe it helped to bring him peace in the end.

She fanned through the massive read, her heart fluttering as she did.

Her eyes picked up words and sentences along the way. *Horn-rimmed glasses... I think he's dangerous, I think he hurts people... pulled the trigger... It was me.*

Until she stopped at the last page, and her eyes fell onto the last line.

Just remember, this world's a crazy place, and everyone has a cross to bear... some are just heavier than others.

Sadie started to cry. She brought his memoirs into her chest and hugged them as if they were him. It took a moment to realize what she was doing, then she pulled them away to make sure she hadn't damaged them.

They were still in good enough shape. But seeing the wrinkles and trails of her own tears run through her father's ink, made her realize that she wasn't yet.

Sadie got up from her bed and opened the closet door. The top shelf was littered with books and boxes; the closet floor had piles of discarded clothes. After being there for two years she still didn't feel settled in enough to organize. She put a stepping stool down in front of her and stood up on it.

Aunt Ellen and Uncle Peter never went through her stuff, she knew that. She didn't think they'd even stepped foot into her room without her there. Sadie always shut her door when she left, and when she came back everything always seemed to be where it was.

The box she was looking for was marked *S-Crow* in bold lettering. She pulled it out from underneath other boxes carefully, not to cause a ruckus, then got down and brought it over to her bed.

Sadie knew it was strange what she kept inside of it: keepsakes from a time worth forgetting. She opened the box and first saw her father's eyes looking back at her through grainy black and white print. Above his head read the words: *Lead Suspect in Serial Case.* She looked at his doughy expression momentarily then put the clipping aside.

Underneath it was a pile of other newspaper cutouts, all to do with her father. They were arranged in the box chronologically—the only thing in her room in order. When she flipped through them it told her a story. It was the tale of a man, framed for crimes he didn't commit but knew them intimately. The last clipping had a picture of her and Diane wrapped in blankets. Diane was bleeding black blood; Sadie's complexion was even whiter than the newspaper could allow.

The headline read: *The Crow Serial Case Ends in Blood: Sanford Crow Save His Daughter.*

It made Sadie smile every time she read it. But then she would remember the gun to his head, Sadie shutting her eyes, her father's voice saying, "*No more,*" the explosion in the room—the sound of her father's death.

She took in a long deep breath, telling herself the phrase her mother used to say to her. *Smell the roses and blow out the candles.* She exhaled and knew it was a phrase she would tell her own kids.

She looked back in the box and emptied out the remaining artifacts: her mother's sobriety chip, her father's watch, both of their wedding rings. When the box was empty she took her father's memoirs and placed them neatly on the bottom, then carefully covered them with everything else.

She looked over at her desk and saw the roll of duct tape she used to hang posters on her walls, much to her uncle's chagrin. She grabbed it and went back to the box.

When she shut the lid, the last thing she saw inside of it was her father's eyes again, innocent through the tiny slit of cardboard. She'd never taped it up before, but something told her it was the right thing to do. She stretched the tape over the box and sealed it shut.

Sadie didn't know when she'd be ready to open it again. Maybe in a week, maybe in a year. Maybe never. All she knew was that there was no rush. She was only eleven-years-old after all. Time was on her side.

Author's Note

This book grew out of a fascination with how the past echoes forward and how the things we inherit shape who we become. While this story is entirely fictional, the emotions of its core are very real: the pull of memory, the weight of family, and the question of whether we can ever truly outrun who we are and where we come from.

Thank you for spending time in this world with me. I hope Sanford Crow stays with you long after the final page.

Until next time.

— Mike Lemieux

Acknowledgements

This book would not exist without the support and encouragement of many people, and I am deeply grateful to all of them.

First and foremost, thank you to my wife, Britt, for her love, unwavering support, and belief in me. Your knowledge and the path you paved helped make me a better writer.

Thank you to Garrett DeTemple for his thoughtful feedback and invaluable help during the editing process.

To my parents, thank you for always encouraging my love of storytelling and for supporting me every step of the way.

And to everyone who offered encouragement along the journey, especially my readers on Wattpad, thank you for believing in this story.

Mike Lemieux is a writer of mystery, thriller, and horror fiction. His work explores the darker edges of family, purpose, and identity, often blending psychological suspense with emotional depth. *Sanford Crow* was a 2022 Watty Award winner, recognizing its impact with readers worldwide. He lives in New York with his family, always working on the next story.

www.ingramcontent.com/pod-product-compliance
Lightning Source LLC
LaVergne TN
LVHW100512110826
845146LV00002B/609

* 9 7 9 8 9 9 4 9 1 8 7 0 8 *